WE KILL KILLERS

WE KILL KILLERS

S. T. ASHMAN

DEDICATION

I want to thank Sallie and Jayla for giving Agent Vallery Rose a voice. I also want to thank all my other amazing editors and readers for making 'We Kill Killers' a reality!

Kate... I can't wait to meet the baby. ☺

CONTENTS

PROLOGUE

New York 1981

The winter wind lashed mercilessly against the young boy's face, cutting through his skin like a blade. As his teeth clattered uncontrollably, a deep, desperate wish took root within his broken heart: that both his parents were dead.

Clad only in a dirty T-shirt and underwear, he stood on the slippery stairs of the backyard porch. His bare feet had turned an alarming shade of blue, while his ears throbbed from the cold.

"Put the knife down, you bitch!" his father's raging voice echoed from the house in Slovenian.

"I'll kill you!" his mother screamed, a threat made so often that its familiarity was chilling.

Even at his tender age, the boy couldn't understand why such broken people would choose to have children. Their pitiful lives were a series of devastating choices, each worse than the last, including that of having kids.

The jarring slam of the porch's storm door was quickly followed by the violent shatter of glass somewhere inside the house. In an instinctive reaction, Mojca pressed his eyes shut. Footsteps approached from behind, igniting a paralyzing fear within him. Escape seemed impossible, as if he was caught between his violent father and intimidating mother.

"Mojca, it's me," whispered the familiar voice of his older brother Anton, who nudged Mojca's eyes open. Standing before him, Anton gently guided Mojca's slender arms through the sleeves of a worn coat.

In a kinder world, Anton, hovering between youth and adulthood, would be somewhere else. Maybe on a date at the mall or secretly puffing his first cigarette behind a corner store with friends.

But this wasn't a kinder world. Not for them, anyway. So, Anton was here, by Mojca's side, as he had always been.

His brother's comforting smile warmed Mojca even more than the snug fit of the dirty boots and pants that Anton quickly dressed him in.

"Let's go ride on the train, okay?"

Anton's voice was so calm, one would never suspect that their parents had been dangerously close to murdering each other just moments before. But Mojca played along, faking a soft, sad smile.

Hand in hand, they navigated the grim streets of 1980s South Bronx, making their way to the 167th Street train station—the epicenter of American ruin.

They passed the homeless, cocooned in makeshift beds. Rusted bodegas, buzzing liquor stores, and shady pawn shops lined the gloomy streets. Not even the biting winter winds could cover the nauseating stench of urine and shit. A group of men loomed at the side of a street—probably gangs selling crack to zombie-like creatures, their vigilant eyes darting, ever-watchful for the cops.

The train station was just around the corner, and the inside warmth felt like a friendly hug.

As they climbed over the ticket barrier, Mojca realized that Anton had forgotten his coat. Given how things had unfolded earlier at home, this wasn't exactly surprising.

Mojca cast a hesitant glance back in the direction of their house, worry and uncertainty evident on his face.

"I'll be fine. It's warm on the train," Anton assured him.

"But . . ." Mojca began, "your pills. What if—"

His words were cut off by the shouts of two drug addicts getting into a fight. Just a typical Saturday morning in the Bronx. Around here, every moment felt like a living hell.

"Come on, let's go." Anton tugged Mojca by the hand onto the cold train platform.

They had done this countless times before, but today felt different to Mojca. He couldn't quite explain it, but it felt like the darkness that had always lingered at the edges of his life was suddenly encroaching, ready to finally swallow him.

Determined, Mojca paused.

"What is it?" Anton asked.

Mojca couldn't quite find the words. Everything was the same as always, but today, the shadow of mortality felt more palpable, its cold breath on his neck like a warning from the afterlife.

"I . . . want to go home." Mojca's voice was firm.

Anton's forehead creased. "We can't."

Discouraged, Mojca dropped his gaze to the stained concrete floor of the station, its discarded gum and scuffs. Deep down, he knew his brother was right. They couldn't go back until one of their parents was arrested or left the house for a few days to go on a drinking spree. This pattern was all too familiar.

But in that moment, as crazy as it was, their home seemed like the better option to Mojca. Better than that horrific feeling in his gut, at least.

Anton gently tugged Mojca along the platform. "I'm cold, Mojca."

Glancing at the approaching train, Mojca wanted to protest again, but Anton's quivering, blue-tinged lips silenced him. For the first time, Mojca noticed Anton's swollen eye. It was almost half-shut. Clearly, his father had gotten a hold of him while he was fetching Mojca's clothes.

"Are you a brave warrior or a scared princess?" Anton asked, smiling as he fished out Mojca's necklace from beneath his shirt. He gently pulled it free, exposing a small stone ankh symbol on a worn leather chain—a gift from the Metropolitan Museum of Art during one of their free admission days for families in need. Fascinated, Mojca and Anton had spent hours at the Egyptian exhibition, lost in discussions about life and death, the gods living in the stars, and the powers that the Egyptians believed they wielded.

Anton nodded at the necklace. "What do I always tell you?"

"That there are many stars up there with special powers, and someday, one of them will shine down on us," Mojca recited.

"Yes, that's right." Anton tousled Mojca's hair just as the train roared into the station.

As they boarded side by side, Mojca tightened his grip around his brother's hand, realizing one stark truth: that without his brother, he was utterly alone.

Bover 1981
Leah

The early rays of the sun were still soft and weak, barely illuminating the thin layer of snow on the ground. I sat on the orange couch by the living room window, watching my parents in the driveway as they loaded more suitcases into the back of their station wagon. Their breath was visible in the chilly air, rising in soft puffs. My mother ignored me, not sparing a single glance in my direction. She usually did that when she sensed she'd done something wrong. Not that she felt guilty—I was sure her contempt for me would turn into relief the moment they pulled out of the driveway and I was out of sight. But deep down, they both knew that leaving their child alone for weeks wasn't something their friends would do. My father's expression made that clear.

My mother was in the passenger seat, filling letters into a magazine puzzle, when my father paused before sliding into the driver's seat. He caught my gaze. Shame was etched across his face. But all my mother had to do was clear her throat—loud and annoyed—and my father got in the car and drove off.

I never knew how long they'd be gone. If they went to our small ski cabin at Stowe, they'd be gone for about seven days. If it was a road trip south or west to warmer weather, it could be weeks. A good indicator was the amount of non-perishable food they left behind. A scan of the pantry this morning suggested this trip would be a very long one.

I stared at the empty driveway a moment longer, then turned and walked to the piano in the small dining room. It had belonged to my grandmother and was completely out of tune, but it was the only thing in the world that provided me with distraction.

I sat and sank my little fingers into the keys, striking them aggressively. Then I started Chopin's Étude Op. 10, No. 12 in C minor, also known as the Revolutionary Étude. I ran my hands forcefully up and down the length of the keys as if the loud, angry roars of the music were my only voice.

As always, time blurred when I played, and eventually, I found myself sitting in the rays of the afternoon sun. My hands throbbed with pain, and blood from my wounded fingers speckled the keys.

Calmly, I rose and walked into the kitchen to get some Band-Aids and a glass of water. I rarely felt hungry. The thought of perishing was almost a relief to me, but in the end, I always forced myself to eat.

I was halfway through my cheese sandwich when I heard the giggle of children outside. At first, the sound was joyful to my ears, the warmth of their laughter cutting through my endless emptiness like no music ever could. But as I approached the living room window, I knew the group of kids gathered on the street wasn't here for comfort—they were here for torment.

"There she is, the witch girl," one of the girls yelled before hurling a snowball against the window. It burst upon impact, scattering snow dust across the glass.

"Get her!" yelled one of the boys, launching another snowball.

The group of kids started a relentless attack, throwing more and more, laughing and screaming until the first rock hit the window. It struck with a sharp crack, leaving a hole in the glass and hitting my forehead.

The group instantly ran off, laughing and screaming.

My first concern wasn't the blood trickling down my face. Instead, it was the broken window. Would my mother feel anger? Would she feel rage? Or would she wish I were dead again? Was there even a difference among these three? Which emotion would make her hate me less? Distinguishing these feelings was incredibly difficult. I vividly recalled the day the psychiatrists diagnosed me with severe alexithymia. The condition blurred my ability to understand my emotions and those of others. That same day, my mother coldly confessed she wished I had never been born. The specialists credited my exceptional musical abilities to Savant syndrome, but my mother, indifferent to the arts, saw me as nothing more than a mistake—a burden placed in this world to torture her.

As I stood there, watching the kids bolt down the street as if they were being chased by the devil himself, I couldn't help but wonder if anyone else in the world felt this hollow emptiness deep inside.

Chapter One

Boston, Now

Under the silvery glow of the moon, the quiet graveyard was pierced by the distinct sound of metal meeting earth. Across the scene, the moonlight draped eerie shadows that danced and shifted with every movement. The men's methodical shoveling joined the restless sway of tree branches in the night wind. White beams of flashlights added an artificial touch. They illuminated the fresh mound of dirt and the tombstone inscribed with the words:

Emanuel Marin. Born 1998, Died 2023. Loved & Loving Son. He is now with his beloved mother.

The warm breaths of the three men formed misty clouds as they unearthed the coffin. Their shovels dug relentlessly into the soft earth, each scoop revealing the darker, damp soil below.

When the first shovel hit wood with a muted thud, all movement ceased. The three men locked eyes. The skinniest among them, looking to be in his late forties, quickly made the sign of the cross, murmuring something in Italian.

The bulky man of the trio shook his head, his voice dripping with a mix of mockery and a Boston-Italian accent. "Seriously? You kill without blinking, but this has you wetting your panties?"

"It's holy ground, alright?" the skinny man snapped back.

"Would you two shut up?" the tallest interjected as he knelt on top of the walnut coffin, clearing from it a thin layer of dirt. He pried open the top, revealing a face hardly recognizable anymore, its skin a patchwork of green and brown, dried out and sunken in places. The foul stench that emerged made all three turn their heads and gag.

"Father, forgive us. We're just doing our job," the skinny one muttered, his face twisted in disgust. He got a saw from a black duffle bag and passed it to the tall man, who was kneeling over the corpse again. Eyeing the situation, he nodded in approval as his eyes narrowed from the odor.

"I think I can cut out the heart without opening the rest of the coffin."

"Then do it," the shorter one urged. "If we can get that shit cremated soon, we can be done with this before dawn and never talk about it again."

CHAPTER TWO

Rome, Italy

Leah

The blue and red lights from the police escort cut through the dark streets of Rome like a cavalry launching its attack. My limousine was part of a caravan transporting Europe's most powerful politicians. Every street was barricaded, with countless pedestrians raising their phones to record this event of a lifetime. Traffic had been redirected, allowing us to sail through red lights as though we were a plane in the endless, free sky.

I glanced at one of the Italian military snipers atop a tall apartment building and wondered if my silhouette was in his sight as we thundered by.

Before long, we rounded the final corner and arrived at our destination: the mighty Colosseum.

Illuminated under a starry sky, it stood as a testament to the long-forgotten glory of the ancient world. On an ordinary day, the Colosseum stood as a breathtaking reminder of ancient glories. But today, it was poised to etch its greatness into history once again, having been transformed into an energetic concert arena.

As the caravan approached, a massive crowd cheered. Metal barriers held them back from the main entrance. Awaiting us was a lavish red carpet flanked by a battalion of cameras, their flashes as blinding as lightning. Circling above the arena, news helicopters were like vultures on the hunt.

For a moment, I was awestruck, marveling at the fact that the Italian prime minister had actually pulled this off. When Emanuel passed away, I canceled my Europe tour without explanation. The sudden cancellation of my only overseas concerts in a continent that loves classical music as much as Americans love the Super Bowl struck its people with profound disbelief. Especially at a time when Europe itself struggled to hold on to its dream of unity.

The French prime minister personally called me, offering me the chance to play at Versailles. The Greeks followed with the Epidaurus Amphitheatre, Spain with the Sagrada Familia, and the UK, much to the outcry of post-Brexit Europe, with Wembley.

I rejected them all and directed my assistant to send a message to the Italian prime minister: I might consider playing at the Colosseum—not just using its exterior as a backdrop like at other performances but utilizing its heart, resurrecting it from its grave of ancient glory.

Even I couldn't hide my surprise when, the next day, I received a photograph via email depicting an army of engineers walking the Colosseum. The subject line read: We have a deal.

It was a task of gigantic proportions.

But the outcome was a masterpiece: fifty thousand seats, a central stage that seemed to echo the battles of ancient gladiators, and front-row seating reserved for Europe's elite.

Staring at this wonder of time in front of me, I adjusted the silk scarf draped over my naked shoulder. My dress, tailored exclusively for this occasion, was crafted from the finest black chiffon. The back revealed my slender frame, devoid of undergarments. The sides featured a slit extending to my upper thighs, showcasing a delicate thigh chain made of gold and diamonds. At the back, a prominent bow with a long train added a touch of nobility. This garment was an intersection of ancient Roman style and modern sex appeal, conceived solely for this event and costing me a whopping $200,000, not counting the jewelry. It was an unspoken truth that today's spectacle demanded unparalleled grandeur. The Colosseum wouldn't settle for anything less. Europe wouldn't settle for anything less.

"Could you drop me off at the back entrance?" I asked my driver in rusty Italian.

The middle-aged man glanced apprehensively in the rearview mirror, his eyes darting out the window to the procession of Europe's caravan of politicians. Ultimately, he made the right choice and veered the car aside. "Of course . . . La Imperatrice."

I stood beneath the enormous stage, feeling the presence of ancient gladiators who had once prepared in these depths to face their fate above. The Hypogeum, the Colosseum's intricate subterranean maze of tunnels and chambers, had housed both gladiators and wild animals before their turn in the arena.

From above, thin beams of light seeped through the cracks of the temporary stage, piercing the darkness to cast an ethereal glow around me. It was as if I had stepped into an eternal underworld.

The orchestra had just concluded Beethoven's 9th, and the applause reverberated through the structure, causing the ground beneath my feet to vibrate.

I bent down, took a handful of dirt in my hand, and squeezed it. For a fleeting moment, I felt as if I could hear the distant screams of the souls once sacrificed here.

"You have outdone yourself, La Imperatrice." Luca Domizio's voice resonated from behind me. "What you've achieved here . . . it's a marvel that will etch itself into history, never to be forgotten or replicated."

When I turned, I saw him clad in a pristine, hand-tailored white tuxedo. His fingers brushed the cold walls where gladiators and slaves had once stood. He belonged to the class of men who aged with grace, radiating a powerful presence that silently cautioned others against challenging him. His hair was a mix of black and silver and neatly combed back, complementing his long nose and thin lips.

His wide eyes reflected awe. "To witness this . . . here . . . bravissimo, La Imperatrice. Truly, bravissimo."

My gaze shifted upward. Through the stage's gaps, I caught fleeting glimpses of the orchestra members departing. I always performed solo; the risk of another musician ruining the performance was too great.

"I'm not fond of that title," I remarked, my voice devoid of emotion.

"You've revived the era of Rome's great emperors," he countered in a respectful tone. "It's their way of celebrating you. No woman since Maria Callas, The Divine, has been given such an honor. Calling you 'The Empress' is a fitting tribute considering where we stand, don't you think?"

As I reflected on this, I realized that emperors were often ruthless murderers. "Perhaps," I conceded hesitantly.

He nodded.

"Do you have it?" I asked, letting the dirt slip from my grasp.

"Yes." From his pocket, Luca produced a golden locket. It looked grotesquely opulent, swathed in diamonds and gold, each detail screaming of lavish extravagance.

"You shouldn't have." I fixed my gaze on the locket as its diamonds shimmered in the ambient light filtering in from the stage above.

I reached out to grab it but hesitated inches away. How could I ever dare to touch him again after he had died because of my mistakes?

Still, I allowed my fingers to graze the gold surface. Emanuel's gentle smile flashed before my eyes.

Pulling back, I handed Luca a note with the details of the resting place of Emanuel's mother at a cemetery outside Rome. As a first-generation immigrant, she had expressed her wish to return to Italy during her final weeks so that she could pass away surrounded by her four sisters. Emanuel had always told me that someday he'd reunite with her. It was his heartfelt wish.

Now he would.

"Could you have the locket buried at this grave?" I asked.

Holding the locket in one hand and the note in the other, Luca studied me, a hint of curiosity in his eyes. When I offered no further explanation, he tucked both items into his pocket. "A sad love story? Is that what this is all about?" With a sweep of his arms, he encompassed the grandeur of the Colosseum. "I didn't know you had a romantic side." He smirked playfully.

"I'm afraid my answer would leave you disappointed then," I replied.

Guilt and regret over Emanuel's death haunted me. The events leading up to it, my own blunders, tormented my sleepless nights. Reliving every mistake that led to this, over and over, threatened my sanity.

But no . . .

Emanuel's death hadn't transformed me into the stereotypical grief-stricken victim. I hadn't suddenly found faith in the afterlife or God. But

Emanuel believed in it. So, honoring his beliefs by reuniting him with his mother felt like the least I could do. After all, who was I to insist that my perception of the world was the only truth?

"Miss Nachtnebel." A young stage worker called for me.

I stepped into the dark corridor of the tunnel system.

She spotted me instantly, with a large crew of stagehands in tow. "It's time. We're ready when you are."

I acknowledged her with a nod and followed, leaving Luca behind.

We navigated through the ancient tunnels like famous gladiators, heading toward the massive stage entrance that had withstood the test of over two thousand years. With each step, spontaneous applause erupted from the concertgoers waiting for me in the hallways. Our group grew rapidly, coming to resemble the tail of a massive, applauding comet.

"Thirty seconds away," reported the stage worker into her headphones. Anxiety laced her voice.

As we neared the gate to the stage, the crowd around me grew rapidly into a large mass of people, their voices rising to manic shouts, their hands reaching out in a desperate attempt to grab at me.

"Bravissimo!"

"Bella!"

An older Italian woman, tears streaming down her face, managed to briefly grasp my arm. "La Imperatrice," she sobbed, as if our connection would bestow a blessing upon her like the touch of a saint.

Bodyguards swiftly aligned themselves into two protective lines flanking me, shielding me from the tidal surge of the frantic crowd.

"Twenty seconds," the woman ahead of me relayed into her headset as we approached the final tunnel to the stage. The tunnel's end radiated with a luminous light like a gateway to the beyond. "Three, two, one," she counted.

As we climbed the last set of stairs to the stage, all movement halted—except mine.

"Europe, your La Imperatrice has arrived!" a commentator announced ecstatically through the speakers of the mighty Colosseum.

In a breath, I transitioned from the shadowy passageways to the brilliantly illuminated stage of one of the seven wonders of the world. The gigantic arena erupted in an overwhelming cacophony, with tens of thousands leaping to their feet in an impassioned display of excitement.

The male commentator's voice resonated through the speakers: "The Colosseum lives again!"

For a moment, I stood there, taking it all in. Flowers started raining down on the stage, thousands of them, before I'd even touched a key.

Under the watchful eyes of its leaders, Europe had made a spectacle of this event, and the results were overwhelming. In the crowd were people dressed like ancient Romans, screaming and hollering as if this were a World Cup final. I wasn't a fan of such drama, yet I played my part.

With elegance and determination, I approached the applauding European delegates placed to the left of the stage, not far from my grand piano. I recognized them, all from the news and some from my concerts in Boston. Leaders from France, Germany, Italy, Spain, Portugal, Greece, the Netherlands, Norway, Belgium, Austria, Croatia, and Poland, a few kings and queens, the Pope, and the rest of Europe. They were all here for this classical version of the American Super Bowl.

Catching fleeting images of myself on the colossal screen strategically placed high above the temporary stages, I stopped before them and fluidly swirled the train of my dress. I dipped my head toward them—a gesture of respect but devoid of submission.

Then I turned to all four directions of the ecstatic crowd and expressed my gratitude with four similar nods.

The arena resounded with chants of "La Imperatrice," as though I had emerged victorious from months-long games of life and death in ancient Rome.

I paused for a moment, a fake smile on my lips, then gracefully made my way to my piano and took my seat behind it.

It was my first and only concert abroad. Europe's elite had spent ridiculous sums for their rare stage seats. But a glance at the politicians reminded me of the true message that this spectacle was conveying to the world. It wasn't solely in my honor. It was also intended to demonstrate that Europe, after years of struggles, stood united through one of the most magnificent events in its modern history.

And I was OK with that, as I, too, had come here with a hidden agenda. I had come to celebrate not Europe's light but its underworld.

For something priceless in return.

Liam

Rain blasted against my apartment window as if it were trying to break through. I sat on the couch, staring at the TV, my arm wrapped around Josie, who was absorbed in funny kitten videos on her tablet.

"What a concert!" the commentator announced euphorically.

On the screen, Leah was standing in the middle of the mighty Colosseum. Flowers were being thrown onto the stage as if it were raining there too.

"Angela, you've been quiet for some time now," the male announcer said.

"Yes, Bob . . . I'm just speechless, to be honest," answered Angela, the female commentator. "This was undoubtedly the most spectacular event I've ever had the honor of witnessing. To be here tonight and watch the Colosseum come to life like this . . . I'm fighting back tears."

"A feeling many probably share with you. They say that tickets sold out within a second of going live," Bob said.

I stared at the screen, my eyes fixed on Leah. She looked stunning in that black dress. Josie and I had caught only part of her performance after we'd returned from the mall, but it was the best I'd ever seen. Villain or not, this woman was truly one in a billion. Larsen was an asshole. He'd gotten what he deserved, but he sure as hell was right about that.

"Dad," Josie said, putting her tablet aside. "Can we watch the movie now?"

I was still glued to the TV, watching Leah accept roses from the Italian prime minister as the crowd cheered. Would Leah be able to make it to our meeting this weekend?

I pulled out the flip phone from my pocket.

"Earth to Dad!" Josie said.

"What, sweetheart?"

"You said we'd watch that new anime after the concert." She nodded at the TV.

I let out an exaggerated sigh and quickly texted Leah *MNY*, then put the phone on the table. "If you think," I said, turning to Josie and raising both hands, imitating claws with my spread fingers, "that I'd rather watch some big-eyed, neurotic cartoon characters with my daughter than one of the most important classical concerts of our time..." Josie started giggling the moment I tickled her side. "...then you are absolutely right!"

We both laughed as Josie wriggled under my attack like a worm on a hook.

Leah

My fingers flew over the aged piano keys in front of me as I played Liszt's "Grand Galop Chromatique," Cziffra's Version. It was known as one of the hardest pieces ever written if played at its intended speed.

The notes of Liszt's masterpiece echoed over the heads of Europe's political powerhouse and their fifty thousand guests as I delivered an immaculate performance of this extraordinary test of a pianist's capabilities. If every note was played correctly—which, due to the technical inability of the player, was the case less than 0.01 percent of the time—the piece would mimic the sound and rhythm of thundering hooves.

I entered the piece's intense finale at two minutes and forty seconds. My fingers turned into a hurricane, every single one of them tirelessly playing across the entire span of the keyboard, pushing the limits of my reach and control with precise strokes unmatched anywhere in the world. The treacherously wide stretches at a relentless pace required everything I had. I was renowned for being the only pianist in history—next to Liszt himself and Georges Cziffra—to play this piece in under three minutes and five seconds.

I played it in two minutes and fifty seconds.

Many years ago, MIT students employed a new software to detect the accuracy of musicians. They used it on the biggest names in music

Nobody matched my speed and accuracy.

Nobody.

Their study catapulted me to the top of the classical music world overnight. A star was born. A machine in human form.

I was sweating as I finished this madness of a piano piece. I played it seldom and only at the end of my concerts. I hated the feeling of sweat dripping from my forehead onto the keys, creating a slippery mess and endangering my accuracy.

With a last stroke, my hands hammered the end of the piece. A second of silence passed. Another.

Then the crowd of fifty thousand erupted into chaos. The air vibrated with chants and thunderous applause. Their voices melded into a harmonious roar, chanting "La Imperatrice," hailing me as their divine empress.

Yet . . .

Amid this frenzy, I stood completely still, an island in a stormy sea. I listened and observed, feeling an overwhelming sense of emptiness, a profound solitude that contrasted starkly with the chaos around me. Despite being the epicenter of one of the biggest events in the history of the European Union, I felt utterly alone.

Leah

The Colosseum faded behind me, its ancient stones still echoing the applause and melodies of the evening. The balmy Roman air enveloped me, mingling the scent of traffic and an earthy aroma.

Ahead, a gleaming black limousine stood in stark contrast to the illuminated Roman ruins in the background.

"Miss Nachtnebel!" a young assistant to the Italian prime minister called out, rushing after me.

I continued walking, but she managed to catch up.

"Miss Nachtnebel," the pantsuit-clad woman huffed, catching her breath.

I stopped to face her.

"The prime ministers and their guests have another gathering now. I apologize for the confusion."

I was about to answer her when my flip phone buzzed in my pocket. *MYN?* read the message from Agent Richter.

It made sense; I was still in Rome, and we were scheduled to meet this weekend at our usual spot. The *Meet Yes No?* inquiry was justified.

Y, I quickly texted back, then slid the phone into my purse. Finally, I turned to the waiting assistant, my face emotionless. "Please convey my deepest apologies to the prime ministers and their special guests, but I have other commitments. Thank you."

"W-what?" the young woman stuttered, her face reflecting utter disbelief.

Earlier in the evening, I had dined with the prime ministers and entertained their guests, consisting primarily of Europe's most influential manufacturers. After the concert, there had been a champagne reception. The prospect of yet another event with the stifling entitlement of the ultra-rich was a daunting as my next commitment.

"I said cancel it," I asserted with calm authority and resumed walking.

A tall man in a black suit got out of the passenger seat of the limousine and opened the door for me.

Inside, in the back, Luca Domizio glanced at the stunned assistant. A hint of amusement played on his lips.

"Drive," I instructed as I got in. I didn't share Luca's joy. A scandal like this could ignite global backlash—maybe not enough to destroy me but certainly enough to be extremely bothersome.

The limousine journeyed for about thirty minutes before the urban sights of Rome transitioned to the tranquil Italian countryside at night, with its rolling hills and iconic cypress tree silhouettes.

We ascended a gravel path leading to a majestic Italian castle whose façade glowed under gentle golden lights. A rustic dinner setting awaited outside, tables graced with grapevines, candles, and sumptuous Italian spreads. The bright sound of laughter filled the air as children darted among the tables, occasionally earning reprimands from the adults. Meanwhile, discreetly stationed security personnel in sleek black suits surveyed the scene.

As the limousine stopped, a diverse group of Italian men and women ceased their conversations and looked straight at us. The men, radiating both anticipation and respect, began to approach the vehicle, keen to welcome us.

I cast a wary glance at a grand piano positioned beneath an olive tree and, more importantly, at the gathering of Europe's top mafia dons. Their presence in these modern times was a testament to the enduring corruption that existed within global political systems.

"What am I doing here, Luca?" Frustration tinged my voice.

"Bellissima, you know exactly why you're here," he replied, a cunning smile gracing his elegant features as a security guard opened our door.

We remained seated.

"You're indebting me to you," Luca continued, his grin broadening. "A debt far beyond providing you with a dead junkie's fingers for false fingerprints or stalking FBI agents for you. A debt so profound, only I could repay it. And whatever it will be, you'll collect on it someday, whether that's in weeks or years. Or am I wrong?"

A lock of silver hair cascaded onto his forehead, emphasizing his intense gaze. I stayed silent, shifting my attention to the approaching group of mafiosi.

Luca chuckled. "Oh, my La Imperatrice." He stepped out and extended his hand to assist me. "May the gods who created you be eternally blessed."

Accepting his gesture, I emerged from the car. "Or the underworld they reside in," I countered. I faked a smile as an elderly mafioso, his skin weathered with age but his eyes sharp, gently took my hand. With a respectful nod, he pressed his lips to the back of my hand, the gesture exuding an old-world charm.

"Makes no difference to me," Luca interjected, taking his place beside me. "I was never afraid of the dark."

CHAPTER THREE

Liam

I was standing at the end of a weathered wooden dock, the gray sky casting a depressing shadow over what should've been a sunny fall day.

The growl of a bike caught my attention. I turned to find a light-colored dirt bike, its rider encased in a red and black leather suit. The bike skidded to a halt at the end of the dock. For a moment, the person just sat there, staring at me from behind a dark helmet visor.

My hand instinctively moved to the gun in my chest holster. Then the rider pulled off the helmet to reveal herself: Leah, strands of hair tumbling out of her lazy bun. She clutched her helmet and rode the dirt bike at full throttle down the long dock, coming to an abrupt halt just a few feet from me. Damn, she knew how to handle those things.

She dismounted with a smooth grace and stepped beside me. I caught a glimpse of her deep green eyes. Then my gaze shifted back to the waves crashing against the dock's old foundation.

"I didn't think you'd make it," I said.

"Didn't you get my text?" she replied.

"I did."

A brief, awkward silence followed. These meetings were still so weird to me, especially out here, next to this rundown old factory sprawled across a shitload of acres north of Boston.

"That was quite a concert. Maybe one of the most spectacular things I've seen on TV."

"The Colosseum did most of the work," Leah countered.

"Won't you need to lay low after pulling off such a spectacle?" I asked.

She shook her head and stepped even closer, entering my personal space and catching me off guard with her proximity. Her perfume filled my senses: an elegant floral scent with notes of yasmin, white peach, bergamot, and cedarwood. "For a short while, maybe. But the sort of people who attend my concerts aren't the type to stalk me for TikTok videos or want to read about me in trashy magazines."

I nodded. Thinking about it, I realized that I could walk past any classical superstar on the street without recognizing them.

"Do you have the files?" she asked, her voice as calm as ever.

"Yes." I handed her the folder with the reports and pictures from Emanuel's crime scene at the train station. "The photos are quite—" I started, wanting to warn her of their graphic nature.

However, she was already looking at them with an emotionless expression as if she were checking the weather.

I cleared my throat, attempting to be sensitive. It was hard to know what she was thinking. "I'm sorry about what happened to him," I continued. "I . . . eh . . . left his case with the police. I thought it best not to draw attention or have people wonder why the FBI was involved. The police wrote it off as just another case of a homeless person pushing someone in front of a train."

"Good," she said as she turned and made her way to a weathered wooden bench close by. As she sat there, her piercing green eyes scanned the reports and pictures. I watched her in silence before cautiously taking a seat beside her. Everything about this felt odd, especially considering I was sitting next to a serial killer of serial killers. A whirlwind of questions raced through my mind as her expensive perfume enveloped my senses again.

Who was she really? And how did she end up this way?

Was a storm of emotions raging behind her composed exterior as she sifted through the gruesome pictures? Or did she really feel nothing at all?

My eyes fell on the picture in her hands: Emanuel, his head and left arm severed cleanly by the train.

Jesus.

"I'm . . . so sorry," I mumbled again.

She remained silent, then shifted slightly in her seat. "You mentioned a note?"

I nodded. "One of the reports mentioned it. It was clenched in his fist, but those idiots lost it."

Her lack of surprise told me she knew the messy procedures of law enforcement all too well. "Does the report mention what was written on it?"

"There's a picture of his hand with the note. That's how I found out about it. I think it said something like—"

"Leros," she cut in, pulling out the close-up of Emanuel's hand with the blood-soaked note. Her eyes narrowed, and for a fleeting moment, something dark flickered in them.

"Do you know what it means?" I asked.

"Yes. It means nonsense."

"Nonsense?"

"Yes."

I frowned as Leah's expression darkened even more.

"Were you able to get a picture of Patel's autopsy?" Her voice had shifted and was now slightly lower.

"Yes." I leaned forward to retrieve it from the back pocket of my pants and handed it to her. "Sorry. I just got it this morning from the closed files. Work has been crazy, and this new agent, Rose, it's like she's spying on me for McCourt. Every time I turn around, she's right there."

Leah barely glanced at the picture before suddenly rising and handing it back to me. "It's not him," she declared, then walked to the dock's railing, where she gazed at the enigmatic expanse of the ocean.

"It's not who, Leah?" I asked.

"Patel," she said. "Patel isn't the Train Track Killer."

I sprang to my feet and joined her, the picture still in my grasp. "What? What do you mean Patel isn't the Train Track Killer?"

It looked as though she was collecting her thoughts. "Patel's shoulder. It should have a bullet wound."

I frantically examined the photo of Patel's bluish body on the steel autopsy table. "But there *is* a bullet wound, right here on his chest, at his heart," I protested.

"I know. I put it there," Leah admitted, openly disclosing how she had killed Patel. "But I also shot the Train Track Killer in the shoulder the night he dropped Anna on the tracks."

The gravity of her words hit me like a punch, and I stumbled back a step. "But . . . there's no bullet wound on Patel's shoulder," I said, stating the obvious.

"Precisely," she confirmed.

I took in a deep, shaky breath. "Are you trying to tell me that the Train Track Killer—" I couldn't even finish the sentence.

"Is still alive," she finished for me, turning to look straight into my eyes.

It took a moment for me to steady the sudden whirl of dizziness that clouded my thoughts. But then it set in. All of it. "Fucking Christ, Leah!" I scoffed. "Do you even realize what that means?"

"I do. And it makes sense when you think about it. Patel's profile never matched that of a genius serial killer. He was a brainless, sadistic follower."

"Maybe Patel didn't match the profile of a Hannibal, but what about all the other evidence?" I countered. "Anna's DNA was found in his van, and her grandmother's blood was also found all over him, confirming him as her killer. Anna testified it was him who killed her grandmother. Are you saying he was innocent?"

"Far from it."

Thank God. The relief came before nausea could hit.

"Patel did kill her grandmother and was most likely there when Anna was kidnapped the first time. His vehicle was probably also used for that. But he wasn't the man I met in the woods that night. The missing bullet wound confirms it."

A moment of silence passed. "He was working for him," I finally said in a weak voice. "It does make more sense that way. Patel was a struggling psycho, yes, but a genius?"

"Not so much," Leah confirmed.

"Goddammit."

She bit her rosy lower lip, an unusual gesture for her. "I've suspected for weeks that I made a mistake," she said. "But now it's confirmed. The Train Track Killer has outsmarted us."

Frustrated, I ran my hand through my hair as my eyes stared into nothingness.

"My daughter!" I suddenly exclaimed. "If this son of a bitch is still alive, I have to get her into protective custody ASAP."

I frantically patted down my pockets, searching for my phone, only to remember it was back at the apartment—ensuring I couldn't be traced. As I turned to sprint off, Leah's grip on my arm halted me. I froze, my gaze dropping to her small hand, clad in a leather glove. Touch like this was a new thing for her. Us.

"That won't be necessary. He won't hurt her," she assured me in a low, soothing voice.

"We don't know that. He killed Emanuel."

"Emanuel was an adult. The Train Track Killer has never harmed children. Not once. He must see them as innocent, almost sacred, maybe a reflection of his own painful view of childhood."

I stared into her eyes, wrestling with her words. Gradually, the tension in my muscles eased, and the dread of losing my daughter diminished. I trusted Leah. Trusted her instincts. But I had to be sure.

"Anna was barely a woman, and he tried to kill her."

"Anna is nineteen," Leah countered.

"Exactly. Still a kid."

A faint smile flickered across her lips. "Many men would consider Anna in the prime of their lust-driven pursuits."

I frowned. "Well, those old bastards have some soul-searching to do."

Her smile briefly widened, then disappeared. Under my watchful gaze, she slowly removed her hand from my arm, staring at it as if questioning why she had let it linger there for so long.

"Regardless, your daughter is safe. Which is more than I can say for us. But then, if he wanted us dead, it would have happened already."

"So, you think he knows who we are, and that we're on to him?"

"Most likely, yes."

"That makes no sense. Why leave us alive but kill Emanuel?"

Leah's gaze returned to the waves. "I . . . don't know."

It felt like an admission of failure.

We stood in silence, lost in thought, listening to the relentless crash of the waves.

"What do we know about him besides the fact that he's one of the smartest sons of bitches I've ever come across?" I asked. "And that he doesn't hurt children?"

"He's more than just smart." Her eyes darkened with intensity. "He's a genius. One in a billion. Probably highly successful and powerful, maybe even with a family of his own. He counted on me juggling too many chess pieces at once and starting to slip up. And he was right about that."

I caught the harsh self-criticism in her tone. "Leah, this isn't your fault."

"Of course it is," she shot back.

A pause lingered between us once more.

"Do we have any leads? Any clues we can pursue?" I asked, desperation seeping into my voice. "What about the symbol he leaves at the crime scenes?"

"The ankh."

"Isn't it the Egyptian symbol of life and death?"

She nodded. "I had a meeting scheduled with an Egyptologist in DC. I didn't follow through because I thought we had identified the killer with Patel's capture."

"We should follow up on that now. Do you want to meet with this expert, or should I?"

"I will. On my way back from Ocean City."

My expression darkened.

Ocean City. Fucking Harvey Grand.

"So, we're really doing this?" I asked hesitantly.

"Of course." The certainty in Leah's voice was astonishing. "Is he still in Ocean City at the Caribbean Dreams Inn?"

I took a deep breath and exhaled slowly, preparing myself for what lay ahead. "Yes," I finally said. "The inn is booked until the end of the week. He just got another advance from his publisher."

"The timing is perfect. People don't expect me back from Europe yet."

"Is there no other way?" I asked.

"Of course there is," she said, "but it all depends on what you're hoping for. We could accept the outcome of our broken justice system—a system where a man who killed dozens of people and was found with more evidence than Dahmer gets to whore around, gamble, and then write a book about it. But will we accept what happens next?"

"Which is?" I probed.

"I assume you know the difference between a sociopath and a psychopath?" she asked.

"There are many, but overall, a sociopath is an out-of-control savage while a psychopath is a calculated genius."

She nodded. "We both know what Harvey Grand is. A thirteen-year-old could have dumped his Googled poison mix into a public well. Harvey even used a credit card to purchase the supplies and didn't even bother to disguise himself. This man is a sociopath with the IQ of an average pig. To him, it's always been about attention, rage, and financial gain. Once one of those diminishes, he'll strike again, probably in the same manner, seeking the same result. We all know he'd end up in prison when that happened, but by then, more people would have paid the price for the unimaginable luck life has bestowed upon him."

I leaned over the old wooden railing, staring into the ocean.

"There were women and children among the victims," Leah added.

"There were," I confirmed, balling a fist. Leah was right. Families were mourning at their loved ones' graves while this monster was gambling and snorting coke in casinos across the country. "Let's get him," I said, my voice laced with determination. "But no Harris crime scene, you hear me? The image of Harris's face tied to that tree in the woods still haunts me at night."

Leah pushed off the railing beside me. "Don't waste your dreams on a piece of shit like Harris. They don't deserve to live on through us."

I met her gaze. "I mean it, Leah. We'll use drugs. It worked with Harris, really threw our investigation off. Grand has a long history of substance abuse. Nobody will question an overdose."

Her eyes narrowed briefly—was it disappointment at missing out on the thrill of torture? Or did my commanding tone unsettle her?

Eventually, she nodded. "Drugs," she conceded, then turned and walked over to her bike. "Do you know how to ride a dirt bike?" she asked, gracefully swinging a leg over one side.

I raised an eyebrow. "I grew up white and poor. What do you think?" Confidently, I approached her bike, examining it closely. "Looks like this bike was meant for someone much heavier. The suspension's too stiff for you. Must be hard to control." I pointed out the insufficient sag.

A wide grin spread across Leah's face, showing a mix of admiration and amusement. "Impressive, Agent Richter." She pulled a piece of paper from the bike's storage bag and handed it to me. "These are coordinates for alternative meeting locations. Memorize them and burn the paper. If you ever think you're being followed, don't return here. Text me a different meeting location using this map, and ride a bike through the woods to reach it. No calls."

I accepted the map as a mix of astonishment and worry crept in. She'd thought of everything. If Leah ever turned against me, how in the world would I outplay her?

"What about Anna?" I asked. "Is she safe from him as well?"

"He hasn't killed her yet, though that doesn't mean we're in the clear. As I said, she's not a child, and she was already on his list."

"I need to talk to her ASAP," I said.

"That won't change much. I've already spoken to her."

"To Anna?"

Leah nodded. "I wasn't sure he was still alive, but I warned her, nonetheless. I offered her a substantial sum and a fake passport from her country of choice, but she declined."

My head snapped back in surprise. "Why the hell would she do that?"

Leah shrugged. "Probably for the same reason most make foolish choices."

I raised an eyebrow. "Which is?"

"Matters of the heart, of course."

"You mean she met a guy?"

"Or a woman. This is the twenty-first century, Agent Richter," she teased with a smirk.

"Yeah, yeah. Man or woman, the foolish girl still needs protection."

"She made her choice. And explaining to law enforcement why you're protecting her could severely complicate things, especially if the FBI catches wind that the Train Track Killer is still out there."

"I'll figure something out. Blame it on a copycat or something."

Leah raised an eyebrow, doubt shadowing her features. "If he really wants her dead, the only way to ensure her safety is to eliminate him or send her away. Far enough for him not to bother with it. A simple patrol car outside Anna's place won't cut it."

I cursed under my breath, hating everything about this situation yet knowing Leah was right. "Then why not go public with it? Announce he's still alive. Put everything the FBI has behind this."

"I'd advise against that. Parts of the investigation would leak to the media, and we'd be openly at war with him. Not wise when you don't know who your enemy is or what motivates him."

I mulled over her words.

Leah watched me carefully, then put on her helmet. "At least wait until I've handled this other matter. Then do as you wish," she said, her voice wavering slightly. "And keep that gun with you at all times," she added, kicking down the kickstarter lever to revive the engine. "We're up against someone who might be cunning enough to take us both down. Just because it hasn't happened yet doesn't mean we're safe. I'll reach out after Grand is neutralized and I've met with the Egyptologist. Let me know if you find anything else."

I nodded, watching her ride off into the distance past the decaying factory complex and disappear down a narrow trail in the woods. I sighed as the weight of our reality sank in. The whole situation was utterly surreal.

The Train Track Killer was still out there, slipping through the FBI's grasp, outsmarting the most brilliant mind I'd ever known. My new reality rang with the clarity of a bell in a graveyard. I needed Leah more than ever. It wasn't just about Anna or the countless others in the crosshairs of the Train Track Killer; it was about me too. She had become my sole ally in a game in which I'd crossed the point of no return. But could I truly place my trust in someone who regarded the dismembered remains of her former lover with less engagement than someone scrolling through reels on Instagram?

But what other option did I have? Leah Nachtnebel wasn't a hero, but in an era when darkness brought order to justice, a villain of her caliber was exactly what the world needed. She was the most ingenious person I'd ever met. As things stood, she was our only hope in capturing one of the worst killers to walk the earth.

CHAPTER FOUR

Leah

The darkness provided my only solace as I stood in the moldy closet of a room at Caribbean Dreams Inn, a decrepit seaside motel in Ocean City. It was around 3:00 a.m., two torturous hours after Harvey Grand had stumbled back from the casino, completely wasted. My senses were assaulted as I witnessed this five-foot-five abomination fucking two drug-addicted prostitutes he'd brought along. Their inability to hide their contempt was evident, their moans of fake pleasure a pathetic attempt to continue. One of them was so high she fell asleep with his dick still in her mouth and inadvertently bit down on him. Enraged, the yellow-toothed piece of shit struck her and broke her nose. Blood streamed down as it hung grotesquely to the side. But she was so high that she barely seemed to notice the pain and passed out on the couch with a wide grin.

The other prostitute, a bony figure with bruises all over her limbs, remained silent, clutching her next hit as Harvey decided to take her doggy style. With a pitiful grunt, he dismounted. Then she, too, succumbed to the heroin, collapsing on the filthy couch with a vacant smile.

"Stupid whores almost used all the smack," he cursed, scavenging through the debris on the table—empty beer cans, used needles, crumpled chip bags, and loose bills. I watched in disgust as Harvey cooked the leftover heroin on a spoon over a candle, drew it into a needle, and shot it into his vein.

There was nothing genius about Harvey Grand. A man who'd lucked out with an aunt who had married into a wealthy family and was capable of affording lawyers who played the justice system like a child played with a toy.

I lingered for a few more moments, then cautiously edged the closet door open and stepped into the room. Cloaked in a black coverall and booties, I was a ghost, leaving no trace of my presence. My steps, silent and deliberate, carried me past the couch on which the two unconscious prostitutes were sleeping. The scene was a bleak testament to the wickedness I was about to end.

Approaching the grimy lounge chair, I stopped in front of Harvey. His head was tilted back, his wide-open mouth revealing uneven yellow teeth.

Shaking my head slowly, I acknowledged the simplicity of the task at hand. This oceanfront motel was the perfect setting for an "accidental" overdose. Harvey had been partying and sleeping with prostitutes for days, and the motel's ground-floor layout and bathroom window, facing the dark beach beyond, made it easy to enter and leave unnoticed. Nobody would question anything.

Suddenly Agent Richter's voice echoed in my mind: "No Harris crime scene."

I fixed my gaze on Harvey with a mix of disgust and resolution.

"Use drugs," Richter had advised.

A wry smile touched my lips as I delved into my coverall's pocket and withdrew two syringes—one filled with a clear liquid, the other filled with a caramel-hued substance.

I set the caramel syringe on the cluttered coffee table and administered the clear liquid into the median cubital vein in Harvey's arm, precisely where he'd injected his last hit of heroin. Swiftly, I withdrew the needle, securing it safely in my pocket with the cap reattached, ensuring I left no evidence behind.

The moment the Narcan—a medication negating the heroin's effects—coursed through Harvey's system, his eyes snapped open. He gasped for air as though he were rising from the grave.

"What the fuck?" he spluttered as his bloodshot and bewildered gaze locked onto me. The drug had cleared the opiate fog but left the alcohol haze untouched. "Who the fuck are you?" he slurred, confusion written all over his face.

I mustered a seductive smile and picked up the other syringe from the coffee table. "I'm Cindy, remember?" I gestured toward the two unconscious women on the couch. "Jenny called me. Said you were looking for more fun. Twenty for a blow, fifteen for a hit of smack." I waved the needle before him.

He wiped his mouth, which was a mess of saliva, and leaned in sluggishly. "Why you dressed like that?" he mumbled, reaching for the syringe I held just beyond his grasp.

"Got a cleaning gig later at the Sea Lion Motel," I cooed, my voice dipped in fake allure. "Lean back, let me take care of you. That makes fifteen plus twenty for the blow, yeah?"

His response was a grotesque grin. He smelled like semen and whiskey, yet I knelt between his legs, which were spread open in anticipation. "You've gotta try this." I leaned closer, whispering the lie with practiced ease. "Right here, I mean." I pointed at his neck. "In an artery. Hits you ten times harder, sends the gold straight to your head, arms, even your dick."

Harvey's grin widened, lulling in excitement. "Fuck yeah, bitch."

"Good boy," I whispered back, my gaze and steady hands fixed intently on the delicate skin of his neck near his collar bone.

What I didn't share with this sociopathic asshole was that I was aiming for his right common carotid artery, intending for my special mixture to bypass his heart to avoid dilution. Finding arteries was a challenge; unlike veins, they weren't visible, and despite my extensive, costly private education from physicians in the art of anatomy and medicine, my first attempt missed. Harvey flinched as I withdrew the long needle before swiftly repositioning and trying again. This time, I hit my mark. The needle's resistance against the strong flow of blood confirmed it. Bright red blood backfilled into my syringe, mingling with the caramel liquid. I pushed the plunger, injecting the mixture into Harvey's neck. Then I stepped back, watching him closely.

He reacted with a growl of pleasure, his body tensing in anticipation. "Fucking bitch, yeah," he groaned, gripping the armrests of the lounge chair. But his ecstasy quickly shifted to surprise. Then shock. Then horror.

"What the fuck is—" he choked out, his complexion turning a fiery red, his eyes bulging.

"Krokodil," I stated coolly, watching as he collapsed to his knees and clawed at his throat. "A little parting gift from the families of Newcastle. They didn't appreciate the poison you put into their water. And, frankly, neither did I. So the emphasis is on *parting*, I suppose."

Harvey's screams, initially choked, erupted while his red face conveyed pure terror. It was as if flames were engulfing his entire body— which, in a way, they were.

"I modified the recipe, adding more paint thinner and introducing hydrofluoric acid. That explains the platinum needle and special gloves," I said. "This mixture is extremely hazardous and will cause internal corrosion. I also mixed in a blood thinner to ensure my cocktail spreads quickly throughout your body, targeting as many areas as possible until it finally attacks your heart. How do you like it?"

Harvey's screams morphed into a ghastly wail as the drug began corroding his insides at his neck and face. Raw, exposed tissue emerged before my eyes as patches of skin and red flesh seemed to dissolve into the air, transforming him into a figure straight out of a zombie apocalypse.

"I lcccccelp!" he shrieked, staggering to his feet. In a clumsy motion, he clutched at the nearest prostitute, the one with long blonde hair. She jolted awake to the nightmare of his melting visage and chest—a horrifying blend of red flesh and white bone laid bare.

The woman's frantic scream matched his in intensity as she scrambled away, pulling Harvey with her. He maintained his grasp on her hair as they fled past the large dresser, where I swiftly concealed myself, and out the door. Harvey stumbled along, dragged like a blind man by a service dog. He maintained his grip until he tumbled over the porch steps. The abrupt fall yanked a large strand of hair from the woman's head.

The screams drew a few curious onlookers to the courtyard. Their initial intrigue turned to terror as they witnessed the macabre scene unfolding before them.

Lurking in the shadows of the motel room, I observed as Harvey's last moments unfolded on the grimy concrete of the motel's walkway. A frantic crowd gathered around him. Their desperate cries for help filled the room.

I was about to make my way toward the bathroom window through which I'd slipped inside when I paused beside the prostitute with the gruesomely twisted nose. She had miraculously slept through the entire show. Overdose, or just a deep high?

Gently, with gloved hands, I checked her pulse. It was steady and slow. The situation with her nose wasn't as encouraging; it was jarringly sideways and covered with blood. Even if she made it to a hospital, without top-notch medical care, which I doubted she could afford, it would never look the same. An outstanding plastic surgeon could fix it later, but a woman like her wouldn't be on the client list for something like that.

Her only other option would be for someone knowledgeable to snap it back into place before the swelling began. That would need to happen immediately.

On impulse, I realigned her nose to its natural position.

I didn't stop there. Quickly, I pulled her underwear back up, then put the table's cash into her purse.

As the chaos outside escalated, I slipped through the bathroom window and onto the dark, deserted beach, where the night air—cool and salty—surrounded me. The rhythmic crash of waves and the moon's reflection on the water cast a tranquil spell. Shedding my coverall, I walked up to the edge of the high tide.

Why had I intervened on behalf of the prostitute? Why had her misfortune suddenly become my problem?

The wail of distant sirens intruded upon my thoughts, pulling my mind to Agent Richter. Had that act been for him? A bid to sprinkle a dash of humanity over my actions tonight, knowing this case would inevitably land on his desk?

Harvey's gruesome end replayed in my mind. Richter wouldn't approve, of course, yet part of me reveled in the justice of it all. If I was indeed softening, even if just for Richter's sake, it changed nothing about the aftermath. I wasn't a hero or a knight in shining armor. I was the darkness that hunted monsters, and a single act of kindness to a prostitute wouldn't elevate me from the depths.

That was fine by me.

At the end of the day, my feelings on the matter were ambivalent.

Chapter Five

Agent Vallery Rose

"Come on!" Agent Vallery Rose huffed loudly, gasping for breath as she landed another blow on the punch bag. This was followed by a forceful side kick. The large red bag, suspended from her basement ceiling, was the final challenge in her rigorous morning routine. For Rose, excellence was the only acceptable outcome in every aspect of her life.

"Come on, I said one more!" she urged herself, sweat flying from her ebony skin as her fists and feet moved with increasing ferocity. "I said," she grunted with each punishing kick as if chastising herself for even considering fatigue as an excuse to stop. "One." Another determined kick. "Moooooore!" Her final kick sent her to her knees.

Pausing, she leaned forward, trying to catch her breath as she rested her hands on her thighs. A fleeting image of her brother smiling during a sunny day at the zoo crossed her mind before thankfully disappearing.

After a long shower, Rose dressed in her crisp suit pants and white shirt, her gun securely in its holster. Breakfast was the usual affair: organic eggs and gluten-free toast with a cucumber-spinach-apple smoothie, consumed in solitude at the kitchen table of her quaint three-bedroom single-family home in Roxbury. The only sounds were the ticking of the kitchen clock and the clink of dishes being placed in the sink.

As a college graduate with a good job, she could have moved to a suburb with farmers markets and bicycle lanes. But her childhood memories of a loving mother and brother anchored her to every corner here. It wasn't the safest of places, yet she stayed, devoting her free time to community projects and her garden.

After donning her blazer and smoothing down a strand of her bob, she attended to her Glock 19 Gen 5—a top-tier handgun reflecting the FBI's standards for excellence. Every morning and night, she checked the ammunition, locked the slide to the rear for a visual inspection of the chamber (clear) and then cycled the slide to ensure it moved freely. Satisfied with its functionality, she reassembled the gun and holstered it. With a final, contemplative look in the hallway mirror, she reminded herself in a quiet but determined voice, "We get to see what happens only if we don't give up."

With that, she stepped out, ready for the day.

She had barely left the home and made it past her beloved flowerbed with its blooming rose bushes when she saw a parking ticket on the windshield of her black SUV, which was parked in her driveway.

Muttering curses, she pulled it out and waited for—

"Rooooooose!"

The urgent call from an older neighbor across the street amplified her annoyance.

"Rooooooose!" called out the older white man who was limping across the quiet street. Rose tried to ignore him and get into her car. However, he caught up quickly and prevented her door from closing by wedging himself between her and the handle. The smell of cigarettes filled the car.

"You see this, Rose?" With visible frustration, he pointed at the parking ticket in her hand. "Another one, Rose. They gave me another one."

Leaning back in her seat, Rose muttered something inaudible. Then she spoke up. "Billy, please stop putting your parking tickets under my windshield wiper. How many times do I have to tell you this? I'm not a traffic cop. I work for the FBI."

Billy placed his hands on his hips, his demeanor turning defiant. "And that makes you blind to injustice?" he challenged.

Rose exhaled, offering him the ticket. "When it comes to parking violations, yes. Besides"—she raised an eyebrow at him—"I've warned you about parking in front of the hospital when you go to your appointments."

"It's a spot reserved for individuals with disabilities. I'm a disabled vet," Billy retorted.

"And I thank you for your service. But that spot is for ambulances," Rose clarified. "To save people's lives, you know. You're lucky they squeezed by and didn't tow you."

Billy mumbled a disgruntled reply before snatching the ticket with a sharp yank.

Rose shut her door and started the engine, but Billy knocked urgently on her window. She rolled it down, frowning. "Damn it, Billy, I'm going to be late."

"It's Kevin," he said, a hint of defensiveness in his voice as he presented a black backpack to her. "He didn't come home last night. That boy is nothing but trouble."

With another sigh, Rose accepted the backpack, realizing this would make her late for work. But unlike the parking ticket, this problem was of genuine importance. She knew exactly where to find Kevin, who had lately been spending too much time with the B street gang—a choice that had destroyed his good grades.

Rose drove to the local 24/7 corner store, directly in view of a group of young men sprawled on old couches in the adjacent empty lot. As she parked her car, her gaze briefly met that of Hassan, the shop owner, who nodded with concern toward the group. She understood the gesture wasn't out of fear but rather to indicate Kevin's whereabouts.

This part of the neighborhood, one of Boston's last remaining projects, was familiar territory for those. She had grown up here, and she was well aware that, despite the hardships, many in this community banded together. They wanted to protect their youth from a nation governed by the wealthy one percent who didn't give a shit about the demise of the other ninety-nine. The community was a mix of young and old from various ethnic backgrounds. However, they had one thing in common: the struggle to survive and pay the bills.

Backpack in hand, Rose got out of the car and made her way toward the group. Almost instantly, the men averted their eyes and mumbled inaudible curses. She knew nearly all of them—men and women from all sorts of backgrounds, but all too deep in the criminal justice system for a simple school diploma to make a difference. In Boston, gangs usually formed based on where they were located, differing even from one street to the next. In Rose's area, a few gangs were racially mixed, mirroring the neighborhood's diversity. This mixing was boosted by the fact that young folks of different backgrounds hung out together in school and local spots.

"Come on, Kevin. Let's go," Rose said firmly to a teen dressed in jeans and a hoodie. "I don't have time for this." She presented the backpack as if it were incriminating evidence in court.

Kevin ignored her, looking at his phone as if she weren't there.

"Dude, it's Nario's little sister," one of the guys muttered to Kevin before shifting his attention back to his phone. The others disengaged, quietly scrolling on their devices.

Rose furrowed her brow at Kevin. "At least have the decency to face me when I'm talking to you, Kevin. Otherwise, I won't let your ass stay with me the next time your grandparents kick you out."

Kevin finally turned, a hint of remorse on his face. "What you doing here, Rose?"

"Getting your ass to school on time."

He shrugged in defiance. "Why bother? My school is a joke. Up in Beacon Hill, their kids get salad bars and MacBooks. My piece of shit school is stuck with metal detectors and PFAS in the water fountains. I don't care about no diploma. There are other ways to make money."

Rose nodded. "Salad bars and PFAS, huh?" The hint of irony in her voice inspired a few grins among the group. "Other ways to make money. I see," Rose mumbled. "Well, if you want to throw your future away over a salad bar and quick cash, then by all means, go ahead. Just do me a favor and don't walk around acting like it's big news that rich people don't give a shit about us small people."

She stepped closer to the group, her presence commanding. "Because, Kevin, we already know that there isn't a salad bar or a MacBook waiting at school for you or anybody else around here. But nobody's going to fight your battles for you. You gotta do that on your own, like all the other kids in your class. Does that suck? Hell yeah, it does. But guess what? That quick cash you make right now won't be worth much when your ass sits in jail, will it? So stop the excuses and get in the car."

Kevin hesitated, scanning the group for support that didn't come.

"Go, man. School is important. We'll catch up later," Vito said.

Rose locked eyes with Vito. A higher-tier gang leader in the neighborhood, he had earned a lot of respect from the younger guys. He was in his late thirties and had outlived more than one gang shooting. The hardship of a life of violence was evident in every inch of him.

Finally, with an eye roll and a series of handshakes, Kevin took the backpack from Rose and headed toward her car. Rose felt a fleeting sense of relief, as she was aware this could have gone differently. She nodded to the boys and returned to her car.

"You know he's right," Vito called out to her as soon as Kevin was inside the car.

"Of course he is," she shouted back, "but we get to see what happens only if we don't give up."

Sliding into the car beside Kevin, Rose sighed. She would be late for work—a fact that unsettled her. That nagging sixth sense in her gut warned her that today wasn't a day to be late. And her intuition was almost never wrong.

CHAPTER SIX

Liam

"And don't you fucking dare talk to the media! None of you. Everything goes through me first," warned McCourt's voice through the phone. I leaned forward, resting my elbows on the desk, which was cluttered with papers. Heather, Cowboy, Martin, and a few other agents were packed into my cramped office. They stood before me, their expressions a mix of anticipation and shock.

"Understood. No one's speaking to the press," I said, giving Cowboy a stern look. "Not a word. I promise," I pressed, my gaze hardening.

Cowboy, trying to play innocent, mouthed a *what* as he raised his hands. Yet this same "innocent" man had blabbed for a low-budget documentary about the College Snatcher, posing in front of a cheesy black cloth backdrop like he was Charles Bronson reborn. McCourt had quietly suspended him for a week, making me play babysitter. Meanwhile, McCourt watched closely through Vallery Rose's scrutinizing eyes.

She entered the room, her forehead creased with concern. "What's going on?" she asked.

Heather put a finger to her lips, signaling for silence.

"Liam, I need that bastard taken care of quietly," McCourt barked, his voice echoing across the room. "No drama. No hiccups. Like a beautiful Sunday stroll with Granny through Boston Common."

"Yes, sir," I responded.

McCourt ended the call without another word.

"Can someone catch me up?" Rose asked as the others began to grumble to one another.

"Harvey Grand. Remember him?" Cowboy asked.

"The well water poisoner?" Rose asked.

Cowboy's grin widened. "He overdosed in Ocean City, partying with drugs and whores."

I watched Rose closely, gauging her reaction.

"Holy shit," she said, hands landing on her hips.

"Nothing 'holy' about it," Heather chimed in. "We've been told his body is in a pretty rough state."

"From the drugs?" Rose asked.

Heather shrugged.

"We're still putting the pieces together," I said, rising. "They confirmed his identity after matching his prints with those we have on file from his time in jail. McCourt wants us to head there immediately on a military plane, retrieve the casket, and deliver it to his aunt somewhere near Boston. The exact location's still undisclosed."

"Why the hell would we do all that with taxpayer money?" Heather asked.

I pinched my lips. I'd wrestled with that exact question the moment McCourt had given me the instructions to retrieve Harvey Grand from Ocean City.

It almost pained me to admit this—almost—but the thought of Harvey being dead gave me an unsettling feeling of peace. He couldn't harm anyone else ever again.

"Harvey Grand was never convicted of any crime," I explained. "His family is fully aware of the accusations against him and expressed concerns about the safety of his remains if they were transported back without protection and under public scrutiny. They've provided evidence of threats to their personal safety."

"So, in short," Cowboy interjected, "the bastard's aunt was a Marilyn Monroe lookalike in her prime and married into one of the wealthiest, most powerful families on the East Coast. Now they're stealing government resources to quietly bring back the body as if nothing ever happened, all because they've lined the pockets of half of DC with campaign donations."

I frowned. Cowboy's crude summary was spot on, but my focus was on minimizing office drama. McCourt was more volatile than ever. His ambitions to become the next FBI director had found new life amid the dissatisfaction in DC with the current director, Helen Finch. Since then, he'd doubled down, staying mostly at the office in DC and weaving a network of informants throughout the FBI to report directly to him. Agent Vallery Rose was his eyes and ears in Boston.

"Thanks, Cowboy," I said, my tone heavy with fatigue. "Why don't you coordinate with Hanscom Air Force Base for our transport? They're briefed and ready to fly us out to Ocean City to collect the body. If everything goes smoothly, we'll be back before our shift ends."

Cowboy snapped a quick military salute and made his exit. I wasn't thrilled about bringing him along, but he wasn't the sharpest tool in the shed, which could be an asset given my arrangement with Leah.

"Heather, Rose, you're coming with me," I continued. "The rest of you, back to work. We've got full support from the military and the local Maryland police, so there's no need to turn this into a spectacle."

"What about the Bay Reaper?" Heather asked. "I was supposed to meet with the Cape Cod police this afternoon to interview a potential suspect."

Damn. I had completely spaced on that. Some lunatic in a skull mask was out there stabbing people along the bay, earning himself the media nickname Bay Reaper. Thankfully, there were no fatalities, but he needed to be stopped. Now.

"Take Martin with you," I directed. "I'll manage with Rose and Cowboy."

Heather and Martin nodded and departed with the rest, leaving me with Rose.

Her gaze lingered on me, probing. "So, we're really doing this? Getting Grand for his rich aunt?" she asked.

"I'm afraid we don't have much of a choice."

"It'll look like we're guarding his remains. The remains of a mass murderer."

"We're safeguarding the public around those remains," I countered. "Harvey Grand made plenty of enemies. If someone attempted to attack his coffin, it could endanger others."

Rose folded her arms, her stance firm. "Everyone here sees this for what it is—a powerful family abusing their influence."

"Maybe," I conceded. "But McCourt's orders were loud and clear, literally, and we'll follow them. This operation stays as quiet as possible. And if, by some chance, someone does target the coffin, we'll be there to handle it. Public safety is our top concern."

Her stance seemed to soften slightly, though I was taken aback by the fact that she'd questioned McCourt's orders, especially given her role as his informant.

As I began tidying the papers on my desk, I noticed Rose hadn't left. Her gaze was fixed on me, expectant. "Is there anything else?" I asked.

Rose pinched her lips. "I . . . overheard an agent coordinating a patrol car for Anna Smith when I walked in."

Shit.

"Yes?" I prodded, feigning ignorance. Until now, nobody had questioned it.

"Well, the Train Track Killer is dead, so . . . why?"

I shuffled the papers into a manila folder, deliberately avoiding eye contact to downplay the situation. "A threat was made to her life. Probably just some teenager messing with us, but better safe than sorry." I looked up just as Rose was about to speak again. "Where were you this morning?" I asked.

Immediately, I regretted it. No one here needed micromanaging except maybe Cowboy. Typically, I didn't question comings and goings; my agents had their reasons. But whatever Agent Rose was chasing with the whole Anna thing needed to stop.

Her expression shifted from inquisitive to embarrassed. "I . . . was dealing with something personal."

"Next time, please call. I need to know where my agents are during duty hours."

"Yes, sir. It won't happen again. I promise."

"Thank you." Rose turned and exited.

As I watched her leave, my thoughts raced. How had Larsen managed this dance with Leah without getting caught? Most of the details of this new collaboration with Leah remained shrouded in mystery.

Harvey Grand's downfall ensured the world was now a safer place, and the fact that Leah had gotten out safely was equally comforting. But the stress of our secret operations weighed heavily. A cunning agent might start connecting dots and Tillery Rose could very well be that agent.

Cowboy's presence at the door caught my attention. "That's not how you make friends, you know." He jerked his thumb over his shoulder in the direction of Agent Rose.

"This isn't high school. We're not here to make friends. We're here to stop psychopaths and sociopaths."

"Wait, is there a difference between the two?"

I sighed. "Cowboy, whatever you're here for, can it wait? Because today is quite—"

"You need to hear this!" he interrupted, full of joyful energy. The way he stomped in was annoying as hell. I leaned back in my seat and watched as he sat across from me. Silence fell as he grinned, barely able to hold back.

I shrugged. "Sooooooo, you gonna spill the big news or what?"

"You'll never guess."

"You're right about that, so just say it now, and I mean right this second." My patience had run thin.

"Alright, alright," Cowboy said. "I just got a phone call that blew my mind."

I straightened in my seat, as would anyone who was hiding a second identity as a killer of killers. Had Leah gotten caught?

"We all got played," he said, grinning. "Right here in Boston, under our noses, lives one of the worst serial killers of all time."

Every inch of my body tensed. Would Cowboy bring us down?

"The Boston Strangler..." he finally said.

I sank into my chair, relieved. Then his words hit. "The fucking what?" I countered.

"The Boston Strangler," he repeated. "Never heard of him?"

"Do you think I grew up under a rock? I'm from Boston. Of course I've heard of him," I said. "His case involved a series of murders of women in the Boston area between 1962 and 1964. The victims were mostly older women who were raped and strangled. Albert DeSalvo confessed to the murders while in custody for other crimes, but no evidence conclusively linked him to any victims until a DNA test in 2013 connected him to the death of Mary Sullivan. Yet quite a few people believe there might have been a second Strangler because DeSalvo's stories don't add up for all the victims."

Cowboy nodded enthusiastically. "Yup. I'm one of those many believers. And not only did that second Strangler get away, but he actually still lives here in town." He leaned over my desk. "Right under our noses. Like some twisted fairy-tale ending for a sick fuck. Who knows? He might kill again, for all we know."

I sighed. "The Boston Strangler, part two."

"Mm-hmm."

"And somebody called you, huh?" I asked.

He nodded. "A tip."

"A tip," I repeated.

He nodded again, his eyes filled with sparks.

"Cowboy..." I sighed loudly. "Even if there were a second killer, the Boston Strangler killed in the early sixties."

"So?"

"So..." I sighed again. "Let's just say, for the sake of argument, that whoever murdered those women was in their twenties back then. How old do you think that person would be now?"

The wheels turned in his head. I watched his excitement slowly turn to disappointment. "Old?" he asked, like a school kid guessing the answer to a teacher's question.

"Very, very, very old," I said. "Too old to kill anyone. Most likely even dead. Sorry, buddy. Is there anything else I can help you with?"

Cowboy frowned and stood. "Too bad. I grew up watching documentaries about him. The guy is a legend in all the worst ways. I really hoped he'd get caught."

I sympathized with Cowboy. This work could be draining. "We have to focus on those we actually catch," I said, also rising. "And you're doing an amazing job making that happen. I'm glad to have you on the team."

His eyes lit up with pride, and he smiled, about to leave.

"The Strangler..." I tossed out.

"What about him?"

"Just out of curiosity, what did the tip say?"

"Oh, yeah. Some woman called and said her dad talks in his sleep about strangling women. Maybe he's old enough to actually be the guy?"

I shook my head. "He'd most likely be over one hundred years old. Even so, it's a stretch to assume an old man's nightmares make him the Boston Strangler two-point-oh."

Cowboy listened carefully.

"Let's keep this between us," I said. "We have enough to worry about. I don't want any fake news causing panic and distracting us from our current mission. The media would be all over us."

"You can count on me."

"Thanks."

As Cowboy left, I sank back into my chair. Of course, I'd follow up on this lead. It could be nothing, or it could be everything. Most cold cases are solved by tips like this, no matter how many years later it happens.

So, was this how it worked? Leah needed me as much as I needed her. I'd offer most of the leads; she'd take care of them like a dark knight.

If any of this information about the Boston Strangler was even remotely true, the only choice we'd have wouldn't be a warm and fuzzy one. But I could live with that.

CHAPTER SEVEN

Leah, Boston 2003

I watched closely in Doctor Silver's high-end wound care clinic by the Boston harbor as he amputated a severely infected toe. "It's crucial to remove all the dead tissue to prevent the infection from spreading and compromising the healthy areas," he explained, dropping the severed toe into a metal tray. It landed with a clinical clink.

As he prepared for the next incision, Doctor Silver offered me the scalpel. Calmly, I took it in my gloved hands and followed his instructions precisely to remove the next toe.

"Remarkable work," he said after a moment, admiration evident in his tone. "None of my students have ever demonstrated such precision."

After the procedure was done and the patient gone, I handed him a yellow envelope filled with cash and promised to return the following Monday.

The typical Boston weekend buzz of people danced around me as I walked down the street near the harbor. Then, out of nowhere, the sound of a police patrol cut through the vibrant atmosphere. The officer had pulled over a minivan.

What appeared routine escalated in seconds. From the open window, a shot rang out at the officer before the van accelerated through a red light and plowed into a crowd crossing the street. It mowed them down like a bowling ball sweeping through a set of pins. The van's violent journey ended in a construction zone, where it crashed into a large excavator. The surrounding screams were chilling.

I bolted over to the van and found the driver, who reeked of alcohol, clutching his neck. Blood spurted around a large shard of glass embedded in his flesh. The passenger, an older woman, was dead, her head crushed by an excavator's shovel, which had broken through the windshield. In the back seat, a little girl cried for her parents, oblivious to the real tragedy around her. Her mother was right next to her, unconscious.

"Mimi," the girl whimpered, calling for her grandmother, apparently not knowing the woman was gone. "Daddy and Mommy don't answer!"

My gaze shifted to the man in the front. I briefly swept over the street, taking in the chaos and victims, before returning to him. He was the villain in this tragedy: a man led astray by booze and selfishness, willing to risk everything to avoid the consequences of his actions, even if it meant killing his own child.

"I'm not going back to prison," he gasped, blood bubbling from beneath his hands as they clutched his wound.

I glanced at the unconscious woman in the backseat, wondering why she had stayed with this man despite the threat he posed to her and their child. Had childhood trauma locked her in a cycle of misery, causing her to risk a bleak future for her and her daughter with a man who didn't deserve their love or loyalty?

"I'm not going back to prison," he repeated, gasping through the blood. Even now, he cared only about himself. It was pathetic and disgusting . . . not worth another moment of my time or anyone else's.

"I'm not going back to—"

"You won't," I interrupted, harshly.

"Ma'am, step away from the car! This man is dangerous," a police officer yelled in my direction.

Quickly, I surveyed my surroundings, noting the ring of officers encircling the vehicle, guns aimed at us from a safe distance. Then I redirected my attention to the bleeding man. "Close your eyes," I instructed the little girl.

"I'm scared."

"Don't be," I said. "Darkness is your friend in dark times like these."

Finally, she complied, sobbing softly.

Without a second to waste, I pressed both hands on the glass shard, driving it deeper into the man's neck. He grabbed my wrists the moment he realized I was there not to save him but to ensure his end.

"Don't fight . . ." I whispered into his ear while pressing the glass deeper, cutting myself in the process. "Let them go."

After a few more twitches, he was motionless, his eyes wide with terror, staring right at me.

The police were at my side moments later. "Ma'am, step back!" they shouted.

"He's dead," I told them.

Their attention quickly turned to the surviving mother and daughter.

As I watched the police carry the mother and girl to safety, an overwhelming sense of justice and satisfaction filled me. It was a new yet profound feeling. I had removed a threat, a monster who posed a risk to others and would have continued to do so if not for my actions today.

As the EMTs rushed to aid the mother and daughter, I slipped away quietly, my part played.

The notion of cleansing the world of monsters felt infinitely more fulfilling than any applause I'd received as a pianist. The little girl and her mother might stand a chance in life again. Was that not justice?

Right then, this act of finality, this intervention, felt like the most meaningful accomplishment of my life. Maybe my life had meaning, after all. Maybe the flawed model that left the factory years ago had intentionally been made broken, setting the stage for a dark yet hopeful path ahead.

Chapter Eight

Leah

My eyes gradually opened, my mind still clouded by remnants of the dream—a vivid memory of my first kill.

I shifted to the edge of the bed, feeling the silk sheets against my bare hips and legs, and gazed out the expansive hotel window of my luxurious penthouse suite in Washington DC. Through the glass, the US Capitol's iconic dome stood as a radiant landmark amid the bustling cityscape. The surrounding gardens appeared tiny from this vantage point, yet they offered a sense of tranquility.

I found myself deep in contemplation. Dreams were foreign to me. I hadn't had them since childhood. But this was the second one I'd had since meeting Agent Richter.

For a moment, my hands almost felt tingly, as if I'd just pushed the glass into that man's neck.

A soft moan broke the silence. The man beside me stretched a muscular arm toward me with a suggestive smile.

I rose and made my way to the large closet before we could make contact. "Thank you. You can leave now," I said, moving to retrieve my clothes from my suitcase.

He sat up, confusion etched across his face. "Now?"

I fetched my purse from the desk and removed an envelope filled with cash. "Yes, now." Handing him the envelope felt as mundane as purchasing a coffee.

He hesitated, his deep brown eyes locking with mine. He was undeniably handsome, embodying the Mediterranean features I favored—a detail well-known to the escort agency. His name eluded me, but at this point, their names were inconsequential. Since Emanuel's death, I never allowed them to linger beyond their purpose: providing me with a brief escape. And this one had overstayed, likely because I'd inadvertently fallen asleep.

"Our transaction is complete," I explained. "Thank you."

"I . . . I wouldn't mind staying a bit longer for you," he offered.

"That won't be necessary. I expect you to be gone after my shower. And I'm quick." I headed toward the bathroom.

The clock on the nightstand read 9:04 a.m. It was highly unusual for me to sleep this late, but then again, dreaming wasn't part of my repertoire either. My appointment with the Smithsonian Secretary, Robert Michaels, loomed at 10:30 a.m., leaving me scant time for breakfast and a shower.

Initially, my interest had led me to the Museum of Fine Arts in Boston to consult with their Egyptologist. However, I shifted my focus when I learned that Emilia Wagner had been appointed as the new Egyptologist at the Smithsonian Museum of Natural History. She was one of the best in the field. Our meeting was scheduled under the pretense of discussing a potential advisory council seat—or, to be more precise, to become a significant donor to the Smithsonian Institution. That would be the most logical explanation for my visit should it ever be questioned. A logical cover was of the utmost importance. Always.

After my shower, I was mildly irritated to find the escort still present. I quickly dressed, donning a bra, a white silk shirt, and a satin cream-colored skirt atop black thigh-high stockings. I'd complete the outfit with black pumps and a luxurious cashmere poncho. Today's makeup would be more natural, complementing my hair, which was neatly tied in a bun.

The escort was still awkwardly standing by the bed, fidgeting like a guilty child. "I'm sorry," he mumbled, our eyes meeting. "But I can't find my phone."

"It was on the couch," I said, watching him rush over and frantically lift the cushions. As he bent over, his sweater rode up, exposing a glimpse of his toned back and the edge of his muscular abdomen.

Instantly, a vibrant heat came to life within me. Psychopaths often sought comfort in lust and sex. It was one of the few things they could truly feel. And I wasn't naive enough to think I was different. But my interests didn't align with those who reveled in violent fantasies. My preference was more run-of-the-mill. I yearned for the intimacy that came with a loving, committed relationship. It was a curiosity that had puzzled me all my life, one that, unlike the logical processes I usually depended on, would likely never be solved.

He retrieved his phone and offered an apologetic smile. "I'm leaving now. Please don't tell the agency I've upset you. They . . . said you're a big deal."

As he walked past, something within me stirred. "Wait!"

He stopped and turned, his eyes meeting mine.

The battle was brief but intense. My craving for another encounter that made me feel alive, the few seconds when I reached that orgasm, clashed with rational thought.

One last time, I thought. *Then he'll leave, and I'll request someone new on my next visit to DC, avoiding any pattern that might attract the Train Track Killer's attention.*

"I'll pay you an additional thousand cash if you fuck me against the glass window."

"What?" He looked surprised, likely more by the abruptness of my request than by its content.

Approaching the window with a view of the Capitol Mall, I outlined my fantasy. "I'll stand here, looking out. You'll embrace me from behind, whisper intimacies into my ear. Act like we're married. Then you'll finger me and tell me how much you want to fuck me. When I'm about to cum, you'll pull my panties down, thrust your cock into me, and tell me that you love me." I turned to face him. "Try to sound convincing. Understood?"

He nodded slowly.

"Good. There's an extra five hundred in it for you if you get it right."

He pursed his lips. "When . . . do you want to do this?"

"Now, of course," I said, positioning myself at the window, adopting the role of an oblivious bride mesmerized by her new beginning. "I have to leave soon."

My driver was waiting by the dark limousine when I stepped out of the hotel. There was no time for food, but hunger was a sensation I had mastered. I was accustomed to waiting for hours on end, standing perfectly still, just as I had done while waiting for Harvey Grand in his rundown motel closet.

Lost in thought, I gazed out the window as we drove past the majestic buildings of downtown DC. Their imposing neoclassical architecture rivaled the grandeur of Europe.

As if last night's dream weren't strange enough, my mother's words suddenly echoed in my head. They were words she had repeated far too often during my childhood: "Are you stupid? I wish you were never born!"

Reflecting on it now, I strongly disagreed with her assertion that I was lacking in intelligence. In fact, I stood firm in my belief to the contrary. Among the many things I might have been, simple-minded was not one of them.

And yet, I could understand her aversion toward me as an individual and my father's silent complicity. My upbringing occurred long before the concepts of attachment parenting and the mental health movement took root. In the seventies and eighties—particularly in small American towns—a family's reputation, and more so a woman's, adhered to very strict standards. The prevalence of face-to-face interactions meant that social perceptions and gossip played a significant role in determining one's community standing. Against this backdrop, my mother, who placed her social standing in our small town above everything else, saw me as a threat to her reputation and, therefore, a threat to her survival. My father, a modest man who'd managed to marry the prom queen due to his own father's successful gas station business, found himself obliged to support my mother's views. He was always walking on eggshells around a woman he otherwise couldn't have dreamed of marrying.

There was no love between my parents and me. We maintained a relationship that was more transactional than familial. I regularly paid them their share from my wealth as though they had invested in my childhood piano lessons like stocks. A very large dividend, so to speak. They were entitled to it in my mind.

Aside from these financial interactions and the obligatory phone calls from my father on Christmas and my birthday—which I reciprocated on their birthdays until my mother requested I stop—there was no contact.

Though our situation might sound heartbreaking, it was a perfectly acceptable arrangement for us.

And yet, here I was, dreaming about my past and contemplating my unusual childhood for the first time in nearly three decades.

"Ms. Nachtnebel," my driver said, pulling me from my thoughts. "We're here." He sounded curt, like he'd tried to get my attention more than once.

Shaking off my thoughts, I glanced up at the National Museum of Natural History. Its grand neoclassical structure and iconic rotunda were a sight to behold. The sun's bright reflection off its white pillars was dazzling.

"Thank you," I quickly said, slipping out before he could come around to open the door for me. "I'll text you when I'm done. Stay close, please."

As I approached a group waiting at the museum's entrance, I recognized the head of the Smithsonian right away. President Robert Michaels was just as his pictures portrayed: a head of neatly groomed hair with silver highlights and eyes that seemed to sparkle with a genuine love for his work, all complemented by a tweed jacket and dress pants. He approached with a smile that was both warm and eager.

His hand stretched out to shake mine as soon as I reached him. "Ms. Nachtnebel, it's such an honor to have you here," he said. "I mentioned to my wife that you might join our board, and she just laughed. I had to show your assistant's email to her to convince her it was real."

I returned his smile as a woman stepped forward.

"This is Mrs. Emilia Wagner, our renowned Egyptologist," he said.

Mrs. Wagner, who had sun-kissed skin and graying hair, wore a linen blouse and khaki trousers. The ankh necklace around her neck caught my eye immediately. The symbol was the same one the Train Track Killer had left by his victims. My gaze lingered on the necklace as she shook my hand with a vigor that spoke of her passion.

Choosing her felt right. If anyone could help me unravel the mystery of the ankh symbol found with the bodies, it would be Emilia Wagner, a true expert in her field.

"That moment when the whole Colosseum chanted 'La Imperatrice,' I teared up," Mrs. Wagner said, her grip on my hand still firm.

I gently pulled my hand from hers. "Thank you, Mrs. Wagner—"

"Call me Emilia," she interjected. "I've been a fan for ages. I snagged a ticket off a waitlist to your Christmas concert three years ago. It was magical."

Mr. Michaels nodded enthusiastically as if to underline her sentiments. "Your music is right up there with discovering ancient tombs," he joked.

"You're both too kind," I replied with a smile.

"I hope you don't mind that we've invited two other potential donors to join our tour?" Mr. Michaels gestured toward two men engrossed in conversation by the grand museum doors. I was initially reluctant, but the presence of Nabil Adel, the real estate magnate, made their inclusion understandable. His portly figure and thinning hair were overshadowed by a grin that carried the unmistakable hint of power-driven lechery. Adel was as notorious for his tasteless opulence as he was for his tax evasion tactics. Or his affairs with models.

My smile faltered as I observed the person beside him. In his mid-forties, this tall, blond man stood out in an impeccably tailored suit and confident posture, mirroring the appearance of an elegant gentleman from a bygone era. He wasn't overly handsome, but his aura attracted attention, somehow enhancing his presence and rendering him remarkably distinguished. It was a rare gift that undoubtedly served him well in business—and most likely with women.

Mr. Michaels led us toward them. "Let me introduce Nabil Adel," he announced.

After a brief handshake with Adel, I turned to the other man.

"And Mr. Jan Novak."

"It's a pleasure to finally meet you, Ms. Nachtnebel," Mr. Novak said, then gestured toward the museum's entrance. "Shall we begin?" His voice was both commanding and melodious, leaving no room for disagreement.

"Of course," Mr. Roberts said, obediently opening the large doors for Mr. Novak, who, unlike Adel, stepped aside to let the women enter first.

The tour of the museum was captivating. It began in the grand entrance hall, from which we moved through the Hall of Mammals. There, we marveled at the array of life, from diminutive shrews to the colossal African elephant. I paused, looking into the elephant's dark, dead eyes. Such a magnificent creature, wasted on us humans.

"It's known as the Fénykövi elephant," Mr. Novak said, coming to stand beside me. "Named after the Hungarian game hunter who donated the hide. They also affectionately call the elephant Henry, from what I've read."

I continued to gaze at the unfortunate creature's eyes, faux yet sad. They reminded me of the eyes of a serial killer's victim. "Killed solely for someone's amusement," I remarked coldly. "How distasteful and absurd to call it Henry . . . *affectionately.*"

For the first time, Mr. Novak smiled. He followed me into the Ocean Hall, where Mr. Michaels was elaborating on the mysteries of the deep sea to Mr. Adel. "You disapprove of violence, then?" Mr. Novak asked.

The irony of his question almost made me laugh. I thought of Harvey Grand and the satisfaction I'd derived from watching another predator dissolve, quite literally. "It's not the violence that disturbs me but the motivation behind it," I replied as I noticed Mr. Adel awkwardly scratching his privates as if no one could see him.

"It disturbs you when it's done for fun?" Mr. Novak asked.

"It's more nuanced than that, but yes, among other reasons," I responded.

Mr. Novak nodded thoughtfully. "Maybe violence is simply in our nature, and we're not so different from animals after all. Many species like cats and dolphins kill for entertainment." He shifted his gaze from the imposing whale skeleton above to a large dolphin model.

"Possibly," I conceded, pausing beside him in front of the dolphin display before moving on to the ancient realm of dinosaurs, where towering skeletons dominated the space. Mr. Novak kept pace with me. "But I would also argue that a species capable of reaching the moon should adhere to higher standards than mere primal instincts," I continued. "Humans have moral reasoning and the capacity for ethical decision-making. This sets us apart from most animals. While certain animals might kill beyond their survival needs, interpreting this as 'fun' could misrepresent their actions. Humans, with our advanced cognitive abilities and societal norms, generally view the killing of others for pleasure as a grave departure from ethical behavior, not as an innate trait."

"Fascinating argument," Mr. Novak admitted. A grin played on his lips as we ventured through the Hall of Human Origins, delving into the intricacies of human evolution.

The group paused before John Gurche's bronze sculpture of a Homo neanderthalensis mother and child. The artwork captured them with profound realism, showcasing distinctive Neanderthal features like their robust build, pronounced brow ridges, and strong facial structures. The mother smiled as she cradled her child.

Mr. Michaels shared a few words about the artist and the sculpture before leading the group toward the skeletons. An eager Mr. Adel trailed behind, inquiring about tax deductions.

I was about to follow when I noticed Mr. Novak lingering by the sculpture. He kept his gaze fixed on it before shifting his icy blue eyes to me. "What do you think we should do with humans who kill for fun? Get rid of them for the good of others?" he asked.

I hesitated, suddenly rooted to the ground. It wasn't easy to catch me off guard; in fact, I could recall only one other person who had managed to do so recently: Agent Richter. The precision of Novak's question struck me, his inquiry as sharp as a scalpel. "Could you clarify your question?" I asked, maintaining his intense gaze, neither of us willing to back down.

Standing a head taller than me, Mr. Novak was an imposing figure. He narrowed his eyes. "Those who kill for pleasure. What do you believe should be done with them? To stop them, I mean."

The gravity of his question remained. It felt as if he could see through the myriad layers of my facade, touching a truth I had kept concealed to most.

I held his stare a moment longer before offering a forced smile. "I think that's a question better suited for Mr. Michaels, not a concert pianist. After all, his halls are the ones filled with death. My own is filled with life and dreams."

A hint of a smile played on Mr. Novak's lips. His intense gaze never wavered from mine.

"Do you have any other questions about the sculpture?" Emilia approached us with hurried steps, her tone that of a worried host. "Did we move too quickly!"

"Not at all," I replied before following Mr. Michaels, bypassing the insect zoo and butterfly pavilion.

"Ah, here we are, the tour's highlight," Mr. Michaels announced, stopping before the grand entrance to the Egyptian exhibit, marked "Eternal Life." The room lay shrouded in darkness, deliberately set to enhance the effect. "It may not be the largest collection in the nation, but we've managed to acquire some of the most prestigious artifacts from Egypt. Loaned to us at a significant cost, so the American public can experience history up close for free, thanks to our generous donors."

Inside the exhibit hall, a dim light shone on the Egyptian treasures, enveloping us in an air of ancient mystery. The darkness highlighted the artifacts on display, their details brought to life under focused beams of illumination. Statues of pharaohs, mummies, and intricate hieroglyphics glowed ethereally, their presence stark against the shadowy ambiance.

"Look at this guy!" Mr. Adel bellowed, his grin wide as if he'd just cracked a fart joke. He was gesturing toward a large mummification display featuring a bull's head and genitals.

I brushed off his childish humor and moved closer to a golden necklace adorned with an ankh symbol made of lapis lazuli gemstones. Its T-shape was crowned with a loop shaped like a teardrop. Inside the glass showcase, it sparkled on a crimson silk pillow like tiny stars twinkling in the night sky.

"Ah." Emilia stepped up beside me, her voice tinged with awe. "The Eternal Kiss. Believed to have belonged to Agathoclea, the favored mistress of the Greco-Egyptian Pharaoh Ptolemy IV Philopator. Stunning, isn't it?"

I nodded. "Is that the ankh symbol?"

Emilia touched the pendant of her own ankh necklace, her fingers tracing its sun-stained contours. "Yes," she responded. "I'm impressed you recognized it."

"What does it symbolize?"

"Most commonly, it's a symbol of eternal life. But its significance can vary with the context. In this instance, we believe it was a gift from Ptolemy to his mistress, Agathoclea. He loved her more than anything else in life. His obsession with her was profound. Legend has it he constructed a magnificent temple for the gods, hoping to persuade them to allow her to join him in the afterlife when he died."

"As in, he planned to kill her upon his own death?"

Emilia nodded. "Such practices weren't rare for the era. Servants were often buried alive with their pharaohs. But Agathoclea and her brother attempted a coup for the throne upon Ptolemy's death. Their plot failed, and she met a grisly end, torn apart limb by limb."

The necklace seemed even more enigmatic as I pondered its history, struggling to connect any threads to the Train Track Killer. "How intriguing. You mentioned it usually represents eternal life. Are there alternative interpretations?"

A wave of pride washed over Emilia's aged face. "Actually, yes."

I leaned in, captivated.

"It's not widely known, even among Egyptologists, but I was fortunate enough to participate in an excavation where we unearthed a rare stone tablet. It depicted a priest's vain daughter, clutching the ankh as though she were gazing directly into it."

While Emelia talked, an unmistakable sense of being watched crept over me. It was just like when I was eight and Laruun had them between cars, chasing after me. I turned my head slightly and immediately caught his gaze.

Jan Novak.

Shrouded in darkness away from the group, illuminated only by the ambient light reflecting off a nearby mummy, he had fixed his intense blue eyes on me with the precision of a predator stalking its prey. Our eyes locked.

I felt momentarily paralyzed.

"So, although the ankh is most commonly associated with life or eternal life," Emilia pressed on, "in this exceptional case, it signifies a mirror. Its form unmistakably resembles an old-fashioned hand mirror. This interpretation is supported by the sequence of its consonants, ʿ-n-ḫ, appearing in several Egyptian terms, including, as you might guess—"

"Mirror," I said, shifting my attention back to her.

She nodded. "We theorize this interpretation could originate from the notion of the mirror as a reflection of one's true essence or soul."

"To highlight the significance of self-reflection of one's current self and beyond? Like a self-analysis or evaluation?"

Emilia pondered this. Then her eyes lit up with excitement. "Yes. Your interpretation really supports the mirror theory from new angles. Would you mind if I shared your observation with some of my colleagues?"

I glanced back to where Jan Novak had been standing. He was gone.

There was something about that man . . . something deeply unsettling. It wasn't like the darkness I'd come to recognize in the eyes of the monsters I hunted. Still, he had a strange quality that I couldn't quite grasp.

"Well," Mr. Michaels said as we returned to the hall where our tour had commenced, "unfortunately, Mr. Novak had to leave on urgent business. But I hope you align with his belief in the importance of preserving our cultural heritage." Clearing his throat, he added, "As you're aware, access to any Smithsonian Museum is complimentary for everyone. We depend significantly on the generosity of patrons like yourself to fulfill our mission of presenting history to the public."

"Is there anything else we get out of this besides tax deductions?" Mr. Adele asked. His tone was getting on my nerves.

Fed up with his rudeness, I discreetly pulled out my phone to text my driver to be ready outside. "Mr. Adele," I said firmly and impassively, "a donation is essentially a voluntary contribution, given without the expectation of receiving anything in return. What you're inquiring about would constitute a transaction, an exchange where goods or services are traded with the anticipation of something in return. It would have been prudent to acquaint yourself with this distinction prior to attending and enjoying our hosts' precious time."

Mr. Adele looked stunned, then pulled out his checkbook in silence.

Approaching Mr. Michaels and Emilia, I extended my hand. "Thank you for the exquisite tour. My assistant will be in touch with the details of the amount of my regular contribution."

Both Mr. Michaels and Emilia's expressions brightened. "That would mean the world to us," Mr. Michaels responded.

I turned to Emilia. "Should I have further questions regarding the ankh symbol, may I reach out to you?"

She nodded enthusiastically. "Absolutely! Please do."

With a courteous smile, I made my exit.

As I descended the steps, my thoughts drifted back to Mr. Novak. His probing questions about the morality of killing, coupled with his intense scrutiny in the Egyptian exhibit, struck me as profoundly unusual. An enigma surrounded him, one that warranted closer examination.

Then there was Emilia's insight into the ankh symbol.

A mirror.

Why would the Train Track Killer want to reflect on himself and his actions? Was he grappling with his identity, searching for himself, or aspiring to evolve into something more formidable or terrifying?

As I settled into the limousine, my conviction to consult Agent Richter solidified. I knew I had to talk to him. After giving him some time to process the situation with Harvey Grand, of course.

I had no doubt that what he encountered in the autopsy room would disturb him.

CHAPTER NINE

Liam

Cowboy, Rose, and I stood alongside the pathologist in the oppressive silence of the Green Cross Hospital morgue, where a pin drop would have resounded as if it were being played through a megaphone. Harvey Grand's body, or what remained of it, lay splayed on a cold embalming table. The stark metal surface was a sharp contrast to the eerie stillness of the lifeless form it bore. And *form* was indeed the right descriptor for whatever the hell lay before us, as *human being* no longer seemed a fitting term.

What was once Harvey Grand had been grotesquely altered by the acid. The remains were partially dissolved, right down to the bone. Certain areas were more severely eroded than others, revealing exposed tissues and discolored, uneven surfaces where the acid had mercilessly eaten through flesh, muscles, and even bone. The eyeless face, retaining mere remnants of a yellow-toothed mouth torn open in a scream, bore a chilling resemblance to something out of an Evil Dead movie.

The room's dim lighting cast long, somber shadows, lending a macabre emphasis to the gruesome spectacle before us.

"What . . . the . . . fuck?" Agent Rose's voice, muffled yet sharp, cut through the silence like an arrow streaking across the sky. Her hand rose to her neck as if to assure herself that she hadn't ingested poison as well.

The atmosphere was spooky, saturated with the antiseptic scent of a hospital.

Overwhelmed, I tilted my head back to gaze at the water-damaged ceiling, my lips tightly pinched in disbelief.

"Well," Cowboy said, "he did like to party."

Rose and I turned our sharp gazes on him. He responded with a what-did-I-do-now shrug.

"Krokodil," interjected the pathologist, a petite woman named Dr. Giselle Lopez.

"The Russian zombie drug?" I asked.

She nodded. "I've never encountered anything like this." Her voice was tinged with professional intrigue. "We're seeing more cases as Krokodil spreads on the streets across America. Acidic burns down to the bone aren't unheard of with this terrible drug . . . but this?" She shook her head. "This batch is something straight out of hell."

Cowboy stepped closer, snapping on a latex glove that had been in his pocket. "Did they increase the paint thinner or whatever the hell could have caused such a severe reaction?"

As he reached toward the body, Dr. Lopez swiftly intervened. "Don't!" She gestured toward visibly corroded latex gloves on a nearby metal stretcher. "You need butyl gloves, or the acid will burn through."

"Holy shit!" Cowboy hastily retreated from the body.

"What the hell did they spike this batch with?" Rose asked, her voice a mix of horror and curiosity.

I observed silently, a gnawing certainty in my mind that this was not an accidental cocktail. Leah knew exactly what she was doing here.

"Holy shit indeed," Dr. Lopez echoed. "I'm still waiting on the full lab report, but there's only one substance I know of that's potent enough to do something like this. And the fact that it doesn't eat through plastic only confirms my suspicion."

"Hydrofluoric acid," I murmured.

"The stuff that ate through the bath tub in Breaking Bad?" Cowboy asked.

Dr. Lopez nodded solemnly. "Drug dealers throw all sorts of things into Krokodil, including paint thinner, but this is absolute madness. I pray to God this was the only batch of this hellish cocktail."

A heavy silence fell again as we stared at the grotesque remains of Harvey Grand. The yellowish pus, the black holes for eyes.

"Why did it spread so much? Shouldn't it have killed him instantly?" Rose asked.

Dr. Lopez gestured toward an area of the neck, just above the collarbone. "You're right. Usually, we only see burns near the injection site. That's because most of the time, users inject into visible veins. They're easy to find. But this unlucky guy somehow managed to inject into an artery. Unlike veins, they pump blood and drugs away from the heart."

"And that causes . . . *this*?" I asked, gesturing both hands at Harvey.

"Yes," she replied gravely. "As I said, arteries carry blood away from the heart. This means the toxic mix kept circulating through Harvey Grand's body even after he suffered one of the most horrific deaths I've ever encountered."

"So, the heart kept pumping the acid throughout his body even after he died?" Agent Rose interjected, her voice laced with disbelief.

"It looks like it. He was most likely already brain dead, but given the severe damage of the acid, the heart must have kept pumping for quite a bit longer."

"How is that even possible?" I asked.

"Dying isn't like in the movies," Dr. Lopez explained, her tone clinical and somber. "During the dying process, different parts of the body cease functioning at various times, not always in the same order. For instance, the heart might keep beating even after the brain has stopped. Or the liver might still function when the intestines don't. In this case, the heart continued pumping the acid through corroded veins, spreading it everywhere. Once the drug reached the heart, it instantly stopped due to the corrosive effects of the hydrofluoric acid. The acid did its own thing from here on for quite a bit longer."

"Did he . . . suffer much?" Cowboy asked.

"Beyond anything imaginable," Dr. Lopez replied, her face reflecting the gravity of her answer.

Once more, the room sank into a silence punctuated only by the distant beeps of machines and the muffled sounds of hospital staff.

As I stood there, gazing at this shitshow called Harvey Grand, a surge of anger welled up inside me. What the hell was Leah thinking? We'd talked about using drugs. Whatever happened to a good old-fashioned heroin overdose or even a shot to the head? Both were merciful by comparison. But more importantly, how could I ever trust her with any information again? If that phone tip about the Boston Strangler led us to him, how could I possibly share any of it with Leah? What would she do to him—cut off his head and place it on a spike at the Children's Museum?

This . . . this was unthinkable.

"Jesus Christ." I exhaled loudly, my sigh echoing my internal battle.

My arrangement with Leah was beginning to make me feel like one of those crazy people who kept lions as pets until, one day, Simba got angry.

What had worked for her and Larsen didn't align with my principles. Not in this. Not even close. And there was always the lurking question: Could I end up just like Larsen if I started making waves?

Surprisingly, I felt no remorse over Harvey's death. In fact, when the call came in that a drug overdose victim in Ocean City had been identified as Harvey Grand, an immense sense of relief had washed over me. Leah had a point: An out-of-control sociopath like Harvey was bound to wreak havoc again. Once a monster like him crossed a certain line and was rewarded with a get-out-of-jail-free card and a lucrative book deal on top of that, there was no stopping him, not even with the logic that he wouldn't walk free again. So, Harvey's demise saved innocent lives.

But . . .

I gazed at what was left of his face, where fiery red flesh clashed grotesquely with the yellow-white remnants of wounds.

No, not like this.

Not for Harvey's sake but for my own humanity.

Rose spoke up, shifting the atmosphere entirely. "Eleven," she said abruptly, drawing all eyes to her. "The youngest victim in the Newcastle well case was only eleven months old. His mother, too exhausted to go to the store, made his bottle with boiled tap water instead of bottled water. And now her baby is gone forever."

Shit.

I was a parent myself. My heart shattered.

Cowboy sighed. "Well, she'll be thrilled once she hears that this piece of shit is rotting in hell." A wide grin spread across his face. "Rotting. Literally. You get it? *Rot* in hell."

"That's enough, Agent McCourt," Rose said in a reprimanding tone, beating me to it.

I studied her briefly. The intense look in her amber eyes. The deep frown line between her brows. In moments like these, I found it hard to gauge her stance. Was she relieved at Harvey's demise? Or did she feel deprived of the trial and the justice expected in a storybook-ending court case?

"What happened?" Dr. Lopez asked, her voice tinged with hesitation. "I mean, how did he escape justice?"

Cowboy glanced at me, almost as if expecting me to silence him. However, there was a sense that we owed Dr. Lopez an explanation after sharing this experience with her.

"Some cop screwed us," Cowboy explained. "Before a warrant came in, that idiot searched Grand's home based on some Chuck Norris hunch about the town's nutjob, who happened to be Harvey Grand. He was right about this asshole in the end, but the law doesn't work that way. Not in this country, at least. Right or wrong doesn't matter. The fucked-up wording of the law does."

"Thanks for that . . . colorful explanation, Agent McCourt," I said.

He continued, missing the hint. "His ultra-rich aunt could afford lawyers smart enough to challenge every breath we took. We didn't know about the warrant issue until it all came out. The cops tried to cover it up by forging documents, but the Grand family's million-buck law firm brought all this shit to light. We all agreed to keep this quiet and, of course, to let Harvey walk. That's just how it goes. It's not about the crime you commit but how much lawyer you can afford."

Dr. Lopez looked confused. "How can a single late warrant let a man like him walk?"

"The evidence," Rose clarified, "was inadmissible in court because the search of Harvey's home was illegal. Without it, there was no case against him. There were no witnesses."

"I see." Dr. Lopez paused, lips pursed, then glanced at Harvey's remains with a raised eyebrow. "I guess there might be a God after all."

The loud, insistent ringtone of Cowboy's phone shattered the tense atmosphere in the room. He quickly pulled it from his pocket. As he put the phone to his face, the screen cast a soft glow against his cheek. He listened for a moment, then held the phone slightly away from his ear, cupping the lower half as if it were an old landline. "It's the hospital's reception. Some funeral home, Woods Funerals, is here to collect the body."

I nodded. "Tell them you'll be right out."

"I'll be right up," Cowboy said into the phone and ended the call.

"So, we're not taking the remains back to Boston with us?" Agent Rose asked.

"No, we are," I said. "But the family insisted on having the remains in a coffin instead of some plastic bag."

"A rich-folk-worthy home delivery," Cowboy said. "And we just wag our happy tails."

"All right, can you please bring them down here?" I asked. It wasn't that what Cowboy said was different from what we were all thinking.

However, when you wore the badge, there was a big difference between thinking something and voicing it out loud.

Cowboy exited through the double swinging doors, muttering something under his breath—likely, a tasteless joke.

"Did McCourt say what we're supposed to do after we land with the remains?" Rose asked.

"Yes." I looked over at Dr. Lopez, who understood all too well. "Unless you need me, I have a meeting," she said. "Make sure you sign the paperwork on the desk over there before you leave." She nodded curtly at the desk and threw her oversized gloves in a plastic trash can labeled DO NOT TOUCH. HAZARDOUS WASTE.

"Will do. Thank you for your time," I said and watched her leave.

Rose shook her head, her eyes back on the corpse. Then she walked over and picked up the clipboard with the paperwork. She signed it with a pen attached to it by a small chain.

"His family will collect the remains from a small airport near Newcastle where they've got a mansion they use for summer vacation," I said. "We just hand him over at the airport. It's all them from there."

Rose nodded. "Nice."

With a resounding crash, the double doors flew open and slammed against the door stoppers. They rebounded and collided with an ornate wooden casket adorned with golden handles. It was being wheeled in on a stretcher by two older men in sleek black suits.

"What's up," one of them greeted us with a nod.

"Thanks, guys," I responded. My gaze shifted to Cowboy, who lingered in the hallway and looked uneasy as he used a foot to prop open one door.

"Umm . . . guys?" Cowboy said. "You might want to see this."

Rose and I exchanged anxious glances, then stepped into the hallway. There, we were met by a throng of hospital staff, their eyes fixed on us amid a murmur of curiosity. A man in blue scrubs brandished his phone, poised as though he were expecting a celebrity's entrance.

"Shit," I muttered as we retreated back into the morgue.

Rose folded her arms. "Seems our 'covert operation' isn't so covert after all."

"Should we have clued Dr. Lopez in on the whole FBI confidentiality spiel?" Cowboy's sarcasm was only thinly veiled.

"I doubt she's the leak. She's been in the loop longer than we have," I said, frustration threading through my voice as I raked a hand through my hair. "Goddamn it."

Who leaked this?

"Cowboy, call for local PD backup," I continued. "We're going to need a lot more muscle to get us to the airport."

He was on his phone in an instant.

This was a complication we didn't need. The FBI's involvement was supposed to ensure discretion. No public spectacles, no vitriolic protests shadowing the hearse. Definitely no reporters thrusting their microphones at us. McCourt would be livid if this spiraled out of control.

"What's the situation at the front desk?" Rose asked the moment Cowboy ended his call.

He shrugged. "Just a small gathering of patients and staff, snapping photos of the funeral service. No press . . . yet."

"For now," I added, the urgency clear in my tone. "Can we expedite this?" I asked the funeral staff, who had donned protective gloves and were preparing to handle Harvey Grand's body.

"You can't rush the dead," the older one retorted, unfazed and unhurried.

"The dead won't mind if you become the face of the evening news for carrying the coffin of one of the nation's most despised individuals," Rose retorted. "I'd reconsider that so-called wisdom of yours unless you're keen on becoming a public spectacle."

The funeral staff exchanged looks of concern, then hastened their pace considerably.

"Be ready for potential confrontation," I advised, withdrawing my Glock from its chest holster beneath my blazer. I swiftly checked for a smooth slide action and unobstructed barrel, then verified the trigger and firing pin function with a safe dry fire.

Cowboy glanced my way, his expression one of disbelief. Then he turned to Rose, who was completing her weapon's dry fire check. My eyes locked with Rose's, and an unspoken understanding passed between us.

"A team of optimists, I see," Cowboy said.

"Check your weapon, Cowboy," I ordered, holstering my Glock.

He rolled his eyes but followed suit.

"Let's move, now," I urged as the funeral staff secured the coffin with a hefty lock.

Exiting the room, we were met with chaos. The corridor leading to the elevators was crammed with curious hospital staff, their murmurs punctuated by the clicks of their camera phones. This scene extended all the way to the main entrance.

Beyond the hospital's glass façade, a large crowd had gathered, with patients and onlookers blending into a mass of curious faces. It wasn't a riotous assembly yet, but it was too large a group for what was supposed to be a discreet operation.

Outrage erupted from the crowd.

"Fuck Harvey!" a man shouted.

The words sparked a chain reaction, with other voices amplifying the dissent.

"Why are you protecting this asshole?"

"Shame on you!"

Tensions escalated, morphing into a cacophony of indignant murmurs.

We had barely made it out of the hospital when police backup roared in: a fleet of at least ten cars, sirens wailing and lights flashing. Among them was Agent Wilson, the local FBI liaison who had escorted us here. She had waited outside in her SUV.

"Thank God." I breathed a sigh of relief and directed the funeral and our escort vehicles into formation. "Load him up." Then I approached the lead police vehicle. "Appreciate the swift response. Could you have your team form a protective detail around us? We need coverage front and back, all the way to City Municipal Airport."

"Yes, sir," the officer said quickly. "Sirens?"

"All the way. We need to get the hell outta here ASAP."

"Understood."

I navigated to the SUV in which we'd arrived. On the way, I passed Agent Wilson and her partner, who'd been part of our detail. I caught a glimpse of Cowboy attempting to claim the driver's seat, only for Rose to snatch the keys from him and nudge him aside. This elicited a frustrated "Hey" from Cowboy before he climbed into the back seat with a grunt.

"Let's roll!" I announced to our team. Police cars maneuvered past us to form the vanguard of our procession, akin to the tip of an arrow.

Swiftly, I settled into the passenger seat beside Rose. After a quick exchange of determined glances, she ignited the engine, and we joined the escort of police vehicles carving a path for us.

The blare of sirens from the police cars cut through the city noise, clearing intersections as our convoy hastened toward the airport. From the corner of my eye, I noticed a camera crew from a local TV station trying to tail us from an intersection.

"FBI Escorts Notorious Corpse: Public in Uproar," Cowboy quipped, holding an imaginary microphone to his mouth.

I reached for the handheld radio and eyed the conspicuous white van adorned with a satellite dish. "Can someone intercept them and do an ID check to buy us some time?" I asked.

"On it," came the prompt reply from an officer.

I watched as a police vehicle decelerated, strategically positioning itself to obstruct the media van's pursuit.

Our advance continued, with onlookers attempting to capture fleeting images, seemingly enthralled by the spectacle of our mission. But the swift pace of our escort ensured we made it to the airport quickly.

The metal gate to the airfield swung open as our convoy arrived. We sped down the airfield toward the C-17 awaiting us with its cargo door lowered.

A group of airmen in camouflage-patterned utility uniforms hurried down the ramp to meet us. They included Lieutenant Colonel Jason

Lewis, whose approach was marked by a cool, deliberate stride. He had personally overseen this mission on the military's end to ensure everything proceeded without a hitch. The balding officer, in his early fifties, made his way over to me as I exited the SUV alongside my team.

"Go get him on board," he commanded his airmen, then paused in front of me to survey the extensive police escort. "Making friends already?"

"I guess so," I replied, maintaining a tone of respect. "How soon can we depart?"

Lieutenant Colonel Lewis glanced back at his men, who were efficiently transferring the coffin to the aircraft. "If you're ready . . . now," he said, his voice imbued with his usual confidence.

"Thank you, sir," I said, then turned to Agent Wilson, the lead of the local agents who had supported our mission. "Thank you."

She nodded, her demeanor professional. "No problem. Good luck," she responded before signaling her team to vacate the runway.

I acknowledged the police officers with a wave before hastening up the ramp to join the others.

"Let's get her off the ground!" Lieutenant Colonel Lewis ordered, standing beside me as the airmen used tie-down straps to secure the coffin to the C-17's expansive metallic floor. The aircraft's cockpit, outfitted with advanced instrumentation, lay at the front. Our passenger seating ran along the windowless sides, underscoring the plane's utilitarian design for military use.

"Got lucky on this one, huh?" Lieutenant Colonel Lewis mused, eyeing the coffin. "Kinda wish our enemies would eliminate themselves. Would save this country lives and money."

"No kidding," I murmured, offering the Lieutenant Colonel a respectful nod before settling down next to Rose and Cowboy. We watched the airmen testing the straps. One of the airmen reached for his phone, aiming for a photo of the coffin, but Lieutenant Colonel Lewis intervened sharply. "Is that for your one follower on social media, Sergeant Dorfman?"

The other airmen laughed as Sergeant Dorfman stowed his phone back in the side pocket of his camouflage-patterned utility trousers like a beaten dog. Then they quickly took their seats across from us.

I felt the powerful engines roar to life, vibrating through the mighty aircraft's frame. Its acceleration was steady and forceful, pressing me back into my seat. Soon, the plane took off the ground, transitioning from the rumble of the runway to a smooth glide over open air.

The outside noise diminished as we climbed into the sky, embarking on our short journey to the Portsmouth airport near Newcastle to hand Harvey Grand over to his family.

Nobody really talked during the hour-and-a-half flight. While the engines were louder than those on commercial flights, it was more that the cargo had everybody in a quiet mood, exchanging nothing but quick glances and nods.

Everything progressed smoothly until we began our descent into Portsmouth airport. That was when Lieutenant Colonel Lewis pressed the headset connected to the plane's intercom system against his ear. He looked serious. After a brief exchange, he stood and signaled me to join him.

Unfastening my seatbelt, I hurried to the cockpit, where three pilots in military attire operated the controls, surrounded by an array of buttons and displays. "We have a problem, sir," said the senior pilot, nodding out the window.

My gaze followed his and landed on the unexpected sight below. The small airfield had been swallowed by a vast, tumultuous sea of people. A carnival-like assembly of journalists and protesters had besieged the normally tranquil airport. With each foot we descended, the tension in the cockpit thickened.

"Goddamn it," Lieutenant Colonel Lewis cursed before I had the chance.

Goddamn it, indeed. My mind raced. This was what I'd been dreading. The impending media frenzy and the fallout were inevitable, and McCourt's fury would be unmatched.

"Fuck yeah," Cowboy whispered, his excitement barely contained as he and Rose squeezed into the cockpit. His reaction starkly contrasted with that of Rose, whose gaze fell to the metallic floor, her silence heavy with frustration. Unlike Cowboy, she fully grasped the gravity of our predicament.

"Special Agent Richter." Lieutenant Colonel Lewis turned to me. "Awaiting your orders."

I stood frozen, overwhelmed by the sight of the gathering crowd.

"Special Agent," he pressed, urgency lacing his tone as the airfield loomed closer.

The crowd swelled to the point that we could discern the first of many hostile signs: "Rot in hell, Harvey!"

"Would you like us to land or redirect to another airport?" he continued.

I slowly nodded, the weight of the decision heavy on me as I confronted the daunting reality awaiting us. "Let's land," I said.

There was no need to redirect the flight. Regardless of how our operation had come to light, our next airport would most likely look the same. It appeared we had a mole. There was no other explanation for the press's rapid mobilization.

"You heard the Special Agent in Charge," Lieutenant Colonel Lewis instructed his pilots. "Touch down."

"Yes, sir!"

We left the cockpit to take our seats for the last stretch of the landing.

"This is bad," Rose said, shaking her head. Cowboy, on the other hand, cheerfully pulled out a small Ziplock bag from the inside of his fancy jacket. The bag contained makeup, primarily in the form of powders and similar items.

"Hmm?" He offered some to Rose, whose face was a blend of utter annoyance and disbelief.

"You fucking kidding me?" she asked.

"Cameras always make my skin look oily. Gotta look good for the ladies out there," he quipped, then opened the compact's mirror before applying powder to his forehead.

"Unbelievable," I muttered as we touched down, the craft briefly bouncing before coming to a harsh stop.

The airmen instantly sprinted to the coffin.

"Everything from here on needs to be picture-perfect!" Lieutenant Colonel Lewis practically yelled to his men and women. "I don't want to see a single wave or smirk when you carry this coffin to the funeral car. In fact, I don't want to see a single wrinkle in your uniforms or faces!"

"Yes, sir!" they hollered simultaneously.

With heavy steps, Rose, Cowboy, Lieutenant Colonel Lewis, and I lined up at the ramp of the plane that would open any second. A block of anxiety solidified in my chest. This was a nightmare. A disaster.

"Woo-hoo," Cowboy exhaled in excitement, shaking his legs and limbs as if he were ready to step into a WWE fight ring.

"Fuck me," Rose whispered.

"Badges out!" I commanded, affixing my own badge to my belt. "Keep walking. Not one word to anybody! I mean it."

"You can count on me on that one," Rose said.

"Fine," Cowboy agreed hesitantly.

The creak and groan of the heavy metal mechanism reverberated inside the craft as the ramp of the C-17 began to open. Daylight seeped in, slowly flooding the dark interior of the plane with an intense, growing brightness. With each inch the ramp descended, the muffled noises from outside became clearer—the chants of "Rot in hell" growing louder and more aggressive. The camera flashes started as faint flickers but soon turned into a relentless storm of light, each flash stronger and more blinding than the last.

"Still think I'm on a lucky mission?" I asked the Lieutenant Colonel as we stood side by side in silence like allies ready to make it through hell together.

"I'm more wondering whom I have to thank for making my men and women Shakespeare's Othello two-point-oh. The whole nation will hate on these fine airmen." His tone was low, serious.

"I'd say some rich asshole senator in DC," I countered, "but ultimately, the almighty dollar would be more accurate."

"Fucking traitors," he muttered. "All of them."

"Fucking traitors indeed," I mumbled, thinking of the irony here. The monster everyone was clamoring over was dead because of me, yet now everyone saw me as his protector.

The thunder of bright flashes and sound that erupted as the ramp clanged against the concrete was almost otherworldly. A chaotic nightmare awaited us, and there was no other path but straight through the heart of it.

"Let's go," I said, my voice heavy as the coffin settled into position behind us. "Let's bring this piece of shit back to his swamp."

The airmen aligned themselves, three on each side of the casket, preparing to shoulder the burden of carrying one of the country's most hated monsters back to his family as if he were a fallen soldier who had sacrificed himself for a noble cause. Their gazes flicked back and forth between one another. Not a sound was made as Sergeant Dorfman nodded and removed the American flag from the casket. The flag had been mistakenly placed by one of the airmen who'd been unaware of the true nature of the man whose coffin was strapped to the plane's floor.

Having already positioned Harvey Grand's body directly behind their Lieutenant Colonel and the FBI agents, Sergeant Dorfman gave his team one last look, offering them a chance to reconsider their participation. As everyone nodded in agreement, and with the ramp already halfway open, letting in a flood of bright light that seemed to briefly blind him, he reached into his pocket. From it, he pulled out a sticker depicting a human skull with bony hands giving the middle finger above the bold proclamation "Two Wrongs Can Make a Right."

Then he slapped it onto the casket for the whole world to see—a parting gift from his unit, a sinister greeting sent straight to hell.

CHAPTER TEN

Leah

My head gently tilted over the keys as I caressed the final delicate notes of Liszt's "Liebestraum" on a historic Bösendorfer grand piano. This remarkable instrument had withstood the test of time. The illustrious Vanderbilt family had placed it in the very spot where I now had the privilege to perform.

The venue was the Elm Court Estate, near Lenox, just outside of Boston. The Hubble family, current stewards of the former Vanderbilt estate, had invested a fortune into tuning and repairing the piano, ensuring its preservation within the family. Tonight, however, marked a pivotal moment: The piano would become mine. That was the only reason I'd agreed to entertain the whims of the affluent and influential tonight.

The trade-off was worth enduring the indignity of playing their clown for an evening. I had no doubt that Ronald Hubble, the birthday boy turning one hundred today, agreed to let the piano go only because he knew his time on earth was ticking away.

The Bösendorfer was a masterpiece. Not only was it crafted from an exquisite array of woods like cherry and rosewood, handcrafted in Vienna and shipped across the ocean, but it also boasted an original Claude Monet painting on both sides of the lid. A whimsical interpretation of Mozart's "The Magic Flute," it showcased the dreamy, ethereal landscape of an enchanted forest—a tribute to the opera's mystical themes. The soft pastel colors conjured a realm of fantasy, with delicate flowers abloom in the moonlight, akin to the water lilies Monet often painted, all melting into a surreal, magical scene.

My fingers moved softly, gracefully bringing the haunting melody to a close, capturing the piece's dreamlike essence in this final, reflective moment. Its last notes echoed through the grand hall and over the heads of two hundred and fifty elite.

As I rose to my feet and turned to the audience, my gaze effortlessly found Mr. Hubble seated in the front row. His wheelchair did nothing to diminish the presence of the man who had established one of the nation's largest banks and hedge funds. His profound and murky influence was deeply entrenched in the highest political circles. He was the one percent of the one percent, thriving off the labor of the bottom 99.99%. The true American dream.

After exchanging a few pleasantries, I seized the opportunity presented by the cake-cutting and the comedian's performance to discreetly withdraw from the gathering, seeking silence in the vast estate's garden.

Navigating the grand hallway, adorned with a towering ceiling, I felt my phone vibrate in my purse.

Liam.

He had been pressing for a meeting, which I had strategically avoided. He needed more time to process Harvey Grand, and any rushed meeting could only strain the delicate threads of our relationship.

"May I help you?" asked a waitress in a tuxedo with a level of formality that seemed straight from the nineteenth century.

"I'm just looking for some fresh air," I replied, my disdain for these gatherings evident. Despite the lucrative offers, my performances at such events were rare. The aftermath of the Colosseum had prompted me to scale back even more, opting for a period of low visibility. In the US, classical music wasn't as big as it was in Europe and Asia. That allowed me a degree of anonymity among Gen Z as well as freedom from the prying eyes of journalists hungry for tabloid fodder. Maintaining this obscurity was crucial, even if it meant occasionally performing for the insufferable elite who governed this country like farmers watching over a herd of pigs.

The scent of the gardens wafted toward me on a refreshing fall breeze as I approached a set of wide-open double doors. My path took me through a jarring gaming room where classic pinball machines stood alongside modern video game consoles and a bowling alley. For a moment, I forgot the piercing tunes of eight-bit melodies and the assault of flashing lights as I looked up to admire the exquisitely painted ceiling high above.

The illusionistic fresco masterfully deceived the eye, portraying the ceiling as an opening to a clear blue sky. Angels peered down from their celestial perch, lending depth and realism to the scene. Their expressions radiated innocence and joy.

"It's magnificent, isn't it?" Mr. Hubble remarked, his wheelchair quietly brought to my side by his nurse.

I spared a glance at the frail man in his meticulously tailored suit before returning my attention to the ceiling. "It reminds me of the Camera degli Sposi in Mantua, Italy," I said, my eyes momentarily drifting to the gaming room.

"It's a replica of it," Mr. Hubble said. "Aside from its horrendous surroundings," he added, nodding toward the gaming room with a weary smile. He maneuvered his chair to a spot directly beneath the painting, then craned his neck to gaze upward. "This room was once a magnificent library housing a priceless book collection, including a scroll from the Dead Sea Scrolls. But the grandkids wanted to be closer to their bedrooms, so instead of constructing a game room near the pool house, we demolished a piece of history for . . . this."

Silently, I continued to study the painting. The angels' innocent smiles harmonized beautifully with the serene sky and clouds. Then my gaze landed on a darker figure lurking behind one of the angels. It was a boy dressed in rags. He had short brown hair and a face marred by grime. His large brown eyes peered out accusingly from behind his guardian angel. "That figure differs from the original in Italy," I observed, intrigued.

"Impressive, Ms. Nachtnebel," Mr. Hubble said. "Indeed, it does." With a heavy sigh, he fixed a long, meaningful gaze at me. "I assume you're familiar with my story."

I nodded. The tale was well-known. "You began your venture as a teenager, selling mugs outside grocery stores, mugs crafted from clay by a nearby river. After your father's premature death, you persuaded your mother to sell her home, living in a van with your mother and sister so every penny could be invested in a factory. Years later, you became the leading kitchenware producer in the US and the first to import cookware from China. A fairy tale ending for a boy who supposedly began his career by crafting a mug from dirt for his mother's birthday. From dirt to an empire of gold."

Mr. Hubble nodded. "Back then a ceramic mug cost about fifty cents to manufacture in the US and four cents in China. The profits from overseas manufacturing and importing lower-quality items at cheaper rates provided me with the funding I needed to establish Rising Bank and Hedge Funds years later."

"Making you one of the wealthiest individuals on earth," I remarked bluntly.

He offered a brief grin that faded as his gaze shifted back to the impoverished child whose judging eyes stared down at Hubble. "I was eight years old when I made that famous birthday mug for my mother. I understood even then that we couldn't afford a present on my father's salary as a shoe polisher. She wore her worn-out shoes and the same old dress so that the little we had could be spent on us kids. We were so poor, my sister and I would scavenge wood from dog houses and fences in middle-class neighborhoods during winter for heat." A sad smile touched his lips. "The moment my mother unwrapped the old newspaper from around the mug, tears of happiness streamed down her face. I felt an immense sense of accomplishment. All the blisters and burns from shaping the mug and firing it in a fire pit seemed worth it."

"A touching story," I responded, pretending that his narrative had moved me.

His smile vanished. "If that were the end of it, yes. But you see, nobody knows the rest of the story. My mother, she never drank from the mug. I never gave it much thought until one day when I was thirsty and used the mug to scoop water from one of the buckets in our kitchen. The realization struck the moment the mug became wet—the unmistakable stench of feces. I was shocked, and the mug slipped from my grasp, shattering into tiny pieces before me. Somehow, dog feces must have mixed with the mud I collected." Mr. Hubble shifted uncomfortably in his seat. A hint of disappointment flickered across his face. "How could I have not noticed this? Maybe it was the thrill of my mother's happiness over the mug. Or maybe it was because I was so accustomed to stench and filth that I had become desensitized to it." He paused, then shook his head dismissively. "In the end, it doesn't really matter."

He spread his arms wide, his gaze shifting from me to the fresco above.

"What matters is that standing here, in my grandchildren's million-dollar gaming room, so close to the end of my journey, I can't ignore the truth."

"And that is?" I asked.

His eyes met mine with an intensity that felt like a physical force. "That my entire empire was built on shit."

I maintained eye contact out of respect before returning my gaze to the fresco. Silently, I concurred with his assessment.

Mr. Hubble was a pioneer in the movement that had decimated domestic jobs for astronomical profits. Millions of positions vanished, outsourced abroad to child laborers who worked in barbaric conditions. He had played a key role in shifting the political landscape of our nation to favor inexpensive foreign-made goods. This strategy wasn't just about being wealthy; it was about hoarding it all, leaving scraps for the many while a select few basked in opulence. In his wake, Mr. Hubble had left countless boys like the one depicted on his ceiling, silently passing judgment from above.

"Your silence is deafening, Ms. Nachtnebel," he finally said, his voice frail.

"Silence can be complex and multifaceted, Mr. Hubble," I responded, maintaining my composure as I observed the man whose greed knew no limits. His visage caught the lights of the gaming room as if we stood in the pits of a colorful hell. "But in this instance, you're correct in interpreting my silence as agreement."

His expression shifted to one of curiosity.

I gently smoothed a crease from my silk dress. "While I understand the allure of luxury and support it, the very existence of *billionaires* seems absurd in my view. To amass such wealth without genuine concern for those in poverty mirrors a lack of empathy. Billionaires like yourself often support a political system that solidifies your elite status and supports a cycle of hardship for the less fortunate. My stance may not reflect the outlook toward all individuals of vast wealth, but in your case, you're right: Your empire is built on . . . *shit*." My gaze remained fixed on him.

The shock on his face soon gave way to a bizarre admiration, reflected in the grin on his lips. He opened his mouth to say something but was interrupted.

"Leah!" Luca Domizio's voice echoed through the grand hall. He approached me with a smile and gently placed his hand on my back in a gesture of greeting. He was aware of my dislike for cheek kisses and hugs. "I've been looking for you." Luca smiled at Mr. Hubble. "Blink twice if Ronald has kidnapped you to have you all to himself."

Mr. Hubble laughed. "Luca, I'm afraid this time you're off the mark. I believe nobody could kidnap our most beloved wunderkind. She seems quite immune to my charms, if you really need to know."

"I can't believe we've finally encountered a woman who sees right through your crap. Remember Miss Universe?"

Mr. Hubble chuckled. "How could I forget her? If I laugh on my deathbed, only you, my friend, will know why."

Both men laughed.

"Would you mind if I steal Ms. Nachtnebel for a moment?" Luca asked.

"Only if you bring her back to me," Mr. Hubble said with a grin. "Our conversation was very, well, engaging."

"I'll do my best," Luca promised, then walked out with me onto the terrace. He closed the large double doors as I leaned over the white marble patio railing. Its cool touch soothed my warm skin.

"I knew you had friends in high circles," I said. "But I didn't know how high."

"Most of these friendships stem from my darker days. Some of them are sincere. Others are afraid of me. In any case, as a simple government contractor, I can now openly attend their lavish parties. But you already knew you'd find me here, am I correct?"

I remained silent.

"Something tells me that an innocent evening chat isn't why you asked to speak to me after your concert, is it?" He leaned against the railing next to me.

"No."

He nodded. "They're still talking about you as if it were *their* dying wish that you played here tonight, not Ronald's. The Grand family wants to offer you double whatever he paid you to play at their silver anniversary."

The Grands . . .

I couldn't help but grin. How ironic would that be? And yet, no thanks.

He threw a curt nod in the direction of the great hall. "There must be more wealth in this one room than in all of North America combined. I always thought you despised our nation's puppet masters. Lately, you've surprised me, Leah. First, the concert in Italy, and now this."

He was referring to my history of never playing at these parties before, no matter how much I was offered. Even presidents had to come to Boston to see me. But things had changed. There was an enemy out there far greater than any before.

"I'm adapting to new circumstances," I said.

"I can see that. And I'd be lying if I said it doesn't worry me a bit. Are you in trouble?"

I faked a smile. "Always. Do you know a man called Jan Novak?"

"Never heard of him. But I can ask around."

"Please don't."

It was better to lay low right now. I had nothing on Ian Novak other than a strange feeling. Drawing his attention to me by asking around would not be in my best interest one way or the other.

"But that's not why you called me here," Luca concluded.

"No. I need to ask a favor."

"A favor or repayment of my debt?" He smiled.

"Whatever you want to call it."

His smile faded.

"Will you stand by your word?" I asked.

"Of course. I always do."

I nodded. "I don't know when or where, but someday, an FBI agent will approach you and ask for your help. It's important you do as he says."

Luca's eyes narrowed. "Which will be?"

The floral scent of the vast gardens now felt heavy. "Something that might seem horrific at first, but only you can—"

"No, Leah, not that," he said.

He knew. Of course he did. He was one of the smartest people I had ever met.

"Ask me anything else," he said in a harsh tone. "Anything. Money. This house. Any house. The head of anybody in that room." His finger shot toward the great hall I'd played in only moments ago, where the elite were now conversing over $50,000 whiskey about vacation homes in Europe. "But not that," he added, his eyes scowling as he shook his head.

"I'm sorry. This is what I'm asking of you to release you from your debt. Do I have your word or not, Luca?"

He looked at me in defiance.

"Luca," I said, stepping closer, inches away from him. I could smell his cologne. His body tensed at my proximity. For a moment, he seemed distracted, his narrowed eyes widening. "You've never broken your word. Your word is who you are. You've always said so yourself. Do I have it or not?" I asked again, my hand gently grabbing the white jacket of his immaculate hand-tailored tuxedo.

Agony was evident on his face. He resisted a moment longer. Then, after a light squeeze of my hand on his arm, he finally nodded. With force, he turned away as if unable to look at me for one more second.

I knew my request would hit him hard. Perhaps more so than any other request I could have made. And yet, there was no other way.

"I feel played, Leah," he said as he stared at the garden, his back turned to me. "I would never have asked you for the favor in Italy if I'd known the price of it. You know that."

I pinched my lips, looking at the man whom I had indeed played. All I could hope was that the fallout here would make things easier on him once the time came.

But the Train Track Killer would use all his genius against me, pushing me to the very edge of sanity. Checks and balances had to be in place.

My empire, too, was built on shit.

"I'm sorry, Luca."

He remained silent. I lingered for a moment longer, then departed just as my phone buzzed in my purse.

If this were the moment to feel sorrow, guilt, or shame for my actions concerning Luca, I would have embraced those emotions if I could. But, as had been the case so often before, I found myself unable to feel. No matter how much I wished otherwise, I simply couldn't.

For what it was worth, I did feel a sense of deceit. But a war had begun—a conflict against an enemy vast and unseen, a battle that threatened to obscure my distinctions between right and wrong, good and evil, like a blurry watercolor painting in which one color bled into the next. These were the lines that defined morality, the lines that defined me.

In the context of love and war, as the saying went, all was fair—and in this instance, the same principle applied to the pursuit and eradication of monsters.

Including myself.

CHAPTER ELEVEN

Liam

"Two wrongs can make a right?" McCourt yelled at us, spit flying between words like a rabid dog's barks. His piercing blue eyes bore the look of a man accustomed to command, and his perfectly coiffed silver hair complemented his authoritative stance.

The meeting room of the Behavioral Analysis Unit at the FBI Boston headquarters had never felt smaller. The walls seemed to close in on me as the entire floor's unit crammed into the space. A few lucky individuals had snagged makeshift back-row seats by standing just outside the door; they literally couldn't fit inside.

McCourt clutched a copy of the Boston Globe, its front page featuring an enlarged print of the sticker that had been audaciously placed on Harvey Grand's casket. He brandished the newspaper as though it were a wand and he a wizard ready to declare, "You shall not pass."

"This is the last time—I repeat, the last time—I give you jokers a chance to come clean," he bellowed, slamming the newspaper on the table. The motion rattled the coffee mugs on the table's surface. "Because God, Jesus, Jehovah, Allah, Santa, or whoever else you pray to shall have mercy on your pitiful soul if I find out it was one of my own who did this after I leave this room today!"

A heavy silence fell, punctuated by a stifled cough. I avoided eye contact with McCourt. Instead, my gaze briefly met that of Heather, who had spent most of the meeting staring at the table.

"Senator Wheezer is livid," McCourt continued in a weary yet calmer tone as if he were explaining something painfully obvious to children. "And why is Senator Wheezer livid? Because Senator Wheezer just lost five million dollars in campaign funding from the Grand family. And why does that matter to us, you might ask? Well, let me spell it out for you. Because Senator Wheezer personally requested that the Boston FBI ensure the smooth return of Harvey Grand's body. And when a senator, whose political party has recently approved our request for additional funding for staffing, asks us to do something, do we get it done?" He held up the newspaper again. "Or do we take a big juicy shit in his yard in broad daylight?"

He paused to catch his breath.

"The whole fucking nation is now talking about the Grands. They're receiving death threats. Ruth Grand even had to cancel her trip to Paris, and her grandson has been called a 'monster's cunt' at his private school. And why? Because somehow you managed to turn a confidential mission into a national circus. Before you Einsteins took charge, almost no one knew of the Grands' connection to Harvey Grand." McCourt slammed the newspaper on the table once more. "But leave it to us," he yelled. "The nation's brightest and finest. We'll leak confidential information to the press and ridicule one of the most powerful families in the nation with a sticker that sounds like a bad fortune cookie!"

Dead silence reigned as McCourt caught his breath again. He wasn't done. I knew it was just the eye of the hurricane. I used the brief quiet to check my phone quickly. It read 3:29.

Cold chills raced through me.

The hearing for my never-ending custody battle was at 4:30. I had to leave soon. Really, really soon. And to make matters worse, Leah had been ghosting me for a while. At first, she'd simply denied my requests for a meeting, which pissed me off, considering what she'd pulled with Harvey Grand. But then she'd stopped replying to my texts altogether, which drove me mad with anger and a strange sense of worry. Had the Train Track Killer gotten to her? Was he holding her hostage? Would my car blow up soon? Or would I find her head on my pillow like some sick homage to The Godfather?

Relax, I told myself. It's Leah we're talking about here. And that woman was no one's victim. Not even the Train Track Killer's.

"Last chance. Anybody want to come forward?" McCourt said this in a much kinder tone before his eyes settled on his nephew, Cowboy.

Cowboy, who had been doodling on a piece of paper in front of him, took a moment to realize that everyone was staring at him. When he did, he looked up with lost innocence and scanned the room. "Hmm?" he managed, the sound almost stuck in his throat. His eyes, wide with panic like those of a mouse under a cat's paw, found mine. I quickly shook my head at him, signaling discreetly. He understood and shook his head emphatically at his uncle.

"Are you sure, Theo?" McCourt said, his tone still soft.

"Sure . . . about what?" he replied, hastily covering his doodles.

"The sticker, goddamn it!" McCourt snapped.

"No!" Theo recoiled. "It wasn't me. Of course not! I'm an FBI agent. I wouldn't do something like that! If this is about the smiley sticker that was on my desk . . ." He produced a yellow smiley sticker from his jacket. "It ain't on no coffin. Still have it."

The room buzzed with murmurs and sighs. I rubbed my temples.

McCourt stared at Cowboy in disbelief, then pointed toward the open meeting room door. "Everybody, out!"

Agents hesitated, unsure if this was a trap.

"Now, goddamn it!" McCourt barked.

Everyone rushed to get out as quickly as possible. Already on my feet, I caught McCourt's direct gaze.

"Not you. Rose, Richter, Connor, Martin, and Theo, you stay."

"Shit," I mumbled, checking my phone again. It read 3:57. I had to leave immediately to be only five to ten minutes late. "Sir," I said respectfully, "I really need to go. I have my custody hearing at 4:30 and—"

"Then I recommend you stop bickering and sit down again. This will be over quicker if you do as I say."

I caught the empathetic looks from the others. Missing this hearing wasn't an option. These sessions took months to schedule, and Larsen had been killed before he could help get a new judge. I was officially stuck with one of the most inept judges the bench had ever seen. This judge seemed determined to favor Sara, no matter the size of her lies or demands.

So, I remained standing. "Sir, with all due respect, this custody hearing can impact my rights to see my daughter. I would have called in today, but I wanted to respect your urgency."

McCourt looked at me as if he couldn't believe I dared to defy him openly. "It's your choice, Richter, but if you decide to leave now, you might have to explain to the judge how you plan to support your daughter without a job."

I heard Heather's gasp before Martin's.

May all hell freeze over. Had this asshole really just threatened my job? After everything I had done for this unit?

"Sir." Heather tried to stand up for me, but McCourt raised his finger at her.

"Don't you dare!" he said. "All of you. The situation is bad. Really, really bad. If I end up losing my job because of this, I'll make sure to drag down every bad seed along with me. The FBI deserves only the nation's brightest, not its bottom feeders."

Heather was about to say something else, but before she could get herself in real trouble, I sat down and signaled her to do the same. Hesitantly, she did.

I threw McCourt an intense gaze, which he ignored.

Asshole.

"Where are we with the Bay Reaper?" he demanded. "Elections are coming up for Senator Wheezer, and the Reaper needs to be taken off the streets by any means possible."

Heather opened the manila folder she had tucked under her arm. "We interviewed a suspect, Jason Brown. He matches the description in height and weight and has no real alibi except his alcoholic wife's promise that he was at home with her. Both have a record. Misdemeanors. His sister-in-law called the police on him when she found a skull mask identical to the one used by the Bay Reaper in his laundry room during a visit with his wife. Also, one of the victims released from the hospital, Bonnie Marks, identified him in a lineup. After one wrong try."

"Great. So, that's that, then." McCourt's tense body relaxed for the first time since the meeting had started.

"Not really," I dared to disagree, all eyes on me. "We don't have enough to keep him. The witness didn't reliably identify him. No murder weapon was found, and no DNA ties him to any of the victims."

"So?" McCourt countered. "Agent Connor, when you interviewed him, did he say anything damaging?"

Heather straightened in her chair. "Not to me. The police showed me a confession that he apparently signed after seventeen hours of interrogation. When I met with him, he insisted he signed it just so they would stop. He didn't have a lawyer with him either. There's definitely something wrong about him and the way he acts, but I can't say for sure if it's the behavior of a murderer."

I nervously checked the time again: 4:10.

Fuck, fuck, fuck.

"Open and shut case, if you ask me," McCourt said.

I locked eyes with Agent Rose. Her calm, almost detached demeanor had gained my admiration earlier when McCourt was yelling at us.

"Sir," I said, trying to sound confident yet respectful. "Can I look into the case a bit more? I haven't had the chance to review the new evidence yet." I couldn't sign my name to anything I wasn't certain about. Especially not if it involved framing an innocent person.

"And you won't need to. Focus on helping the AG nail Brown," McCourt replied, gathering his files from the meeting table.

Yes, God, let me out of here.

"Got it," I said, rising to my feet. There was no point in arguing further. I'd investigate the case regardless of what McCourt said. He might be my boss, and he could make my life hell, but ultimately, we all had to follow FBI rules and a code of ethics. Sending innocent people to prison wasn't part of that. "Is the meeting over?" I asked, my legs almost shaking.

The moment McCourt nodded, I turned and ran.

I knew I wouldn't make it on time, but maybe I'd get lucky. Maybe the judge would be late herself. Or, more unlikely, maybe she'd be empathetic to my situation for a change.

As I raced down the courthouse corridor, my footsteps echoed ahead of me. Faded photos of local monuments under dim lights adorned the seemingly endless hallway. I passed several imposing wooden doors, each leading to a courtroom where people's fates hung in the balance, until I halted before one of them.

My breath caught at the sight of my mom sitting on a bench, her figure small next to the old, grand doors of the courtroom. She was wearing her Sunday best, her usual glittering purse replaced with an elegant black leather one. When she met my gaze, her thin lips curled into a sad smile.

"Oh, Liam," she said, rising from the bench to place a gentle hand on my shoulder.

"Please tell me they didn't start yet."

Her silence was like a stab to my heart with a dull, rusty dagger.

"Well, let's go. I'll explain—"

My hand had already reached the door when my mom pulled me aside.

"You're over an hour late."

"They didn't let me out of work, and then I hit commuter traffic."

"I know," she said, her tone soft and understanding for once. "Dan told Judge Ethel Dunbar as soon as you texted him, but she waited only ten minutes. She said that 'she knows entitled men like you.' Then she issued a default judgment in your absence, favoring..."

Her voice broke off as the doors opened and Sarah and her lawyer walked out. She was arm-in-arm with her TikTok boy toy, looking as if she'd just stepped out of a courtroom TV show. Her hair was in a bun, and she wore glasses—with fake lenses—that matched her suit skirt and pumps. Her brown eyes locked on me as a devilish grin formed on her pink-colored lips.

She slowed her pace, her lawyer already walking ahead, unaware. Then she had the audacity to lean in and whisper to me, "Vanilla, Liam. You'll always be vanilla. You were never more than that. Only now, you'll have to be worthless without your child."

I was practically shaking with anger and frustration. If not for my mom grabbing my arm and the fact that Sarah was already moving again, almost halfway down the hallway, I would have lost my cool and called her out for what she was.

A cunning piece of shit who'd thrown her own child under the bus.

"Where the hell is Dan?" I demanded, a little too loudly, as a passing couple looked at me. I searched the hallway for my lawyer. The man to whom I paid four hundred and twenty-five dollars a fucking hour to prevent this very thing from happening.

"He had to go to another trial," my mom said.

I took it all in. How the hell had this happened? All of this. Sara cheating on me. Taking everything. Me working myself to death for a world that had awarded my case to a sexually frustrated old judge who hated men for the same reasons I now hated my ex: getting played.

"It's just all getting so freaking much," I mumbled as my head fell into my hands. My mom's fragile body pressed against me from the side, her thin arms wrapping tightly around me. I was a grown-ass man, but right now, losing Josie . . . I could feel hot tears in my eyes. I felt nauseated.

"Dan said we'll appeal," my mom said. "He says everyone hates that judge. People have filed complaints against her."

I wanted to play this game more than anything else in the world right now. The "let's talk until there's hope again" game. After all, hope was all we had left when darkness swallowed us whole.

But for some reason, my anger sharpened like a knife, and one name was at the tip.

Leah.

I pulled my flip phone out of my coat pocket and opened it.

Nothing.

No calls, not even a "fuck off" text.

I'd had enough. I was sick of being the kind dumbass. I was sick of playing by the rules of decency and kindness when nobody else gave a fuck.

My arms wrapped around my mom, squeezing her tightly. "Don't worry, Mom," I said, realizing she was shaking. "Dan's right. We'll appeal until we get a real judge with some backbone. I don't care if I have to take this all the way to the Supreme Court. We'll get Josie back."

She nodded, sobbing as if she'd been waiting for me to be strong again before showing her own pain.

"Don't cry, Mom. We can still video-call her whenever we want."

She nodded.

"Actually, why don't you go home and do just that? Josie wanted to talk to you about the essay she wrote in school. It was about you."

"Really?" My mom looked at me with wide eyes. The mascara she'd worn so gracefully moments ago was now smeared all over her cheeks.

I nodded. "She read some to me. It was the best essay I've ever heard. She must've gotten that talent from you. No one else in our family knows how to write like a poet."

"I did win an award for a piece I wrote for our school newspaper." My mom smiled again. Good. "Are you coming as well?" she asked as I pulled away from her.

"Later this evening, I will. I have something important to do for work right now."

She frowned, her mouth opening to snap at me—her old self again—when I quickly added, "It's important to have my work in order and great references from my supervisors for when we appeal and get that new judge."

My mom thought about this, then nodded. "Very true. Things need to be in order and look good."

"Exactly," I said. "Come on, I'll walk you to your car."

She nodded again as she wiped away tears.

As I walked her down the hallway, my hand on her back for emotional support, I promised myself two things.

One, I was done being people's little bitch.

And two, "people" included the genius mastermind who thought she had me wrapped around her finger like a puppet on strings, dancing like an idiot to every pull and tug of her whims.

CHAPTER TWELVE

Leah

The moment I stepped into my townhouse on Beacon Hill, I sensed something was off. The alarm system had remained untriggered, yet the unmistakable presence of someone in the house lingered in the air. Ida was likely already asleep or watching TV in her cottage in the backyard, as she would have greeted me right away if it were her.

I reminded myself to stay calm. My body's first instinct was to release adrenaline, which would have been helpful if I planned to run, but that wasn't my intention.

As though nothing were amiss, I switched on the lights in the hallway and walked upstairs to the master bedroom closet, keeping a vigilant eye on the stairway as I did.

No shadow or movement.

Good.

With a smooth motion, I retrieved the loaded handgun from beneath a pile of folded silk pajamas, then selected one of the garments and put it on.

Maintaining a normal pace and holding the gun behind my back, I descended into the darkness of my study. There, I listened intently for unusual noises, ready to aim and shoot at a moment's notice. I was about to turn on the light when a voice broke the silence.

"It's me, don't shoot," Liam said calmly.

For a moment, I remained motionless at the wide entrance to the study. Then I lowered the gun and turned on the light.

Liam was seated on the Victorian wood bench by the bay window overlooking the back garden. He was dressed in gray jogging pants and a sweat-soaked T-shirt. A hoodie was loosely tied around his hips. A black backpack leaned against the bench on the floor.

"A rather risky move, don't you think?" I asked.

"Maybe. But don't you want to know how I got in?"

I calmly made my way to my desk. "The small cat door in the kitchen, of course. You used a wire to unlock the door from the inside. Then you used the law enforcement code for the alarm system to turn it off. What I'm curious about is, if you knew I was armed, why did you wait until I came back downstairs before you identified yourself? A little idiotic, don't you think?"

Liam's face contorted with anger. "I jogged five fucking miles in the dark, and I'm going to have to jog five fucking miles back to my car. So, don't get smart with me now. I waited here for you because you went straight upstairs to your bedroom, and I didn't want to follow you there like some pervert."

"So, you risked a bullet to the head in the name of decency? Next time, I'd prefer you do something you deem morally wrong over getting yourself killed."

I placed the gun on the wooden desk next to a bottle of wine and a set of glasses, then made my way to the large stone fireplace. Liam watched with curiosity as I built a fire from a small pile of wood beside it before taking a seat behind my desk.

"How can I help you?" I asked, reaching for the bottle of wine and pouring myself a glass. My gaze lingered on the empty second glass, the one I had set out for Emanuel months ago but hadn't removed. It wasn't in anticipation of guests but as a poignant reminder of my failure that had led to his death. A promise to myself to try harder next time, regardless of the cost.

"How can you help me? Let me tell you how." Liam held up the flip phone. "Remember this thing?" His tone was tense and laced with sarcasm. "People use it to communicate, meaning it's a two-way street, Leah. Back and forth."

"So, you thought it was wise to break into my house to confront me?"

"Wise wasn't part of the equation," Liam retorted, stepping closer. "But it was a risk I was willing to take to get a few things straight." His expression softened. "And to make sure you were okay. I was worried."

"Worried?" I raised an eyebrow.

He recoiled slightly. "Yes, worried. I've been texting you for almost two weeks. You rejected every meeting request, then completely ghosted me for days. I was losing my mind, checking your social media and the news for any sign of your death. I even drove past your house a few times. The Train Track Killer is still out there, doing who knows what. So, yeah, I was both pissed and worried, if that's all right."

I leaned back in my chair, watching the flames cast a soft glow on his face. He wasn't particularly handsome, at least not in the way the escorts I paid for were. Still, he had a quality that any discerning woman would be wise to value. That quality was worth more than A-list Hollywood looks.

Loyalty and kindness.

Liam had plenty of it in a world desperately lacking in both.

I grabbed the bottle of wine and poured him a glass before he could decline.

He looked at the glass warily for a moment. Maybe he was concerned about leaving DNA, or maybe he thought I'd poison him. But then he took it and settled into the chair across from mine, on the other side of the desk. He opened his mouth to speak, but I was quicker.

"I thought you needed some time to digest Harvey Grand. That's why I didn't agree to a meeting and stopped replying to your texts. I'm sorry it caused you emotional distress. I'll try to be better about returning your texts."

Liam's mouth closed. He appeared to be satisfied. Then he leaned onto the desk, glass still in hand, his intense look returning. "Thanks. Now, regarding Harvey . . ." He sighed, shaking his head. "What. The. Actual. Fuck, Leah. Have you seen the man? I mean, have you actually *seen* what he looks like now? Cuz if you haven't, I'm more than happy to show you some pictures. But let me warn you, it ain't pretty. It's bad. Really, really bad."

I let him speak as I sipped my wine.

"Actually, no. Not bad," he continued. "The right words for it would be fucking horrific, Leah. He looks fucking horrific."

"I'm aware. I stuck to drugs, as agreed, but allowed for some artistic freedom."

"Artistic freedom?" he echoed. "Are you kidding me? McCourt was furious. Not only did I get yelled at for this shit, but if the media had found out how bad Harvey really looked, it could have drawn a lot more attention than the shitstorm we're dealing with now. And I have enough on my plate as is!"

There was more than anger here. I wondered what else was at stake for him.

"I apologize," I said.

There was a brief silence as if he hadn't expected my apology and was now searching for plan B.

"Apologize, huh?" he said, much calmer now, like an erupted volcano with no lava left. "That's not enough, Leah. I . . . I can't work like this. I understand Harvey Grand was a monster who had it coming, but what I saw down there in that morgue wasn't a human being anymore."

"He never was."

"Maybe so, but I'm an FBI agent. I can't do it like this, Leah, and nothing you say can change that. If that's something you can't deal with, well, then we've got a problem."

He looked up, his gaze locking onto mine. The flickering firelight cast a warm glow in his brown eyes, intensifying their depth. It was captivating, peering into them. There was an almost childlike innocence in Richter, a belief in a better world, paired with a steadfast determination to defend his ideals. This combination fascinated me. I'd never seen anything like it.

I reached for the wine bottle, inadvertently sweeping over the gun in the process. Out of the corner of my eye, I noticed he didn't flinch. Perhaps, deep down, he knew I'd never harm him.

"All right," I said, my tone devoid of emotion.

"All right?"

"I accept your terms. For now."

He furrowed his brow, then nodded. "Good. Thank you." He downed his glass in one gulp. "Sorry, I was really thirsty. The jog here was brutal." His gaze swept the study as I leaned over the desk to refill his glass, but he placed his hand over it. "No thanks."

"Water?" I offered.

He shook his head. "But it's nice, meeting in an actual home for a change. That whole meeting-on-a-dock-in-the-rain thing isn't as exciting as movies make it out to be. Can't you get the keys to your abandoned factory near the docks so we can meet there? This is the wettest year on record. After our meetings, I have to wear wet clothes all day."

I couldn't help but grin. "I'll look into it."

His lips twisted into a smile. Then an awkward silence fell upon the room, punctuated only by the crackling of the fire.

"Have you discovered anything new about the Train Track Killer?" I asked.

He shook his head, his shoulders drooping. "No, nothing. I've been monitoring the entire train network from New York to Portland for deaths but haven't spotted anything out of the ordinary. What about you? Anything from your meeting with the Egyptologist?"

I shared his feeling of defeat more than I cared to admit. "Nothing substantial. But I did manage to get some additional insights into the symbolism of the ankh. It's commonly associated with eternal life, but the Egyptologist presented a compelling argument that it might also represent a mirror."

"A mirror? Like a reflection of the killer?"

"A reflection of his true self. Maybe as a preparation for the afterlife."

Liam's gaze drifted off, and a thoughtful furrow formed between his brows. "Or he believes these murders will give him powers or immortality."

I leaned back in my chair. "I've been mulling it over, and yes, that's a possibility. But it's only one theory among many. Maybe the Train Track Killer believes that by revealing his true self and making offerings, he'll gain favor with the gods or whichever higher power he believes in."

"Like some twisted version of the Make-A-Wish Foundation?"

"Possibly. If his victims were human sacrifices."

"And the trains? Why the train tracks?"

That question tortured me. I had no definitive answer. "I can't say for certain. There might be a link to his past. Maybe he lived near a train station, or maybe he suffered a traumatic event involving trains. But it's equally plausible that he simply uses them as a means to conceal his crimes. Train police are underfunded and lack a dedicated murder investigation unit. Moreover, they're notoriously inept at seeking assistance from local police. The train tracks could just be a cunning strategy to remain undetected."

"Which he has, for years."

I nodded solemnly. "We must continue to scrutinize old and new files, but I'm afraid he's currently dictating the play, and we're mere pawns."

Liam clenched his fists. I hadn't intended for my words to strike him as harshly as they did, but the truth can have that effect when it isn't in one's favor.

Suddenly, the black and white cat I'd rescued from Emanuel's apartment leaped onto the desk, nearly toppling my wine glass and the bottle. Initially, the arrangement was meant to be temporary, as shelters were full. However, after my assistant failed to secure a home, and the grim alternative was a for-kill shelter, weeks morphed into months. Now, the cat stood as yet another reminder of the failure that had cost Emanuel his life.

"You . . . have a cat?" Liam's face was etched with a surprised curiosity.

"Not really. It just lives here."

"Rrrrrrriiiiiight," he said.

The cat settled on the desk, scattering fur, which I must confess was a significant irritant. Yet, feeling accountable for its situation, I felt obligated toward the animal. Ida and her family loved the cat, but one of her grandchildren was highly allergic, so the cat couldn't live with them permanently.

"I think it wants to be petted," Liam declared as the cat meowed loudly, its large green eyes fixed on me. Ida was overfeeding it, I concluded from its drooping belly.

"I'm aware," I responded, "but it typically seeks Ida's affection over mine."

Liam struggled to suppress a grin, then surrendered to a full-on smirk. "Well, it won't leave until you pet it. Trust me, I had one of those fur-balls before my ex took him along with everything I love."

His demeanor began to darken, the sadness returning to his gaze, so I quickly interjected, "I don't know the proper way to pet it."

The smirk returned to his lips. "La Imperatrice is unfamiliar with the art of petting a cat?"

His mocking tone irked me. "Clearly, I know how to pet an animal. But my concern is that the cat could perceive my actions as insincere and lacking in genuine warmth. That, in essence, would be unkind. No?"

Liam burst into laughter. "For Christ's sake, Leah. Sometimes a damn cat is just a damn cat."

Before I could respond, he stood, leaned over, and softly clasped my hand. I watched in astonishment as he guided my hand in gentle, rhythmic strokes over the cat's soft fur. The contact, his skin against mine, was thrilling. Or perhaps it was the brief drop in his defenses. For a moment, it seemed as if we'd been close for years.

The only sound in the room was the cat's loud purring as Liam continued to guide my hand. Then the cat bounced off the desk and walked into the kitchen, where Ida had arranged a feeding station in an adjacent pantry.

Liam released my arm and resettled in his chair. "See?" he said, still grinning. "It got what it wanted and then dumped you. Totally normal. Cats are fun creatures, aren't they?"

I remained seated, wrestling with how to process what had just happened. Larsen would never have dared to touch me.

But Agent Liam Richter...

Did the presence of this cat in my home make me appear more human to him? The logic was flawed. History had shown that even monsters like Gacy and Hitler could show affection to animals while committing unspeakable acts against humans.

"Can I ask your opinion on something?" Agent Richter inquired as he retrieved his black bag from the floor.

"Certainly, if it's quick," I replied, rubbing the spot where he had touched me.

He produced a laptop from his bag and placed it on the desk between us. "I'm sure you've heard of the Bay Reaper? He's been all over the news."

"I have, but he's not a typical serial killer. His pattern aligns more with a mass shooter."

"A mass shooter?" Liam echoed, concern filling his voice.

I nodded. "Mass shooters often seek notoriety or act from a vendetta against society, as they desire attention for their personal grievances. Their actions are high-profile, aimed at making a statement in public as some form of revenge."

"Some serial killers want that sort of attention too," he pointed out.

"In rare cases, yes. But serial killers typically operate over a longer period, driven by deeper psychological compulsions for power and control, usually away from the public eye."

Liam turned to the laptop. "This is footage of a potential suspect. His sister-in-law found a skull mask identical to the one used in the stabbings in his laundry room. One of the eyewitnesses identified him in a lineup. His only alibi is his wife, who insists he was at home during the attacks."

I watched the video on the laptop. In it, an older man in military pants and boots was led into a cramped police interrogation room. Two overweight detectives flanked him. "Can you fast-forward to the end?" I asked.

"What?"

"The ending, can you skip to it?"

"Um, sure, but the interrogation was quite intense, and we have a confession. Don't you want to see that part?"

"Not really. I have no doubt about the confession, judging by the two GI Joe police officers in the room. Now, would you mind fast-forwarding to the end?"

Liam's gaze lingered on me for a moment. Then he sighed and pressed a few buttons. "Alright, here you go."

I watched as the older man, exhausted and limping, exited the room, handcuffed, the weight of the world crushing his wide shoulders.

"It's not him," I declared, steepling my fingers.

"All right, Columbo, care to elaborate a bit here?"

"Sure. The man in this video limped into the interrogation room. He has a leg injury that I suspect would prevent him from running long distances or even short sprints. Wasn't one of the attacks by the Bay Reaper prevented by a group of young friends, and he fled on foot? You have to be in good shape to outrun younger men."

Liam looked at me, a mix of puzzled admiration and defiance in his eyes. "He could have faked the limp for the interrogation. Many suspects fake injuries to look vulnerable."

"Which is why I asked you to fast-forward. After hours of grueling questioning, he most likely would have dropped the act if it were fake. However, his manner of rising from the chair, shifting weight to his left leg, and using his arms to spare his right leg seemed genuine."

With narrowed eyes, Liam watched the end of the interrogation several times.

"You could always request a warrant for his medical records to confirm or debunk my theory. Hasn't the FBI interrogated him? Typically, your agents don't rush to judgment without solid evidence, unlike smaller police departments."

Liam leaned back in his chair. "We did interrogate him. Not me personally, but a colleague of mine. I usually trust her judgment, and she mentioned having a bad feeling about the guy."

"Understandable given the nature of the crimes, but I would strongly advise basing judgments on facts rather than feelings. Feelings change. Facts don't."

"I actually agree with you. But McCourt is convinced this man is the Bay Reaper. He's, well, not very receptive to other theories, to put it mildly."

"McCourt is an opportunist. The scandal with Larsen and political changes have put FBI Director Helen Finch in hot water. She's on shaky ground. McCourt knows this is the perfect time for him to step up and become the next FBI Director. But to secure his position, he must prove himself to Congress and the president. With elections on the horizon, he sees the Bay Reaper situation as a strategic asset in key battleground states, including those along the Seacoast. Fear has been a potent tool in both classical and modern political climates since ancient Roman times."

"So, who do you think is behind these stabbings?"

"The TV coverage and eyewitness statements describe a muscular male wearing tactical pants and boots, which suggests he might be ex-military. I wouldn't be surprised if the victims' stab wounds matched the size of a KA-BAR USMC Straight Edge."

"A marine knife? You think he could be an ex-marine?"

"Or an Army Ranger. Why would that surprise you? The government dumps active-duty personnel and veterans the moment they exhibit war-induced injuries. Physical or mental. Many veterans struggle to access adequate mental health services. It's led to a silent crisis of untreated trauma and psychological struggles."

He nodded. "Why do you think he isn't killing them?"

"There could be several reasons, but it's possible he's struggling with dehumanizing his victims."

"You mean he's trying to view us Americans as the enemy but is finding it difficult?"

"Possibly. Soldiers often receive training that encourages them to demonize overseas enemies and their cultures. But considering how veterans are treated by our government, it might not be long before he starts seeing fellow citizens as enemies. Once the first body drops, that's when we'll be seen as the enemy too."

There was a brief silence before Liam packed his laptop away. "Thank you for your insights. I should get going. Josie wants to video-call me at eight, and I still have that damn jog back to my car."

As I stood, I tried not to show it, but Agent Richter had managed to surprise me again. The casual way he mentioned his daughter's name, as if I already knew her, made it seem as though he were speaking to an old friend. I harbored no illusions about our working relationship. Agent Liam Richter likely pegged me as a psychopath, as he should. Yet he seemed to have acknowledged that I wasn't an uncontrollable monster like Harris or the Train Track Killer. In his eyes, I was a human being. It shouldn't have felt as good as it did.

Liam slung his backpack over his shoulder and gave me a faint smile. "No more radio silence," he said.

I nodded. "You can get out through the backyard gate. It's dark and leads to a small alley behind my home."

"Thanks, and . . . sorry for the break-in."

I escorted him to the back door in my kitchen. "Do you know a man by the name of Jan Novak?"

Liam paused, scratching his chin, then shook his head. "No, why? Is he a suspect?"

The memory of Jan Novak glaring at me from the shadows of a dark corner in the Egyptian exhibition during my conversation with Emilia surged forward. His eyes had held a glow that, to this day, remained mysterious to me. "He was at the museum tour," I said.

"Did he say anything suspicious to you?"

Reflecting on our conversation, I recalled the peculiar mix of suspicion and innocence in his words, his probing questions about killing killers. "It's difficult to pinpoint. He's highly intelligent, and certain comments sparked my curiosity."

"I could look into him."

"Can you do so discreetly, without anyone knowing?"

"If I handle it personally, yes."

I nodded "Tι ιιι kιιιιι ιιhιιι you find."

There was an awkward silence. Liam stood in my kitchen, shrouded in darkness, with only the hallway light spilling in. "There... is something else," he finally said.

I waited for him to continue.

"We received a tip about the Boston Strangler."

"The Boston Strangler?" I repeated. "He's dead. Albert DeSalvo has been linked to the most recent victim."

He nodded. "But as you know, evidence suggests there may have been two stranglers, and the second one was never found. An older woman called, saying her father talks about strangling women in his dreams. I traced the call back to Jill Wilson. She's a crime podcast addict and claims to recognize some of the Strangler's victims in her father's mumbling. Her father is Donald Wilson. I looked into his background, and there might be some truth to her wild claim."

"Truth to him being the Boston Strangler?" The information stunned me as much as the fact that Liam had almost withheld it—a sign that trust was now an issue between us. It wasn't surprising, given our work together.

"As crazy as it sounds, yes. Donald Wilson is a retired parking enforcement officer. That son of a gun is old as hell, ninety-three, but besides a recent hip replacement, he seems to be in great health."

I took it all in, every word. Excitement rushed through my veins like lava from a volcano. If this monster were finally brought to justice, it would be a welcome distraction from the Train Track Killer's years of playing me. "Did you look into the parking tickets near the murders to see if his signature is on them?" I asked.

Liam hesitated again, then slowly nodded. "They... match."

My eyes narrowed as a slight grin spread across my lips.

"His tickets can be traced back to several locations of the murders. Even the dates match." Liam studied my face. "He also had a rape charge and a few domestic violence arrests. I could get a DNA test done."

"No. I'll take care of it."

"Leah..."

"I said I'll take care of it. I'll reach out once I have the locations of the missing bodies."

Another moment of silence hung between us. Neither of us spoke.

"Let me know when it's done," he finally said, then departed.

I lingered, watching the door through which he had just exited. I had promised Liam to restrain myself, for now at least. But when faced with a killer, could I truly hold back? I'd never made such a promise before, and the gratification of making monsters endure their own torment was one of the few joys in my life.

So, when I confronted the Train Track Killer or the Boston Strangler, would I honor my promise? If I couldn't, what did that say about me? That I was a monster myself? A threat to Agent Richter and others? Someone he had to eliminate?

The pact I had made with Luca Domizio provided a strange solace. If Liam ever deemed it necessary to act on it, I would trust his judgment completely. It was oddly comforting. There was a certain allure in knowing I would meet my end before becoming a true monster myself.

But for now, I had to plan and execute my next rendezvous with a killer. And, given his age and infamy, there was no time to waste.

When I saw Jill Wilson sitting at her cluttered desk in the living room of her modest three-bedroom in Mattapan, I knew this mission was rushed and riskier than usual. In the old days, I would have taken Donald Wilson away from his house, tortured him slowly until he confessed and revealed the locations of any missing bodies, and then tortured him more to make him pay. But given my promise to Richter and the broken trust between us, such a *modus operandi* wouldn't be wise in this case. I couldn't operate without an ally in law enforcement. The tip from a broken-hearted daughter that led me here tonight was proof of that.

Jill was absorbed in a true crime podcast about John Wayne Gacy on her computer while a dating reality TV show murmured from the television. It was 10:46 p.m. A quick scan of the room revealed an older woman who had devoted every inch of herself to her children and grandchildren. Pictures of smiling faces were everywhere. Yet the absence of any photographs of Donald Wilson—a man with domestic violence and rape charges—suggested he had shattered his family just as such men usually did.

I quietly made my way along the wall until I found a shadowy corner where I could watch undetected. I observed the woman with curly silver hair as she drank coffee. People who consumed coffee at this hour did so to stay awake—either to avoid nightmares or simply to savor the silence of the night. I knew Jill wasn't seeking silence.

We both listened as the podcast recounted John Wayne Gacy's love for his childhood dog, Prince. Growing up in a violent home with an abusive father, Gacy had found solace in his relationship with Prince. This bond was shattered when Gacy's alcoholic father killed the dog. Gacy buried Prince, stealing flowers for the grave, and was said to never be the same.

"It makes you wonder if a monster could be saved after all, or at least be taught right from wrong before their soul is swallowed by pure evil," I said, breaking the silence.

Jill flinched and sprang to her feet, staring straight at me. I wore a face mask and was dressed in a dark coverall.

"You were right about your father," I continued. "He's a monster who killed many women."

"Who are you?" Jill demanded, frozen in place. Panic and fear twisted her face. The podcast continued playing in the background.

"It doesn't matter," I replied calmly, stepping out of the darkness. "I won't hurt you."

Her gaze flicked down the hallway, where her father was sleeping in a room next to the room where one of her granddaughters slept.

"Quite risky to have the girl here with him around, don't you think?"

Jill stared at me for a moment before bolting for her cell phone on the couch.

"No doubt, the police belong here," I said as she fumbled with her screen. "But before you call them, consider what the world will say and do to your family once they discover the monster this house harbors."

Jill froze, her eyes wide in shock. Her gaze locked on mine.

"As I said, I'm not here to hurt you. I'm here to work with you to make things right—things you, your children, and your grandchildren shouldn't suffer for."

A tense moment passed before Jill tossed the phone back onto the couch. "It's true then?" Her voice was low and weak. "He really killed all those women?"

"Not all of them," I said, "but many, yes. Deep down, you know what he's capable of. He did horrible things to you and your mother, and he'd do the same to your kids and grandkids if you let him."

A tear rolled down Jill's red cheek. Another tear followed it. "I don't have to look very deep to know what this man is capable of. He never made a fuss about hiding it."

I nodded. "Yet you care for him in his final years and let him near your kids."

Jill shook her head. "I'd never let him hurt them. He wasn't allowed near us until about a year ago, after his hip surgery went wrong and both legs were amputated due to a bad infection. He ended up in a wheelchair. When the hospital called and told me I was his emergency contact, I wanted to hang up. But when they told me that they'd found him homeless on the street..." Her voice faltered. "I couldn't say no." She shook her head in disbelief, her gaze dropping to the floor. "They said he'd pass soon. But here we are. I don't know how he keeps going. We all thought he was on his way out, so I granted his wish to die in his childhood home. This house belonged to his parents before my mother took it in the divorce. But I guess darkness gives you more strength to live than light does. He'll probably outlive us all."

I stepped closer, slowly, cautiously. "He won't make it till morning."

Jill's head shot up as she met my eyes.

"I'll put an end to this monster. Here. Tonight. The only question is whether you'll look the other way for the sake of your children and grandchildren or fight me for a monster who doesn't deserve another second on this earth."

Jill's tears flowed more freely until she was weeping into her fist. How anyone could still care for a man like this was a mystery to me, but then again, love itself was foreign to me.

"Captain Fuzzy," she said, her voice weak. "That was the name of my father's cat. A stray. He was the only creature my father ever spoke of with warmth in his eyes. My mother told me how my father used to torture and kill other cats in the neighborhood, pierce them with sticks. Then he'd go home and cuddle Captain Fuzzy all night. Captain Fuzzy meant something to him, maybe something some would even call love. How bizarre." She pressed her fist tightly against her lips again. "These poor women, the way he speaks about them in his sleep . . . I don't think a man like my father could ever be saved, not after he crossed that line of evil. Maybe a long time ago, when he was just a boy—before my grandfather beat the last bit of love out of him. If anybody had saved him then, maybe these women would still be alive. Now it's too late."

Slowly, with the walk of a broken woman, she made her way back to her desk, to the podcast that had been running the entire time.

"I'll check on him in the morning like I always do." Tears were still streaming down her face. "What I find, I'll find."

I nodded and made my way past her into the hallway. There, I stopped briefly. "It'll look like an overdose on his pain medication. If he cooperates, you won't find anything but a man who died in his sleep. If he doesn't, you'll need to tell the ambulance in the morning that he had frontotemporal dementia and that he hurt himself before he killed himself."

Her eyes widened.

I quickly added, "Your granddaughter won't hear anything. We'll be quiet in there."

Jill wiped her tears with a heavy sniffle, then nodded. "Nobody will find out who he really was?" she asked.

I shook my head. "It was selfless of you to call the FBI, but this man has terrorized others long enough. I'll find out where the missing bodies of those women are and send an anonymous note to the police with the locations. I'll tell them the killer died a painful death many years ago. Some families might find comfort in that. But there's no need to destroy your children's and grandchildren's lives over this. The world would treat them unfairly. A monster like your father can be a burden for generations to come."

Jill nodded. I was almost down the hallway when her shaking voice reached me one last time. "Thank you," she said.

"Frontotemporal dementia," I repeated. "Tell them he struggled with thoughts of harming himself." Then I listened for any sounds from Donald's room or his great-granddaughter's room next to it. Hearing nothing, I entered his dark room with my backpack of supplies.

I had a feeling this man wouldn't simply talk, so I was prepared: tape to cover his mouth and prevent screams, a local anesthetic to relieve pain when he was willing to cooperate, and ammonia mixed with water to wake him up if he passed out from the pain. I still needed him to write down the locations of the bodies, so killing him right away wasn't my goal. Fortunately, I didn't need any injections to kill him; a little digging into his most recent prescriptions revealed that Donald had enough fentanyl patches to do the job for me. He had ten 50 mcg/h patches—more than enough to kill him several times over.

It wasn't the death I'd wished for him, but with a little luck, this monster would resist and grant me some foreplay before the drugs carried him into hell.

I'd already decided on the method I'd use to make him talk. His legs were gone, but the weapon he'd used against those women was still intact. By that, I meant the weapon between his missing legs.

Cutting it off with scissors would be a hell of a way to persuade him to cooperate.

Agent Richter trusted me not to leave a gruesome scene, but surely he wouldn't mind a small detail like this if it meant we'd be able to recover the missing women for whom many families had been searching their entire lives.

CHAPTER THIRTEEN

Agent Vallery Rose

Rose spotted the black FBI SUV the moment it rounded the corner. She was unloading another pallet of water bottles from the donation van in front of the homeless shelter when Agent Richter pulled up beside her. Setting down the water, she walked over to him.

"I guess now I know two people who might beat the odds and make it into heaven," Richter remarked, his tone a blend of jest and admiration.

"Let me guess. The other person is you?" Rose quipped.

"Me?" Richter chuckled, shaking his head. "No way in hell. I meant my daughter."

"I see. Well, if volunteering a few hours at a shelter were all it took to avoid those flames, we'd have more than four volunteers today," Rose said.

Richter scanned the surroundings—the individuals sitting alone, clutching their belongings, their faces etched with resignation. He nodded toward a woman in a dirt-stained pink ski jacket who was digging a hole by a bush in the front yard. "What's she doing?" he asked.

Rose followed his gaze and sighed when she saw the scene. "Goddammit," she muttered under her breath, then shouted, "Cynthia! Please stop digging holes in the front yard."

Cynthia looked up, then scurried away.

Rose sighed again. "It took me hours to fill those back in last month."

"Why is she doing that?" Richter asked.

"Because our system kicks those with mental health issues to the curb," Rose explained, "and because she believes she's creating tunnels for hobbits. But what can I do for you?"

"Do you have a moment to spare?" Agent Richter asked. "I want to show you something."

Rose checked her phone. "We start handing out meals in two hours."

"You'll be back in one."

"It's my day off."

"I know. That's why I'm offering to trade you an hour today for a whole day off later."

She pondered this for a moment, then nodded and got into the car.

Rose sat in the driver's seat next to Liam, her gaze fixed on the Cape Cod jail. It was a typical East Coast detention center: a discreet brick complex set apart by its small, secured windows and controlled entry points.

Silence had swallowed the car as they sat there observing the entrance.

Among the many thoughts crowding her mind, one stood out: Why on earth had Richter involved her in this side mission? He was well aware of her role within his unit—and the reasons behind it.

Dragging her along felt counterintuitive, and Rose hated unpredictability—in situations and people alike.

"So . . . any family in the area? Agent Richter ventured. "Any hobbies?"

It was another subtle probe, another attempt to connect. "No," she replied, shutting down the conversation. If Agent Richter expected her to open up like a chatty housewife on a daytime talk show, he'd be disappointed. And if he thought she didn't see through his tactics, he'd be even more disappointed. "McCourt will be really pissed about this, but you know that already," Rose said, still focused on the jail entrance.

"I do." Agent Richter sounded unconcerned.

"So . . . why?"

He turned to her as if she had posed the most bizarre question. "Why what?"

"Really?" Rose scoffed, more annoyed than amused, but she added, "Sir."

Agent Richter regarded her with a scrutinizing look.

"I see," she said. "May I speak freely?"

He nodded.

"Since you're so interested in me all of a sudden, out of the many things I could tell you about myself, including the fact that I hate bullies almost as much as I hate cheesecake, there's really only one thing you need to know."

Richter maintained his attentive stare. "Which is?"

"That while people were opening doors for you, those very same people either slammed them in my face or tried to get in my pants. I grew up in an America some people choose to deny exists. A shitshow not in some far-off communist country but right here, in front of our middle-class mortgaged doorsteps."

She had barely spoken the words, and there it was: the haunting memory of gunshots, the vivid image of her brother lying on the ground, his eyes wide with panic, gasping for breath, urging her to run as he choked on his own blood.

She shook it off.

"I need superhero strength in this world to survive"—she steadied herself—"so if you think you can play me, you're wrong."

A heavy silence filled the SUV.

"Now, let me ask you again," Rose said, regaining her composure, her gaze piercing. "Why did you bring me on a mission you knew would piss off McCourt?"

Rose was somewhat surprised when Agent Richter, instead of getting defensive, simply nodded. "Fair enough," he replied, adjusting his position. "Let's get to the point, then."

"I'd appreciate that."

He pursed his lips. "What are you doing at the BAU, Agent Rose? Why has McCourt assigned an organized crime unit agent fresh out of the academy to one of the most demanding units on the force, one that usually requires years of field experience? Even Cowboy has several post-academy years under his belt."

Ah, there it was. Rose knew there was a hidden agenda behind all of this.

"Well, maybe I'm the Michael Jordan of the FBI," Rose quipped. "Maybe McCourt noticed that and decided to put me here straight out of school."

Richter arched an eyebrow.

"Fine," she said, returning to a serious tone. "But here's a question for you first . . . Sir. Does it really matter if the assistant director of the FBI wants to keep a close eye on a unit that's just been rocked by one of the biggest scandals in FBI history? Larsen made the FBI look like shit."

"It matters to me."

"Oh, yeah? I pull my shifts like everybody else and, so far, thought I was doing a pretty decent job at it. Or are there complaints I'm unaware of?"

"No, you've done more than a pretty good job, actually. Quite impressive, given your lack of experience. It's as if you've been doing this work all your life."

For a moment, Rose experienced the unmistakable warmth of pride swelling in her chest. Hearing those words—words McCourt could never bring himself to utter—felt incredibly satisfying.

"Then"—her tone softened—"why does it matter what I may or may not do for McCourt?"

Agent Richter's face turned grave. His gaze locked with hers. "I'll tell you why it matters. Because as long as you roll with my crew, I need to know whether you wear your badge for a man whose ambitions might not always align with what's right."

As if on cue, the front doors of the police station swung open. A stout elderly woman, maneuvering a walker in front of her, emerged. She was followed closely by Jason Brown, who limped. Their dirty, worn clothes hinted at a life of food stamps and struggle. In weary silence, they headed to an aged SUV parked nearby.

"Or," Agent Richter continued, his eyes fixed on the man who had nearly been wrongfully imprisoned for McCourt's ambition, "do you wear the badge for the people you swore to protect?"

Rose watched the Browns struggle to store the walker and climb into the vehicle. For Mrs. Brown, the ordeal seemed to be like climbing a mountain.

"Let's be even more frank, Agent Rose," Richter said.

Their eyes met once more.

"If I were to take a bullet for you—as I would for any BAU agent—will my daughter cry at my funeral over a man who did the right thing, or will her tears be shed for an idiot who died for a power-hungry man's footwoman?"

Rose almost laughed. She had to give it to Richter. Out of all the fake people she had met in her life, he truly radiated that certain glow that all those righteous people with overly high levels of integrity seemed to emit. They were a rare bunch. A needle in a haystack full of bullshitters. And yet. If he thought he could bring her here, spit out a few clever words, and make her betray the man to whom she owed everything, he was mistaken.

"Fair enough." She mirrored his earlier words, signaling the start of an understanding. "But how about this? If I promise you that I wear my badge to protect people at all costs, does the rest matter?"

Agent Richter studied her for a moment, then nodded. "No. For now, that's all I need to know."

"Good," Rose said, igniting the car's engine. "Looks like we're good, then. Or is there another stop for me on this little field trip? Maybe Legoland?"

"Nope. We're good. For now."

Liam

I dropped off Rose at the shelter and drove away. I didn't wait for her to get out of sight before I called Cowboy.

"Sup, man?" His voice bounced through the phone as I pulled around the corner.

I shook my head, annoyed even at the way he answered the phone. "Where are you?"

"At headquarters. Looking for potential suspects for the Bay Reaper. Heather did a deep search and found quite a few veterans in the area who fit the new profile."

"Good. Hey, listen, could you do me a favor?"

"What's in it for me?" he said.

"Are you kidding—"

"Relax, just joking. What do you need?"

I got into my car and closed the door, then turned on the engine. "Agent Rose—"

"Our Vallery Rose?"

"Yes. She was transferred here from Organized Crime. Did you know her before you came here?"

"Nope. Never heard of her, but I can ask my uncle about her."

"I'm afraid that's not what I'm going for here." There was a brief silence. In my rearview mirror, I watched an agent walk to his car.

"I see," Cowboy said. "Well, I still got some friends at Organized Crime. I'll ask around a bit."

"Discreetly."

"Of course."

"Great, thanks a ton—"

"So, what's in it for me?"

"Are you serious?" I snapped. "I'm still not sure if it wasn't you who slapped that damn sticker on Harvey's rotting corpse, and you're trying to play me?"

"Relax, kidding again."

I sighed loud enough for him to hear.

"I got this, boss," he said, taking on the accent of some Italian mafioso. "You can trust me."

I shook my head, sighing again. Why the hell was I recruiting Cowboy for help at all? This would blow up in my face. I knew it.

"Thanks. Keep up the good work with the suspects."

"Yes, siiir," he said.

I hung up and pulled over for a minute. The thought of meeting her again was stirring up some stage fright. These meetings with Leah always felt surreal.

On the other hand, as strange as it was, the prospect of meeting her eased the feeling of being buried alive with work and the ache of losing custody of my daughter. Then there was the Boston Strangler. Did she take care of him? Why didn't she let me know like she said she would?

The surreal world she had created, pulling me along, seemed to soothe my worldly pains, of which I had too many to count.

"All right," I said, heading back to headquarters to leave my phones behind and switch vehicles so I couldn't be traced. "Hope the meeting will be inside this time."

CHAPTER FOURTEEN

Leah

As I stepped into the abandoned rope-making factory, the crunch of broken glass under my feet echoed through the vast, empty space. Gray light streamed in through the shattered windows and reflected off the gloomy brick walls. Above, birds startled by my intrusion launched into flight with a flurry of feathers before leaving behind total silence.

I waited almost thirty minutes, but that was acceptable for these meetings. Or maybe Liam simply didn't annoy me as much as Larsen had.

Finally, he approached me with confident strides. "I'm sorry I'm late, but I had to oversee the release of Jason Brown to ensure the police station followed the judge's orders."

I nodded. "You did the right thing."

"Not according to McCourt."

"Probably not. But you don't work for McCourt. You work for the people under his supervision. Supervisors can be wrong. The well-being of the people is never wrong."

Liam straightened. "Thank you."

I nodded. "Does meeting inside the old factory still appeal to you?"

Liam made his way into the large roping hall. Dust covered the factory machines. Beams of light from broken windows cast eerie shadows over old ropes on the floor. The air held a stale scent of mold and neglect.

"It's dry. And these walls do give me a false sense of security. Although the crumbling roof and the restless souls that are probably haunting this place are a negative."

"I'm afraid I don't believe in ghosts," I said.

"It was a joke," he countered with a smile.

I watched him as he lifted an old metal hook from the debris-littered ground.

"Kinda cool," he said. "What was this place back in the day?"

His childlike curiosity was surprisingly entertaining. "An old rope factory. The proximity to the sea made it a great location. But it filed for bankruptcy in the seventies due to intense global competition from Asian countries and a decline in demand for new ships because of the growing popularity of air travel."

He nodded. "The land must be worth a fortune now."

"I purchased the property in the nineties. Before the real estate development boom outside of Boston. As long as people keep multiplying, real estate will be a good investment."

He picked up a few more objects, including an old typewriter, which seemed to give him the most enjoyment based on the time he spent pressing old keys. I watched him until he looked at me, having put the typewriter back on a rusty desk. "I'm sorry, but I didn't find out much about Jan Novak."

That wasn't surprising. Something told me that Jan Novak was a man of much secrecy. "What were you able to find out about him? I hope you were discreet."

He nodded. "Special Agent in Charge comes with some perks, I guess. Cyber got me into the system without logging in under a name. We do that sometimes when the CIA asks us to access information without leaving a timestamp."

"Good."

"Don't praise me yet. There really isn't much about this guy that would raise any suspicion. No criminal record. No speeding tickets. Two kids. He filed for divorce. She fought, wanting to stay together, but ultimately lost. That's it on the dirty side."

"What about his childhood?"

"He was born in New York to Slovenian immigrants in very poor circumstances. Not much there about his family, but once he started college, there's more. Got a scholarship to Penn's Wharton, which is the most prestigious business school in the world. That's also most likely where he met the contacts to land him his first job as CEO of a small investment hedge fund. From there, over several decades, he did a lot of smart investing that launched him into the top point-zero-one percent. He's filthy rich. Bill Gates level."

I already knew he was extremely wealthy, but the *how* mattered. "Were you able to find out any details about how he accumulated such wealth?"

"Pretty standard billionaire crap. Real estate is a huge part of it. So are the several hedge fund groups he owns. He's one of the elite who get rich by investing in stocks when the economy is good and then get even richer by betting against it when the country is struggling. Most of his money seems to be in technology stocks. I couldn't find specifics. The ultra-rich keep their portfolios very private. He also owns a large water distribution company, Waterfina, which is stocked in pretty much every store in the US."

I processed this information with a grain of salt. Not that I had expected much more, but this really wasn't much. "Was there anything out of the ordinary?"

Liam frowned. "Not really. The only strange thing is that I couldn't find much on him in footage from any government-owned surveillance systems. Usually, you can type a person's name into a face recognition search and find something. An airport, toll cameras, public street, something. Not Jan Novak. There's nothing."

"You won't find me on many of those searches either."

"Exactly. You know the techniques to dodge facial recognition. But does he?"

"Techniques? All it takes is a face mask, and those are common after Covid. These days, it's easy to leave no trace."

Richter frowned. "So, Jan Novak is just a germophobe who wears a mask everywhere he goes?"

"Unlikely. He didn't wear a mask at the museum."

"Then he's dodging them on purpose. And he knows how to. Now, why would Jan Novak do that?"

I thought about it. "I don't think he's dodging anything."

"Why?" Liam asked.

"When you typed in my name, I still showed up on some searches, correct? Most likely in front of the Smithsonian Museum near the mall. That whole area is heavily monitored due to its proximity to the White House."

"What makes you think I—"

Forehead wrinkled, I threw Liam a look.

"All right. I did look you up as well." He smiled faintly. "But Jan Novak didn't show up in any of my searches. Nothing."

"How is that possible?"

"I honestly have no idea. There are only a few very high-profile cover agents and some politicians who don't show up in those searches. Their faces have been blocked in the database for their protection."

"Would a billionaire have access to this special, well, treatment?"

Richter ran a hand through his hair. "Hard to say, but why not? I was assigned to escort a mass murderer as if he were a fallen hero, all because his family is a mega donor. So, I guess, with money, anything is possible. But the better question is, why would Jan Novak feel the need for that? I can promise you something like this would come at a price tag that even the point-zero-one percent would think about twice."

We both looked up as another group of birds flapped their wings high above us before settling on the metal beams of the roof.

"I was hoping Jan Novak would turn out to be nothing more than a man with strange ways," I said.

"Do you really think he could be a serious suspect for the Train Track Killer? I mean, that sounds farfetched. A billionaire going out at night to place innocent people on train tracks."

"Farther fetched than a world-renowned pianist killing serial killers?"

He laughed. The sound echoed in the vast hall. It was good to hear, almost comforting. For some reason, it had been on my mind how much Richter was struggling lately. "Touché," he said. "Do you want me to look into him again?"

I shook my head. "I doubt it would reveal more. If it's really him, we're working with a man of utter genius. An old parking ticket won't lead us to a crime scene in this case."

"So, what do you want me to do?"

"Did you find anything on his personal life? Any memberships, upcoming charitable events?"

"I did. But I don't think it's a good idea for you to meet with him again. He could be extremely dangerous."

"It's admirable that you're worried about my safety, but it's unnecessary. Besides, I wouldn't expose myself to such risk."

He pondered this, then nodded. "All right then. He has a membership to a fancy fitness club in New York. He plays badminton there. It's called The Club."

"Good. I'll take care of it," I said.

Richter furrowed his brow. "You'll . . . take care of it?"

"Yes. There won't be any fatalities, if that's what you're concerned about. But it won't exactly be legal either. Still want details?"

"Yup. Sure do."

"All right. I plan to hire a male escort from the New York area to go to the gym's locker room and look for a gunshot wound on Jan Novak's shoulder."

Liam processed this. "Are you sure you got him in his shoulder that night in the woods?"

"Yes. If Jan Novak has a scar on his shoulder, it's crucial we investigate further."

"Sounds like a low-risk operation."

"You're on board then?" My tone conveyed my surprise.

He exhaled deeply. "No, not exactly. But with all the chaos in my life right now, if I can eliminate the Train Track Killer from my worries by hiring an escort to peep around a gym, then tell me how much. Let's do it."

"It's on me."

Liam chuckled. "Do I look like the kind of guy who takes a woman out and then makes her pay for her own escort spy?"

"Is that a reluctant stance on equality?"

As he stepped closer, his smile broadened. "Damn it, Leah, can't a man just act like a man sometimes?"

I wanted to say something like this had nothing to do with manhood or that I was well aware of his low income and high lawyer fees. However, that would have wiped the smile off his face. I didn't want to do that. But why did I even care?

"I appreciate it," I said. "But it would be better not to leave any money trail that could connect us." I hoped he wouldn't insist on paying me in cash.

"Always one step ahead, huh?" he said. Our eyes met briefly. His smile was warm.

"Anything else?" I asked.

He furrowed his brow. Clearly, he wanted to discuss the Boston Strangler—likely the primary reason he had called this meeting. "He's dead," I announced.

"What?" Richter sounded outraged. "Why didn't you tell me? You said you'd tell me as soon as it was done."

"I said I'd let you know once I had the locations of the missing bodies. That's what I'm doing now."

He opened his mouth to object.

I quickly added, "Donald Wilson gave me the locations of the missing bodies. Next week, I'll mail an anonymous letter to the Boston police, providing those locations and letting them know the killer has been dead for many years. It'll sound like the late confession of a munxxxxxx family member of the Strangler."

Richter took a moment to process all this. Then his anger dissipated. "Doing it this way will protect Jill Wilson's family."

I remained silent.

"How did he die?"

"Peacefully. Fentanyl overdose," I said.

Richter nodded, satisfied.

"With a small hiccup," I confessed.

"What?"

"He might be missing his privates. I had to remove them to make him talk."

"Leah, goddammit!" he exclaimed.

"He was all tough and stubborn at first," I said, defending myself. "It was a clean cut, and nothing else happened to him before he drifted into a deep sleep, crossing into hell. He deserved so much worse."

Richter cursed under his breath, then nodded. "Fair enough. I'll look out for the letter. It'll land on my desk soon after the police receive it. The Strangler was an FBI case." He sighed loudly as if he'd truly made peace with the whole thing. "Keep me updated on the Train Track Killer," he added.

"Of course."

I had already turned and taken a few steps when an impulse made me stop and look back.

"The Bay Reaper," I said. "From what I gathered on the cases, it seems there's a significant chance he might escalate his actions soon."

Liam's eyes narrowed. "Like what? Some kind of mass shooting?"

"Maybe."

The abandoned factory lay silent. Liam ran his hand through his hair again. It was a gesture I'd come to recognize as a sign of stress or uncertainty. "I'll assign every available agent to this case."

I nodded. Then I uttered words I never imagined I'd say to anyone— because I never cared enough to say them, and I always meant what I said. "Be careful."

They were barely a whisper, soft, as if they were breaching a dangerous threshold.

"I will," he said.

I turned and left the factory, then stepped into the somber early autumn day. The gray skies seemed to probe the depths of my soul.

Be careful. Why did I care so much?

The words, which might have seemed trivial to others, held immense weight for me. My usual indifference to others wasn't out of spite or narcissism; I had simply been robbed of most feelings at birth, leaving me emotionally detached. To some, I was a walking tragedy—another label attached to me by the judging eyes of the world.

Yet something about Agent Liam Richter unsettled me, prompted me to think and act beyond my norm. Not from any sentimental, romantic illusion but from a deeper, enigmatic concern. It was almost as if I feared he was the sole person capable of anchoring my humanity, preventing my descent into monstrosity. Who would I be if I were to become the very thing I destroyed?

I had convinced myself that I was incapable of inflicting cruelty on innocents, that I derived no pleasure from the suffering of others unless they were monsters, which I deemed non-human. But I had never harmed an innocent person, so how could I be certain of my emotional response, positive or negative? How could I know the revulsion I'd feel, the shame, if I'd never crossed that line?

You're questioning yourself again, I chastised myself.

And that was his fault. The Train Track Killer.

He was a constant battle, an unseen foe, unraveling me slowly but surely. It terrified me beyond words to realize that the power to stop this downward spiral wasn't within me; rather, it was in someone else. It lay in a man who'd awakened feelings in me that I hadn't experienced since childhood. Or maybe ever.

It defied logic, yet the outcome remained unchanged.

Time and again, I found solace in the fact that I had a contingency plan.

Should I ever lose myself, it would be the person I trusted more than myself who would end my misery, saving not just me but potentially many others.

CHAPTER FIFTEEN

The Club Gym, Manhattan

The upscale male locker room at The Club was a sensory symphony, oozing luxury. Steam hissed gently from the showers, creating a soothing, rhythmic backdrop to the black marble floors and walls. Scents of lavender and eucalyptus drifted from the steam rooms, infusing the air with tranquility.

Around him, a few guys were wrapped up in their post-workout routines, moving with the ease of regulars. The metallic clink of locker doors mingled with the steady hum of activity. Dylan, dressed and sporting damp hair from his shower, leaned casually against his locker. After months of blowing a high-profile member, he had finally secured membership to this prestigious club. The steep thousand-dollar monthly fee seemed a small price, especially because the club had just netted him an easy ten grand. And who knew? It might even lead to snagging a wealthy sugar mama or daddy, which was the real reason he had joined.

He flicked through his phone, looking for a picture of the man he was meant to find here. A smirk crossed his lips as he thought about the simplicity of it all, especially because he could have sworn he'd seen the guy before in this very locker room.

Then the shower door swung open, releasing a cloud of steam. A tall man, lean and muscular, stepped out wearing a white towel around his hips. Another towel hung around his neck, partially covering his chest but leaving his shoulders exposed.

Shit.

It was him.

Dylan reminded himself of the rules. *No pictures. And don't talk to him.*

He quickly glanced at the aged photo again for confirmation. Matching the man here with the picture of a young college student from the nineties wasn't easy. But the tall build, blond hair, and slightly crooked nose left no doubt.

It was him.

What freaking luck! He had come during peak badminton hours, and there he was.

Picking up a shoe, Dylan turned toward the man and slipped it on. He just needed a good look at the man's face and shoulder. Though the man was now standing sideways, several feet away, Dylan was certain it was the same person.

Keeping his composure, Dylan put on his other sneaker. He glanced down and then up again, focusing on his real task: checking if the man had any scars or wounds on either shoulder.

From his position, Dylan could tell the man's left shoulder was unmarked. Feeling like some undercover agent, with adrenaline and excitement coursing through him, he grabbed his gym bag and rose. Then he moved to one of the sinks along the wall, as it offered a perfect angle from which to view the man's right shoulder. The reflection in the mirror confirmed his suspicion.

The right shoulder was just as smooth as the left. No scars, no wounds. Just toned, muscular skin.

That was it. Mission accomplished. Ten grand earned.

But something in Dylan stirred—an adventurous spark ignited by too many action movies or a childhood dream of being a cop. The thrill of the man being oblivious to Dylan's mission added an element of the forbidden, a sensation long forgotten in his career as a seasoned escort. He felt like a predator observing its prey or a villain sizing up a victim.

Walking halfway across the locker room, Dylan found himself right next to the man. He was on his way out when he inexplicably stopped. "Good match?" he heard himself say, as if his voice weren't his own.

The man, slightly hunched, straightened up, revealing his impressive height. Maybe six-two or six-three? Definitely a towering figure of authority and sex appeal. "Excuse me?" the man said, turning around, his hands adjusting the towel around his neck.

Dylan gestured toward the badminton racket leaning against the man's locker. "Good match?"

The man's prolonged stare sparked a flicker of panic in Dylan. Those eyes held the commanding presence of someone who knew he stood apart from the rest. "Yes, thank you," the man finally said, smiling. "How . . . kind of you to ask."

Dylan nodded, a wave of relief washing over him. He returned the smile. "Have a good day," Dylan said, making his exit.

The man didn't respond, but as Dylan opened the door to leave the locker room and glanced back, he saw that the man was still there, still watching him, frozen. Then the door slammed shut behind Dylan.

It was odd but not a concern. His mission was a complete success: no scars, and his cover was intact.

That ten grand was as good as his. Life was looking up. About damn time.

CHAPTER SIXTEEN

Agent Vallery Rose

Assistant Director McCourt's waiting room was the epitome of sleek professionalism, adorned with framed awards and a stylish modern vase. His secretary, a short woman with a timid demeanor and neatly cut hair, was engrossed in her computer at her impeccably organized desk. Rose observed her with a mix of wonder and disbelief. She didn't know how anyone could tolerate daily interactions with McCourt. The few hours Rose spent with him each month were more than enough to test her limits despite what she owed him.

The phone's ring cut through the silence. The secretary answered with a stoic face. "He will see you now, Agent Rose," she said, her eyes fixed on her computer screen.

"Thank you," Rose responded, moving toward the door to preempt the inevitable "Come in" response to her knock.

McCourt's office was spacious and imposing, featuring a large mahogany desk. He sat behind it, radiating authority and experience. The room was lined with bookshelves filled with legal and investigative texts, while the walls boasted framed pictures of McCourt with presidents and other notable figures.

The atmosphere was always the same when Rose was summoned here. A solemn professionalism tinged with McCourt's stamp of authoritarianism. His rolled-up sleeves— pushed to the elbows in a failed attempt to seem approachable—fooled no one, probably not even himself.

Leaning back in his massage chair, McCourt gestured for Rose to sit across from him. "How is the search for the Bay Reaper going?" His icy blue eyes bore into Rose as if he already knew the answers to all the questions he was about to pose.

Her hazel eyes held steady, barely blinking under his intense gaze. "Every available man is on it. Special Agent Richter is giving it all we got," Rose replied.

McCourt nodded dismissively. "He'd better, after the fiasco with our main suspect."

"Sir, I don't think Jason Brown was an open and shut case," Rose ventured, maintaining politeness.

McCourt clasped his hands in silence. She'd struck a nerve. After almost two years of these meetings, Rose could write a novel about his moods and body language.

"Oh, yes, I forgot. You threw that 'release party' for Brown together, like pals who run the show," McCourt said, his tone dripping with sarcasm. "Would you enlighten me again, Agent Rose, about all those years of experience in the field that supposedly made you an expert on suspects and their handling?"

Rose remained silent, knowing this was her best response.

"That's what I thought," McCourt mumbled, now pissed. "The entire Boston headquarters watched Richter defy my orders. With elections looming, I've got senators and the president himself breathing down my neck about this goddamn Bay Reaper."

Rose had stopped wondering why McCourt always omitted FBI Director Helen Finch from these discussions. It was clear he considered himself her successor, so he no longer bothered to acknowledge her.

"Sir, are you suggesting we should've kept Jason Brown in custody while the real Reaper is still out there?"

"Jesus, Rose," McCourt huffed. "Of course not! Do you think I'm an idiot? But with elections just weeks away, holding a suspect a bit longer wouldn't have hurt."

"Yes, sir."

A brief, awkward silence filled the room.

"Richter thinks the Reaper might be planning something big, like a mass shooting?" McCourt asked.

"That's correct, sir."

"Do you agree with him? He seems to have an awful lot to shout about this Bay Reaper."

"I do, sir. Examination of footage of the Bay Reaper from various surveillance cameras has revealed that he's getting in and out of different cars with fake license plates. On a few occasions, he had an AR-15 slung over his shoulder."

McCourt sighed, annoyed.

Rose continued. "We're looking for an ex-military male, aged twenty to sixty, with extensive weapons training and a troubled mental health history. I'm thinking he could have had a medical or dishonorable discharge, which made him hate society. Add in some economic hardships and a lack of access to mental health services, and this could be the disastrous recipe for something big, like a mass shooting."

"Good God," McCourt mumbled. "A major event now would be catastrophic, especially after the Larsen incident. If only Richter, that self-righteous brat, would've listened to me. The whole nation knows Brown is free, and the real killer will now feel pressure to act quickly before we find him."

Rose hadn't considered that.

"What?" he said. "Did you get caught up in Richter's noble heroics? I'm not the old idiot you all think I am. I was playing this game when you two were still in diapers. We needed time, Agent Rose. Time we might not have anymore thanks to Richter's damn hero complex. And where were you in all this? I knew a guy like Richter would stab me in the back the moment I laid eyes on him, but you, Rose, I can't help feeling a bit betrayed by you. Which hurts even more considering everything I've done for you. Everything I've risked for you."

Shit. This was bad.

Rose stiffened in her seat. "Sir, I didn't know Richter's intentions regarding Jason Brown when he asked me to come along on the mission."

McCourt's eyes narrowed. Rose always felt like she was navigating a tightrope in his presence. He had given her this life at the FBI. When fate had pulled the rug out from under her, McCourt had been there to prevent her fall. But that didn't mean he couldn't finish what the person who'd pulled that rug from under her feet had started. The roles were clearly defined here: king and peasant. Cat kills mouse.

"I"—she cleared her dry throat—"I called you right after I dropped Richter at headquarters to tell you what happened. If I'd known his plans in advance, I swear, sir, I would've—"

McCourt stood, signaling the end of the conversation.

Rose sat a moment longer, sweating, then rose too. "Sir, I'll do everything I can to find the Bay Reaper before something bad happens."

"Then do," McCourt said, opening the door for her. "Because if this blows up, I know who I'm gonna land on to soften the fall, Rose."

Rose absorbed his words as she slowly made her way to the door. "I won't let you down, sir, I pr—"

McCourt closed the door behind her before she could finish her sentence.

Rose caught the secretary's glance before the woman returned her gaze to her screen.

This was bad. Really bad.

Rose had known the trip to the jail with Richter would anger McCourt, but she had underestimated how much.

She had to find the Bay Reaper, no matter what. Otherwise, the next time she was called to McCourt's office, it might be to kiss her badge goodbye.

Chapter Seventeen

Liam

The relentless clacking of keyboards and murmuring voices formed the new background noise in my life. Urgency filled the air at headquarters, evident even in the hectic way agents sat and rose from their desks. McCourt had okayed pulling agents from the Critical Incident Response Group and the Counterterrorism Division. All were now assigned to catch this guy before he wreaked havoc at some fall festival, of which the Seacoast had no shortage. Not even the news of the death of a suspect in the Boston Strangler case, along with the locations of the missing women, could keep the media or anyone else distracted long enough to shift focus from the Bay Reaper. As sad as it was, the Strangler was a nightmare of the past; the Reaper was the present threat to anyone living on the Seacoast.

I stood by Heather's desk. Cowboy leaned over, listening to her phone call, while Martin ran a search on a potential suspect.

A local resident had handed in her doorbell security footage of the Reaper's attack on a young college student on a Sunday evening in New Bedford, a small port community.

"And you think John Hunt's alibi is solid for Sunday the fifteenth, around 9:31 p.m.?" Heather asked a local detective about the possible suspect.

I watched intently as Heather, phone in hand, nodded and then shook her head at me.

"Damn it," I muttered as she hung up.

"Not him," she confirmed. "Hunt was at an AA meeting. They've even got him on camera entering the church."

"Guess that means we're on to the next suspect on our universe-sized list," Cowboy said. "You know," he continued, furrowing his brow, "it's actually pretty damn sad how many suspects we've got. These brave men and women gave so much for this country, and now they're potential terrorists because no one gave a shit when they came back from war."

We let that sink in, a moment of shared, silent sadness hanging between us.

"Isn't that the goddamn truth," I agreed, reaching for another file from the towering pile. The photo of a middle-aged army vet met my gaze. His dull and weary eyes, along with his three-day beard and unkempt hair, spoke volumes about his battle with life.

"Oh, look who's finally here," Cowboy said as Agent Rose settled into her desk next to his.

"Are you the new punch clock, Cowboy?" Agent Rose shot back.

"Wait, we've got a punch clock at BAU?" Cowboy asked, genuine concern in his voice. "Because if we do, I just want you to know that those afternoons I left early I—"

"Can you be quiet just this once?" Heather interjected. "And go check out that suspect in Roxbury. We don't have time for this."

Cowboy leaned back in his chair in protest. "I already told you, I don't want to go alone. We never go solo. It's one of the most important rules of law enforcement. Never engage alone."

He had a point, but the overwhelming number of suspects made it impossible to send agents in pairs for initial questioning, especially with local police fighting serious staff shortages.

"We're short-staffed like everybody else," I said. "But I respect any agent's request for a partner. Better safe than sorry."

Rose scoffed. "We're dealing with a potential disaster of unknown magnitude, and you need someone to hold your hand? Just avoid entering anyone's house, and call for backup if things get sketchy."

"Amen," Heather said, marking a rare moment of agreement between them. Not that Rose cared, but Heather was quite open about her feelings toward McCourt's mole in our unit.

"There's no shame in playing it safe," I said loud enough for surrounding agents to hear.

As the unit refocused on their work, I felt my flip phone vibrate in my suit pocket. I discreetly checked it. A text from Leah. I hoped it confirmed Jan Novak had the bullet scar on his shoulder, making him a suspect in the Train Track Killer case. The blunt "No" in the text felt like a punch to the gut.

Damn it.

I realized the room had gone quiet. Cowboy was scanning for a volunteer to accompany him. With no takers, I let out a loud sigh, disapproving of such blatant and childish hostilities toward Cowboy. Annoying as he might be, he was now one of us.

I turned to Martin. "Martin, would you do us the honor of accompanying Cowboy?"

"Me?" he asked, looking up from his computer with the innocent expression of a child caught off-guard.

"No, Martin, not you, the other Martin sitting in your chair," I countered. "Now, would his highness please be so kind as to assist us in this matter?"

Martin got up without another word, grabbed his jacket, and followed Cowboy out the door. I could hear Cowboy in the distance, asking Martin if he'd seen the Vice documentary about competitive goldfish racing.

As I made my way to my office, the weight of stress bore down on me. I still had to visit three potential suspects today. It was a burden I had to carry alone, like most agents right now. On top of that, McCourt was so ɪʜ ɪ ʃ ɪɪ̠ʏ my ɪ̠ʏ ̣ʟ̣ it was hard to tell where my ass began and his head started. Then there was Leah and me, grappling with the Train Track Killer case, devoid of leads. Worst of all were the godawful phone calls with Josie crying because she wanted to see me while Sarah stood like the Great Wall of China between us.

It was hell. Absolute hell.

With the next family court appointment still three months away, I had to beg Sarah to see Josie face-to-face. At first, Sarah had flat-out refused. When Josie cried non-stop for two days, Sarah had accused me of turning our daughter against her. Ultimately, though, she had given us three hours a month.

I sat at my desk to quickly type the daily report for McCourt. I knew it was simply a way for him to cover his ass if things went south.

Just then, someone knocked at my office door. "Come in," I called.

It was Heather, who walked in with her usual composed demeanor. "A bit edgy today, huh?" She settled into the chair across from my desk.

"What makes you think that?"

Heather raised an eyebrow and nodded at my chest. "You're stashing pens in your chest pocket again."

I looked down, noting six pens there. "Damn it," I mumbled, emptying it.

"And you were a douche to Martin," she added.

"I know. I'll apologize."

I was about to ramble an explanation, but her deep, empathetic sigh stopped me. "I can't even imagine what you're going through right now," she said, her voice soft and comforting. It was the same tone she used with agents on the floor when they needed it.

"We'll catch him before he targets families at some pumpkin patch," I said.

"That's not what I was talking about." Our gazes met. "I have three little monsters myself, remember? Most days, they drive me crazy. Sometimes, I dream about running away to an island all by myself, far from the chaos. But every time I'm actually away, even right now, I miss them. I'd die of a broken heart if I ever lost one of them."

A sad smile crept onto my lips. "I gotta stay positive. I've got another hearing coming up."

Heather nodded and smiled gently. "You'll ace it. And if not, you can always escalate it to the Massachusetts Supreme Court. Get it out of that cunt's hands."

I couldn't help but laugh. "Heather."

She shrugged. "What? I'm a woman. I know a bitch when I see one. That judge needs a boning bad. Let someone mentally stable decide families' futures."

We both chuckled.

A loud knock interrupted us. It was Rose, who stepped right in. The urgency in her face alarmed me.

"What is it?" I asked.

"Another attack. At the Port of New Bedford."

I rose quickly. So did Heather.

"Which hospital is the victim . . ." Heather asked, but her voice trailed off when Rose's face twisted.

There was no hospital this time. He'd finally done it.

His first kill.

"Shit," Heather mumbled.

"Gather every available agent and send them to the Port of New Bedford," I said. "And radio the officers on site not to touch anything."

"Yes, sir," Rose said as she turned away. Heather followed her.

I fetched my rain jacket with the bright yellow FBI lettering on the back. Then I grabbed my flip phone. I clenched it for a moment before stuffing it into my pocket and making my way into the wind and rain. The summer had turned on us Seacoast folks again, leading us into one of the gloomiest falls on record. One full of rain, dark clouds . . . and deaths.

Liam

I led my team of FBI agents down a rain-slicked dock shrouded in dense mist. Fishing vessels, moored on either side, bobbed slightly in the murky gloom. The scene was illuminated by the flashing blue and red lights of numerous police cars, their colors painting vivid reflections on the boats and dock. The intense gazes of the fishermen followed my team all the way to the end of the pier. We stopped in front of the body of a deceased fisherman in his twenties. A soaking-wet cigarette lay not far from his lifeless hand. His yellow rain jacket was stained with blood. His shirt and fishing pants had been cut open, revealing a large, gruesome incision from his lower xiphoid process all the way to his pubic bone. His intestines grotesquely spilled out. They'd likely fallen as he stood during the attack.

Heather, Rose, several police officers, and my agents surrounded the body in solemn silence. In the distance, a boat horn sounded. Meanwhile, seagulls began to peck at the corpse. They were hastily shooed away by anyone nearby.

"Anything new on the Reaper?" I asked, breaking the silence.

A police officer cleared his throat. "A fisherman from one of the lobster vessels reported seeing a man in a skull mask running away just after a loud scream." He pointed toward a rugged-looking boat bobbing in the water. Its crew stared at us.

"I'll gather any possible surveillance footage," Heather said.

"We should interview everyone who was on the dock that night," Rose added.

I nodded. Those were all logical steps, but as I stood there, facing the grim reality of the Bay Reaper's first official kill, I knew it wasn't enough. "Any other ideas? No matter how small or strange they might seem, they could be vital," I said, still staring at the body.

The group fell into a contemplative silence.

"We're running out of time," Agent Rose said.

I looked into the victim's lifeless eyes. Rain drenched his face, and his mouth was agape in a silent scream that mirrored the terror of his final moment before the darkness took him.

"Yes," I murmured under my breath. "We are."

Reluctantly, I reached for the flip phone in my pocket. It was a move I dreaded, asking the unthinkable. However, we needed to stop the Bay Reaper, and for that, I had to turn to her—the smartest person I knew. Our agreement was far from what I was about to make of it.

It was a desperate measure and a lot to ask, but with lives at stake, how could I not?

Chapter Eighteen

Leah

My fingers flew over the keys of my prized new Vanderbilt Bösendorfer, adorned with Monet's forest painting on its lid. I was deep in the spiel of Beethoven's "Appassionata," a piece as dramatic and intense as the piano itself. My right hand darted with quick arpeggios, while my left pounded out solid, rhythmic bass notes. Beethoven's genius lay in his ability to culminate these energetic keystrokes into a final, gripping chord—a fury that was now mine to unleash upon the Boston Symphony Hall audience.

This piano, my dramatic companion, would've justified Hieber's push for pricier tickets if I'd agreed to it. The stage glowed warmly, a stark contrast to the shadowed audience.

As always, the audience included Luca, who was seated in his personal first balcony box. Ever the epitome of elegance in his immaculate white suit, he bore a stoic expression.

As applause and my name echoed through the hall, Luca gave nothing away. No claps, no typical red rose. His gaze held mine for a moment in a silent conversation before he vanished from the balcony. In that uproar, our new, unvoiced understanding was clear.

I pitied him and this situation.

Though I didn't agree with or relish his anger, I understood it perfectly.

Turning to the crowd, still basking in the glow of the Vanderbilt, I caught a glimpse of a familiar face.

Jan Novak.

Like a shadow against the bright stage lights, he sat in the far back row, not clapping, just watching me with those intense eyes, like he'd done during our museum encounter.

As I stood, meeting his stare, the curtains closed. I peered through the satin folds, the applause still thunderous. But when I looked again, Novak's seat was empty. I wondered if I had imagined it all.

I leaned over the leather seats of my Maibach and tapped Mark's shoulder, signaling him to pull over. He had steered us down a dead-end road behind the Veteran's Memorial Pool, close to the Charles River. The atmosphere of the park at night was mystical and lonely. Shadows gently danced as moonlight filtered through the trees.

A dark figure hurried over. I rolled up the tinted divider window, cutting off Mark's view, and opened the back door. Agent Richter jumped in, clearly out of breath.

"Sorry, had to jog here," he panted, fanning his sweat-soaked gray T-shirt. Drops of sweat ran down his exposed arms—not the bulging muscles of a weightlifter but the lean, natural strength of a fit man.

I watched closely.

There was something erotic about a fit man covered in sweat, his toned skin glistening.

"How far did you jog?" I asked, texting Mark to take a spin around the city.

"Three miles," Richter huffed.

"Then you're out of shape," I remarked.

He shot me a look. "I bet I'm in much better shape than your old buddy Larsen. Why didn't we meet at the factory?"

"You said it was urgent, and I'm too tired after my concert to drive all the way out there. Besides, there are homeless and drug addicts lurking around the factory at night. I'm not up for dealing with that right now."

Richter glanced at the window where Mark sat on the other side. "Can he hear us?"

The Boston night scene unfolded outside my window as my Maibach pulled onto the city roads. Streetlamps cast a warm glow, mixing with the headlights of the sporadic night traffic.

"He's deaf. Plus, I pay him too well to talk even if he could hear us."

"Right. Well, good," Richter said.

"So, how can I assist you tonight, Agent Richter? I assume this isn't about the Train Track Killer?" I sounded weary. After my concert, I was mentally drained, and Jan Novak was still lingering in my thoughts. What did he want from me?

Richter didn't answer, so I turned to him. He sat up, fixing his gaze on me. "I . . ." His voice trailed off. His lips pinched as he looked away, then back at me. "I need your help."

His raw, vulnerable honesty surprised me. So did his words. Never had I been asked for help like this before. I had no close family relations, social ties, or friendships, and my relationship with Larsen was certainly not one in which he could ask for favors.

Now here I was, sitting across from this sweat-soaked FBI agent with average facial features, highlighted by the dim light of my luxury car.

And he was asking for my help.

In a rare moment, my forehead creased. "What sort of help?" I tried to clear my head.

Money?

Political favors?

Or was he asking me to kill someone? That seemed the most logical, given the nature of our relationship. Shockingly, I wasn't necessarily opposed to the idea.

Agent Richter tensed, the gravity of his worries evident in every inch of his body. "The Bay Reaper claimed his first kill. A male fisherman on the New Bedford docks, gutted like a hunting trophy."

I let the information run through my head as I recognized the core of his request for help. He wanted me to help him solve a case unrelated to our agreement of killing serial killers. His notion was understandable, and yet in no shape or form was our relationship that of a detective couple solving crimes together.

"I think there might be a misunderstanding regarding the scope of our arrangement, Agent Richter," I said.

He frowned. "There isn't. I get our arrangement, really. And I promise you, I'm not trying to turn us, whatever *we* are, into some kind of twisted version of Sherlock Holmes and Dr. John Watson, but I need your help, Leah, I really do. This guy . . . he's about to do something big. You said so yourself. And I need to stop him, or else—"

His voice faltered as if he was exhausted.

I observed him closely: the nervous bounce of his leg, his eyes darting out the window and then back at me. His anxiety seemed fitting for an FBI agent on the verge of a mass shooting. One who was also battling an unreasonable ex in court for custody of his daughter. And then there was me, a black mamba promising not to bite.

"You're right to assume that he's planning something on a larger scale soon," I said, maintaining my composure.

Richter looked at me. He nodded. "We've managed to trace him back to his vehicles on several occasions using neighborhood and traffic camera footage." He extracted a rolled-up folder from the side pocket of his jogging pants and offered it to me.

For a moment, I hesitated as if accepting it would cast us into a partnership I neither had time for nor desired.

But then, in silence, I took the folder and pulled out a few crumpled photographs. They showed a man hiding his face under a mask and baseball cap. He was driving various car models, each with a different license plate.

"This is about all the information we have," Liam said. "No one hears or sees much when he strikes. A fit man around six feet tall, dressed in military pants and boots, wearing a skull mask and stabbing people."

I scrutinized the photos: him entering a white SUV, a black truck, a family van—each vehicle brand-new. "The plates are fake?" I asked.

"Yes. It's unclear whether he owns these cars or steals them. The times of the incidents don't match any regional car rental agencies' logs. The makes and models are among the region's most popular ones, but we were able to rule out car rentals. Privately owned vehicles are a different matter.

No law enforcement in the world has the resources to consider all these vehicle models as suspect descriptions."

I narrowed my eyes at the photos before returning them. "I have to admit, he's clever. By choosing these particular vehicles, he's exploiting the very dilemma you outlined. It's impossible to narrow down suspects when he's rotating through the country's most popular car models."

Richter's expression clouded with defeat as he took back the photos, his gaze falling heavy.

"But this tactic will hold up only as long as no one uncovers what he's really doing here," I added quickly, unsettled by his defeated demeanor.

"Which is?" He looked at me, a glimmer of hope flickering in his eyes.

"He's exploiting the lemon law," I said.

"The lemon law? You mean the federal legislation that allows consumers to return defective vehicles?"

I nodded toward the pictures he held. "All those vehicles are brand-new, this year's models, except for the van, which is from last year but still considered new if it came directly from a dealer's lot."

"How can you tell just by looking at the pictures?"

"I have a photographic memory. Car advertisements are among the most prevalent on TV and in magazines. An obnoxious yet subconsciously effective marketing strategy."

Liam looked at the pictures in his hands. "Why would he abuse the lemon law to get new vehicles so frequently? Why not steal them? It would be much easier."

"It's easier but riskier too. This man has dedicated considerable time and effort to the logistical aspects of these attacks, hence the fake plates and car switching. Stealing brand-new cars would be too risky for him, given all the work he's invested. New vehicles are traceable if stolen."

Liam nodded. "But if you buy the car, you're the registered owner, and no one would be searching for it. And if you opt out of dealership title handling, you get a grace period to register the vehicle yourself." His tone lightened as if a weight had been lifted. "That's why our searches for stolen vehicles and rental cars turned up nothing. He's been buying them outright."

"Then, after using the car briefly, he tampers with it just enough to suggest a factory defect and returns it under the lemon law," I said.

"Which grants him the right to a full refund or a brand-new car. Just like that, he's set for his next operation. He could be playing every car dealer along the coast," Richter said, a hint of admiration in his tone. "He's driving around in constantly changing, unregistered cars with stolen plates. If he were ever stopped by the cops, he could play ignorant, providing evidence he had just purchased the car. The cops would assume the plate was a dealership error and tell him to register it within thirty days." Richter's eyes widened, a hint of surprise flickering across his face. "What the actual fuck. I've never seen anything like this in all my years."

"He's cunning, which is a disadvantage for you. Especially now that he's made his first kill."

Outside, a raccoon led its offspring into a commercial trash bin in a dim alley.

"Contact all dealerships within a reasonable radius and inquire about recent lemon law claims," I said. "That's how you'll find your suspect. Time is of the essence. He may have already prepared for his large-scale attack."

Richter shifted uneasily. "I need to get back to the office. Is there a darker park closer to the community college? I don't want to make that run again."

I looked at him with slightly narrowed eyes. "The community college? You're parked near Boston Community College?"

He looked caught. Rightfully so. There was only one reason for him to park at the college, which was out of his way.

I nodded. "I see. May I ask how often you're spying on Anna? She's taking classes at the community college, isn't she?"

He sighed. "I'm careful. I promise. The patrol cars protecting her never see me."

"You need to stop this," I said firmly. "Your worry will draw attention."

"Maybe rightfully so," he countered. "I can't just sit back and watch Anna get killed by the Train Track Killer after everything we've done to protect her."

"Hence the police protection, which already seems to draw attention from Agent Rose. Am I not correct to assume that?"

He remained silent.

"You need to stop this. She made her choice, and you're doing all you can to protect her. If others find out the Train Track Killer is still alive and you were trying to hide that fact, it will make things more difficult for us."

"I understand that," he said, "but I can't just do nothing. Can't you try to talk to her again? Tell her to get the hell out of here? She won't talk to me. Last time she saw me, she turned around and left."

I texted Mike to head toward the community college. This was what I got for working with people with actual hearts. "I will if you promise you'll stay away from her college."

180

Liam nodded.

"Good. Any updates on the Train Track Killer? Or Jan Novak?" I asked as the car executed a U-turn.

"Nothing."

"Are you certain?" I pressed, defeated.

"Sorry. I'm trying, really. But didn't you say that Novak was missing the gunshot scar?"

"That is correct."

Richter's eyes flickered with confusion. "And you're sure it was the Train Track Killer you shot that night? Maybe there was a third person involved, another lowlife like Patel."

I shook my head. "It's difficult to explain, but the man I encountered that night . . . it was the Train Track Killer. I'm certain of it."

Richter frowned. "If you really shot him, and Novak is missing that scar, why is he still a suspect?"

I looked out the window at a homeless man getting into his tent in front of a supermarket. "No monster I've pursued comes close to the Train Track Killer. This man . . . he's one of the most intelligent and cunning people on the planet. He makes no mistakes, never falters. Each action is meticulously calculated, refined. And now we're both trapped in his web. Novak has a certain energy that I can't explain. And I'm *almost* never wrong."

Agent Richter absorbed the information. "Leros," he said, invoking a word Emanuel and I had once cherished privately. "I didn't want to ask back then, given your recent loss, but what does it mean?"

"I've told you, it's old Greek for 'nonsense.'"

"I understand that, but I meant, why that word? What message is the Train Track Killer trying to send by using it?"

The car slowed as we approached a red light.

"It's not about the word's meaning," I explained, "but the fact that the Train Track Killer knows about it. It was an inside joke between Emanuel and me. He sent that message to tell me he's watching." I nearly smiled, remembering the absurd origin of the word, the day Emanuel rescued a kitten and mused about sending messages from the afterlife. "Emanuel said if he died before I did, he'd send a word only the two of us would understand, a sign from beyond. I'm a woman of logical thinking and science. To underline the absurdity of this belief, I chose the word 'leros,' old Greek for nonsense."

"But . . ." Richter struggled, "how could the Train Track Killer possibly know?"

I faced him. "That's the great mystery here. I thought maybe he'd paid someone to follow me that night or listen in on my conversation at the dinner table. But I had the waiters from the night of my dinner with Emanuel interrogated, quite convincingly, and none admitted to being bribed to listen to my conversation with Emanuel."

"But how else could the Train Track Killer know the word?"

A chilling silence enveloped us as we both lost ourselves in thought.

Finally, I spoke. "As I've said, the Train Track Killer is unlike anyone you've encountered or will ever encounter again. That includes myself."

"I was hoping Jan Novak would give us more," Richter said.

"He still might. Maybe he's not the person he portrays himself to be."

"What do you mean?"

"He attended one of my concerts."

"Jan Novak?"

I nodded. "Tonight. And I'm trying to understand why he's suddenly taken an interest in me."

Richter's lips twisted into a knowing smile. "You realize a man might seek a woman's attention for reasons other than murder, especially if the woman is as—" He paused, reconsidering his words. "I mean, is a renowned pianist."

I found it disappointing that Richter had held back his initial thoughts.

"Don't be ridiculous," I countered. "Of course I know that. As a woman, I'm all too familiar with your predatory kind. I understand my value all too well. I represent the perfect trophy for men like Jan Novak. Yet there's something elusive about him, something beyond mere conquest or sexual desire."

Richter's grin broadened. "Do you want me to beat him up?"

I nearly laughed at his absurd humor, but a smile sufficed.

The car slipped into another dense silence as Mark navigated the dimly lit street behind the community college and then came to a stop.

Richter remained seated, thinking. "Leah?" His tone was soft, laden with sincerity.

Our eyes locked.

"Would you . . . I mean, the Bay Reaper—"

"No," I replied firmly. "Not as things stand with him as of now."

"But isn't he, I mean, a killer?" he persisted.

I smoothed out a wrinkle on my dress. "I hunt monsters, Agent Richter."

"If he does what we suspect, doesn't that make him one?"

I shook my head. "This is different. The monsters I hunt were born with a darkness so deep there is no hope. Only darkness can welcome them back into the hell they slipped from. Their souls are empty. Their hearts beat for them and them alone. Even what they claim to love is only there to serve them. But this one . . . your Reaper. This one was made by us. He joined the military to make a difference, but he was disillusioned by the very society he aimed to protect. Returning home, he didn't find the embrace of a grateful nation or the helping hand he needed. He found only neglect. The system that was supposed to be his safety net failed him. Your monster wasn't born a monster. He was turned into one by our nation's collective indifference."

Agent Richter's expression was a mixture of sorrow and contemplation. "Then let's hope there's something of him left to save."

"I fear it's too late for redemption. But maybe you can prevent him from truly becoming the sort of monster I would hunt. There would be some mercy in sparing him that."

Richter lingered, then opened the door. He paused to look back at me. "Thank you."

I nodded. As he was about to exit, I leaned forward. "Richter," I said.

"Yes?" He halted, his hand on the door.

"This . . . you and me . . . this won't turn into some twisted version of Sherlock Homes and Dr. John Watson." I cited his earlier words. "That's not the nature of our agreement. I can see why the lines might blur, but my purpose here on this earth is clearly defined. By me. And me alone."

He held my gaze, nodded once, and then gently closed the door.

As we drove away into the night, Richter stood motionless, watching us merge back into the city's illuminated expanse.

CHAPTER NINETEEN

Liam

In the crowded command center of our Providence FBI Field Office, I stood with Cowboy, Rose, and Martin. They were at my side like loyal knights at a modern-day round table. The air was heavy, tinged with the scent of sweat, strong coffee, and musky deodorant, laced with the occasional hint of perfume from the female officers. The room buzzed with the presence of every available FBI agent and local law enforcement officer from the Providence area. All of us were armored in bulletproof vests, our faces a mix of focused anxiety and unwavering determination.

Behind me, the whiteboard was dominated by two images of Robert Kirby, a forty-five-year-old ex-Army Ranger who had seen the horrors of Afghanistan, Iraq, and a redacted mission in Yemen. The first photo showed a young, eager soldier, the embodiment of dreams and discipline. Next to it was the current Kirby: a man visibly marked by life's battles, his weary eyes and messy beard telling a story of inner scars and haunted memories.

"Kirby is highly trained in short and long-range combat, skilled in weapons, and a veteran of surviving hostile environments," I began. "The technique he used to gut the fisherman on the docks demonstrates experience in hunting and processing game. He's been through hell, taken several bullets, and even played hero during a suicide bomber attack in Afghanistan, saving two fellow soldiers that day. Medal followed."

There was a short pause. Maybe it was the irony of this hero-turned-villain.

"His family," I continued, "says he sometimes retreats to the woods to cope with mental health issues. It's a pattern they thought explained his disappearance from his construction job six months ago and the spotty contact. Kirby is highly dangerous, so don't let your guard down for a second."

My gaze briefly lingered on the picture of Cindy Boon, Kirby's ex-girlfriend. Her heavy makeup hid her fine facial lines but not the trauma and abuse in her eyes.

I continued, my voice grave. "Last he was seen was by his ex-girlfriend of two years. Put a gun to her head after they'd been drinking all night. Asked her if she wanted to find peace with him or keep walking the flames of hell." Again, my eyes briefly met Cindy's in the photo. Her gaze conveyed the deep sadness of a person too hopeful to quit and too hopeless to believe she deserved love.

"He's extremely cunning and organized. Kirby has been using the lemon law to cycle through unregistered, legally acquired vehicles from dealerships, keeping us off his trail. Until six months ago, he was working construction jobs on and off. He vanished after his mental health and alcoholism took a nosedive post-breakup."

Turning to the Providence police officers, I asked, "Is the perimeter around his home ready to be secured quietly?"

The Providence police chief, a stout man of color in his fifties, gave me an affirmative nod. "We have a team ready. Right before we move in, the team will block off the streets. Wearing the uniforms of the local gas company, they'll advise neighbors to stay inside. Gas leak."

"Amazing work, thank you," I said, nodding appreciatively before addressing the group again. "Kirby lives in an old three-bedroom house on King Henry Lane. He inherited it from his grandmother. We'll approach in unmarked vehicles, keeping it low-key. We have a warrant, so entry will be swift and assertive. One team for each area of the home, surrounding it from all sides first to cut off exit routes."

All eyes shifted to the pictures of the rundown house and yard displayed on the board behind me. My gaze swept over the room and stopped briefly on McCourt, who was quietly leaning against the wall in the corner of the command room. His eyes were on me like those of a spider eyeing a fly in its web.

As if on cue, he pushed off the wall and strode up next to me. "No A-Team bullshit," he announced, his tone authoritative. "If a stray bullet hits old Mrs. Molly pushing her purebred Maltese in one of those ridiculous dog strollers, I will personally make sure the human diaper responsible for this shitshow gets thrown out."

As the tension in the room instantly ramped up, I quietly scratched the side of my head to avoid rolling my eyes at McCourt's 1920s cop drama. But he was the ruler of this land. You either took it his way or got the fuck out.

"This operation goes by the book. Is that understood?" McCourt continued.

"Yes, sir," came the collective response.

"Any questions?" I asked.

A rookie officer raised his hand. "We're supposed to shoot him, right?"

Shit.

I felt for the poor bastard. Cowboy grinned wide in anticipation as McCourt stepped closer, zeroing in on the rookie like a drone locking onto a target.

"I apologize if my A-Team reference was lost on those still being burped when this absurd TV show was captivating America's man-children," McCourt said, stepping closer, now right in the face of the terrified rookie. "So, let me spell it out. With the FBI in charge, this mission won't be a John Wick fantasy. It will be Hermione Granger with a gun and a license to kill. Fucking got it this time, Harry P?"

He took a sudden step back, allowing the young man to catch his breath.

McCourt then addressed the crowd again. "Any real questions?"

The room was dead silent.

"Good." McCourt straightened his necktie. "Then let's go get that son of a bitch before he shoots up a school."

Immediately, the room cleared out.

"The A-Team was a damn good show," Heather said as she passed me on her way out.

"He went too far this time," I agreed. "A-Team is legend."

I was about to head out myself when McCourt shook his head at me and Rose. Soon, only the three of us were left in the room.

"Kill the asshole," McCourt said as soon as the room was clear. "Less paperwork, no sob story in the press about another soldier going to hell. Also, make sure Theo sticks to the back during the raid. If anything happens to that little fucker, my sister will hound me to my grave and continue in the afterlife."

Rose and I exchanged glances as McCourt marched out, not bothering to wait for a response. Her lively eyes brimming with a silent protest against his orders. Then she pulled out her gun and methodically checked it before throwing me a look that screamed, "It is what it is." Finally, she exited the room.

Hot on their heels, I decided that McCourt could go to hell.

I knew what he, and most others, thought of me: Richter . . . the guy from a poor but somewhat decent home, following in cop-dad's footsteps to make him proud. The rule follower.

Mr. Vanilla. Not the hardened cop drowning his old scars in whiskey or seeking hot sex with women whose names he'd forget the next morning.

No.

Richter was a guy who'd go home after work to help with a load of laundry, read to his kids, and then make love to his wife despite the stretch marks and extra pounds lingering after childbirth.

And they were right about that.

But Mr. Vanilla wasn't all of me.

I was also the guy ready to fucking die for a better world and for the people I cared about.

When the loudmouths faltered, I was still standing. In a world gone mad, I was the sanity, the glue holding shit together so everybody else could fuck up and be crazy.

And there was another side to me. New Richter, who worked alongside a genius killer to take down monsters like Harvey Grand. That Richter would do everything in his power to save a guy like Robert Kirby. He'd pay dearly for his crimes, especially the murder of the fisherman, but maybe that could be the end of it—no more bloodshed.

So, yeah. "Fuck McCourt," I said aloud as I caught up with Agent Rose, who threw me a worried look. "If Kirby goes down without a fight, nobody shoots. That's an order," I declared.

CHAPTER TWENTY

Liam

If I had known she was playing "The Swan" from "Carnival of the Animals" at the exact moment we were huddled in the stuffy van en route to Robert Kirby's house, it would have felt like a cosmic connection. A personal soundtrack, as if she knew the path I was on.

I knew nothing of classical music, but my music teacher had played "The Swan" to us back in my school days, and it stuck with me. I found it tragically beautiful. Back then, I asked my teacher if the swan was dying. To me, the melody was serene but filled with profound, unspoken sadness, the end of something once beautiful.

Just like Robert Kirby now.

Or maybe myself.

The van was shrouded in its usual pre-mission silence. Any of us could be the one not coming back.

A young, buff, GI-Joe-looking officer suddenly threw up. We all minded our own business as he apologized into his hand.

I felt my cell vibrating in my pants pocket again. It had been buzzing non-stop since I'd gotten in, so I decided to break my habit of ignoring calls before a mission and pulled it out.

I checked it: five missed calls from my younger sister, Stephanie, and twenty-five texts.

What the fuck.

Panic choked me as I opened the messages. After years in this job, I found that my mind always jumped to the worst. Was it Mom? Josie?

My hands nervously fumbled over the first text, which showed a picture of a woman in her early thirties. Neither pretty nor ugly, she had brown eyes and hair that mirrored her unassuming clothing style.

I read my sister's first text. *We have a fucking sister, Liam!!!*

This made no sense to me, so I continued reading the jumbled texts she had bombarded me with.

Dad cheated on mom, that piece of shit!

This woman found me via some DNA test.

She just showed up at my school, Liam. At my fucking school!

She showed me pictures of dad and her mom. Some childhood pictures. She said we had a brother too, but he died driving drunk or some shit like that.

Liam, call me back damn it! I can't breathe, the panic attacks are back.

I hope dad rots in hell!!! I hate him.

Liam!!!

My head flopped back against the cold metal of the car as my pulse skyrocketed. What the fuck? Was this some kind of joke?

I felt the sweat, the anger, the disappointment, and then the anger again.

"You okay?" Agent Rose's voice snapped me out of it. I looked at her. Her gaze shifted from the phone in my hands then returned to my face. Nobody else seemed to have noticed, as people either prayed or stared at the floor in silence.

"Yes," I lied and tucked the phone back into my vest pocket just as the van slowed down and my walkie-talkie went off.

"One minute to touchdown," crackled a voice.

Inhaling deeply, I unholstered my Glock, feeling its familiar, reassuring weight. Around me, the team prepared their weapons, including shotguns, Rose's favorite. After a tight squeeze in a basement with a shotgun on my first warrant execution, the Glock had become my weapon of choice.

"Thirty seconds!" I announced. The van brimmed with palpable tension. Time seemed to blur. Then, abruptly, the van jerked to a halt, jostling us.

I flung the door open and leaped out into the crisp fall afternoon. The peaceful neighborhood belied the gravity of our task.

A fleet of vans and SUVs converged simultaneously, releasing a swarm of agents and officers. I caught their focused stares and signaled the yard team to surround the house. They moved with military precision, Cowboy among them, as that team was the least likely to see action and could find cover quickly during crossfire.

I led Rose and three other teams. Adrenaline surged through me as we neared the front door. Every sense was heightened; my heart thundered in my chest, my gun aimed, ready for whatever lay ahead.

An officer knelt at the floor, quietly working the lock open with a drill. Within moments, it clicked, barely making a sound.

It was nothing like the dramatic entries you see in movies. We pushed the door open gently, then slipped inside with practiced stealth. The home's hallway was tidy yet dated, with a narrow path flanked by old-fashioned floral wallpaper. I gestured to the upstairs team to move in. We scanned our surroundings, searching for any sign of movement.

Standing guard at the front door, the basement team was set to intercept any escape attempts from the first floor or upper floor. Once those areas were clear, they'd clear the basement.

I led my team into the living room, which had older furniture, all bathed in the soft light from an antique lamp. The upstairs team's footsteps echoed as they cleared each room methodically above us.

The living room was empty, so we swiftly advanced to the kitchen. My heart pounded against my ribcage, and I wondered if it might burst free.

Also clear.

We made our way into what looked like an old dining room. It was also clear but littered with maps and various objects scattered across the aging table. The house felt like a time capsule, as if Robert's grandmother still lived here—outdated, mostly neat except for the clutter of empty liquor bottles, beer cans, and vape pods.

"Upstairs is all clear," came a young officer's voice through my radio just moments before the front door team signaled their intent to enter the basement.

My eyes darted over the chaos: wires, tools, containers of volatile chemicals, and protective gloves and goggles strewn about.

Fuck!

"Don't go downstairs!" I bellowed into the radio, a surge of icy panic gripping me. Without hesitation, I dashed past Rose and the rest, screaming, "Don't go downstairs!"

In seconds, I was in the hallway. For some reason, Cowboy was at the top of the basement stairs. The door was wide open, and other agents were likely descending.

I barreled into Cowboy just as a deafening explosion shook the house. The shockwave catapulted us to the ground. My body slammed against the hard floor. The air turned thick with dust and the stench of smoke and burnt wood. A high-pitched ringing in my ears muffled everything as I rolled onto my stomach, struggling to get on all fours.

The hallway was devastated: walls cracked, a carpet of glass and debris ꜰꜰ ꜰꜰ ꜰꜰ all around.

It was an absolute nightmare.

As my vision cleared, I noticed Cowboy next to me. He was coughing but alive. So were the other agents.

I sat up and looked into space, my gaze finally falling on a family portrait of the Kirbys. It had tumbled from the wall and was now propped against a piece of wood amid the rubble. Sunlight streamed through broken windows, and dust danced in its beams like a flurry of tiny stars over the portrait. The glass was cracked, partially veiling the fading photo of Robert Kirby and his parents at an amusement park. In the photo, young Robert and his parents were joyfully poking their faces through a whimsical face-in-hole board designed to represent a happy dog family. Robert's face appeared in the smallest hole, intended for the baby of the family. His eyes sparkled with the happiness of a child who was going on rides and eating cotton candy with the people he loved. His parents' faces emerged from the two larger holes, portraying the parent dogs.

The words above them, bold and clear, read: "From a happy heart springs a life filled with love and joy."

CHAPTER TWENTY-ONE

Leah

My fingers delicately traced the piano keys, concluding my personal arrangement of "The Swan" by Camille Saint-Saëns. I was on stage, performing a rehearsal run of this weekend's concert. Crystal, the operations manager, and a few stagehands sat in the front row, their eyes fixed on me, awaiting instructions while indulging in the music.

It was strange, but I couldn't shake the feeling that something was amiss. It was as if I'd developed a sixth sense. Suddenly, the jarring siren-like sound of an amber alert cut through the room, emitted from several cell phones simultaneously.

Confused murmurs filled the air as the message was read.

"It's the Bay Reaper," Crystal announced, looking at me through her red-framed glasses. "They've issued an alert for a Robert Kirby and a red pick-up truck, license plate MA3 4BZ."

Marianne, a young stagehand with short hair and a nose piercing, fumbled with her phone. "OMG!" she exclaimed, her face a mix of shock and excitement. "There was an explosion at Kirby's house during an FBI search. Now there's a huge manhunt underway!"

"You're kidding!" Crystal gasped. They all descended into excitement.

I processed this information and then clapped my hands. "Focus, please," I insisted.

Crystal and Marianne looked at me, momentarily confused, as if snapped out of their trance.

"Tell Gregory to retune the piano but this time without the digital tuning device. It makes the notes too perfect. People don't appreciate such sterile precision."

"Yes, Leah," Crystal responded, quickly stowing her phone. "Marianne will go right away."

Marianne shot a "why don't you do it yourself" look at Crystal but then got up and left.

I reached for the cream cashmere jacket beside me on the bench and pulled out my flip phone. Rising gracefully, albeit a bit more quickly than usual, I stepped out of sight behind the stage.

For a moment, I stood there, holding the phone.

A cold tingle ran through my chest. Was Agent Richter injured or, worse, dead? If he was, what a colossal waste that would be. It had taken years to replace Larsen with someone of Richter's caliber. Frankly, I doubted I could find another quite like him.

Richter was a man of integrity, unafraid of facing danger. He was mostly stable and guided by a moral compass intent on improving the world or at least preventing its further descent into chaos. Most importantly, he harbored a naive yet sincere hope in his heart, genuinely believing he could succeed in such a colossal task.

Because of that, he was irreplaceable, especially now with the Train Track Killer still out there.

Was it this realization of Richter's value that sparked something in me?

It was a revelation that not only stunned me but also stirred a flicker of . . . nervousness? Worry?

I picked up the phone and dialed his number. No phone calls ever, we said, and yet here I was.

He picked up.

The unmistakable beeps of hospital machines and background announcements left no doubt as to his location.

"Hello?" His voice was soft, detached from reality.

I stated the obvious. "You're alive."

A pause followed.

"Kinda," he finally responded.

Another brief silence.

"Good," I replied and hung up.

His voice left me with no doubt about his state. The past months would have taken a toll on anyone. Despite his resilience and determination, Richter was human, with his own limits. Something told me that Richter was at risk of rapidly losing steam. With the potential loss of his child, and now, if he'd been injured from the explosion, the combined effect might completely derail him.

The judicial system in this nation was bizarre and deeply flawed. Laws seemed to apply only to the poor, and lady luck was as dependable as a drunk whore.

"Crystal," I called as I returned to the stage.

She instantly stood.

"Please arrange for the attorney general to call me on my cell."

Her eyes sparkled with intrigue. "You mean the United States Attorney General in DC, right?"

I pondered for a moment. "No, the Massachusetts Attorney General."

Low status. He would be more eager to trade favors.

"Sure. I'll call his office right now," she said.

"Thank you," I responded, watching her leave.

CHAPTER TWENTY-TWO

Agent Vallery Rose

"We're working on it tirelessly, sir," McCourt said, his voice dripping with the artificially kind and respectful tone reserved for those above him and the public. He sat behind his large mahogany desk, a barrier between him and agent Vallery Rose.

"I'll do everything in my power to catch Robert Kirby before he hurts anyone else," he said, nodding. "Yes . . . uh-huh. Yes, sir. You can trust me, sir. I understand. Thank you, sir. Thank you."

With that, he hung up, his gaze lingering on the handset he had just set down. Then, with an exaggerated sigh, he said, "What a fucking shitshow."

"I take it that wasn't Director Brooks?" Rose asked.

"Of course not. Helen is finished. She lasted quite a while, given that her nominating party lost the election two years ago. Gotta give the old lady that. But now, the big question is, who'll take her spot once it's official?"

Rose straightened in her seat. "I . . . thought your hard work positioned you well for that role, sir."

"That's what people assumed, yes. But that was before all this shit hit the fan." His tone was surprisingly calm. "Robert Kirby's been on the run for almost a week. A goddamn week. And the whole country's asking one very valid question."

Rose waited for him to continue. When he didn't, she fell into his trap. "What question, sir?"

"Fucking *why*, Agent Rose!" he exploded. "The country wants to know why Kirby's still free, turning the entire Seacoast into a cesspool of fear. What the hell are you guys doing down there? Making TikTok videos? Catching Pokémon around the office? Because it sure as hell doesn't look like you're working on finding Kirby!"

Rose could have argued that every available officer in every law enforcement unit was on this case, pulling night shifts and missing Sunday baseball games. But she knew better than to voice that.

"If Richter had just listened to me." McCourt shook his head. "Or if that person I thought I could trust had reported on him before he fucking freed Jason Brown from jail, we wouldn't be in this mess. At least not at the same time as two swing state elections in my jurisdiction!"

"Jason Brown was innocent, sir," Rose interjected carefully.

"Of course he was, but releasing Brown so quickly forced the real Bay Reaper's hand. The moment that white trash headed home to his bottle and wife-beating, Robert Kirby knew we'd be on his ass in no time. We left him no choice but to act, all while we knew jack shit about him. And the result is one person butchered at the docks and four officers in the hospital from a bomb explosion. One of them missing an arm and a leg!"

While everything McCourt said could be a possibility, it also could be nothing but conjecture. In cases like this, no one could accurately predict what might have happened. Some news stations had actually praised the FBI and argued that finding Kirby so quickly had prevented a larger bomb threat. But those same news stations were now turning on the FBI, blaming it for a missing Kirby with the usual sensationalist headlines that went after clicks and views.

"Sir, is there anything else I can assist you with?" Rose asked.

"Let me think . . . yes. I think there is." McCourt's tone seemed as if he was truly thinking about it, but then he slammed his hand on his desk and leaned forward. "Find! Robert! Fucking! Kirby!"

He sank back into his chair, exhausted.

The room filled with a heavy silence that was oppressive and unbearable. McCourt had a point: The nation was clamoring for them to find Kirby. After a week of fruitless searches, the pressure was mounting, reaching Everest-like heights. It weighed heavily not just on her but on everyone. Yet for Rose, the stakes were personal. Her badge and her position, which hung precariously on the approval of the man before her, now teetered on the edge of his rage.

In a twisted way, she understood McCourt. If his promotion was jeopardized by his agents' actions, it made sense he'd scrutinize his closest ally: her. The logic was obvious, even if ethical matters weren't so clear.

The phone's ring cut through the tension, providing a welcome relief for Rose.

McCourt inhaled deeply, then answered with his forced friendly tone, "Assistant Director Clifford McCourt." His insincere smile disappeared as he rolled his eyes. "Jesus, Bonnie, I've told you not to call me at the office unless it's a real emergency."

A woman's muffled voice barely traveled through the line.

"Theo is an FBI agent, not a member of Congress, Bon. He actually has to work."

The muffled sounds continued, growing in volume.

"No, I can't fetch Jen from kindergarten," McCourt snapped. "I'm the Assistant Director of the FBI, for heaven's sake. Tell Dr. Douchebag to let you off early or I'll have a Medicare audit done on his clinic."

The mumbling on the other end became frantic.

"No, I'm not raising my voice at you, Bon," McCourt said in a tone that mixed frustration with a forced apology. He rubbed his temples as he gestured for Rose to leave.

Rising, she sent a prayer of thanks to McCourt's sister only to feel the weight of responsibility crash back down on her the moment she stepped out.

She knew she had to find Kirby, whatever the cost, or start looking for another job. Which, in her eyes, after everything she had endured to beat the odds and be here, would be the biggest failure of her life—the kind that would haunt her to her last breath.

Chapter Twenty-Three

Liam

The entire BAU floor at Boston headquarters had transformed into the nerve center for the Kirby case. Following the explosion and discovery of weapons and homemade bombs in the rubble of Kirby's basement, the case's importance was unmistakable. Time was our worst enemy. So were the fucking woods. Kirby's truck had been found abandoned near a boat dock on the Merrimack River north of Nashua. With its door wide open and some weapons left behind, it was clear he'd ditched the vehicle in a hurry, almost as if he'd known that it'd be found, but he couldn't care less.

It seemed likely he'd escaped in a boat. Eyewitnesses had seen a red truck hauling a boat to and from the dock within the past few months.

And that was where we were utterly screwed.

The Merrimack River, with its considerable length and numerous coves, tributaries, and islands, offered a labyrinth of hiding places, complicating our search efforts. The river's open and fluid nature made constant surveillance a nightmare, even for an intense manhunt with our level of resources. The fact that the river led to the bay at Newburyport only magnified our challenges.

Perched on a chair at Heather's desk, I delved into the notes from Kirby's therapist. Cowboy and Martin sat hunched at their desks nearby, piecing together the fragmented notes on Kirby's victims found at his home. The notes had been damaged in the explosion, but it was clear Kirby had targeted his victims deliberately, profiling them like a hitman.

Surrounded by a sea of evidence and tips, we focused primarily on Kirby's profiling methods and long, tumultuous battle with mental health. These were our keys to understanding Kirby and, ultimately, finding him.

"This info he's gathered on his victims," Martin said, shaking his head, "I honestly have no idea how he did it. I mean, this is incredible work. The FBI would need a hell of a lot of warrants to gather this much info on people."

"That's the US military for you," Heather said. "We create the best."

"And the most depressed," Cowboy added.

His joke was macabre but true. Kirby's story was a damning indictment of our nation's broken mental health system.

He'd returned home from the Middle East as a shadow of his former self.

Initially, Kirby had fallen into the same trap many veterans did: steering clear of help out of fear of repercussions within the military—a culture where admitting struggle was often seen as a weakness and could cost you everything. But reality hit hard with his first DUI and a series of bar fights. Diagnoses of severe PTSD and a substance-induced psychotic disorder followed. It was then that desperation set in, and Kirby earnestly began seeking help.

What he found was a system in shambles. The laughable wages offered to community mental health counselors had precipitated a crisis. There was a severe shortage of qualified professionals and a revolving door of brave souls willing to tackle the county's darkest problems in return for high student debt and a wage comparable to that of a grocery store clerk—without even the benefit of a store discount.

Self-medicating became Kirby's answer to the haunting nightmares and PTSD: a deadly combination.

"Damn it," I mumbled as I gazed at a photo of a young, hopeful Kirby and then at the broken man our country had abandoned post-war. "These days, a soldier's real enemy isn't in the Middle East. It's right here in his own fucking country." I dropped Kirby's file onto my desk.

Heather, Martin, and Cowboy looked up, their faces a mix of agreement and frustration.

"These bastards in DC send our boys to hellholes to get fucked up for life while their own kids get private schools and vacations in Paris," I spat out. "Why the hell do we still let them do this to us?"

"Bread and circuses," Heather chimed in. "Just like in Roman times when emperors kept the masses calm with free bread and shows. Not much has changed. As long as we have just enough for fast food and cable, we won't grumble."

As we absorbed that, Martin received a call and then hung up with a brief "thank you."

"Local police," he informed us as we all braced to dive back into the case. "A hunter said his cabin was broken into near Concord."

"Is it close to the river?" I asked.

Cowboy rose, phone in hand, and walked out. "I'll be back."

I paid him no attention.

"About two miles," Martin said. "In a pretty secluded area."

I frowned. "Could be something." Though I suspected it was yet another dead end, like the many we'd already chased.

"I'll get a unit out there," Martin said, his voice betraying the strain of stretching our resources even thinner by pulling in another police unit.

The manhunt had been dragging on for days, spanning several states. Support for such a massive operation was dwindling by the minute, from the FBI down to local stations.

"Thanks," I replied, my gaze suddenly catching McCourt approaching us like a hyena scoping out the savanna for injured prey. "I'll be back in a minute," I said as I stood and wove through the maze of desks and chaos, opting for the stairs at the far end to avoid the elevator McCourt was using.

Descending a floor, I headed straight for the Cyber Crime Unit, then made a beeline for a small office at the end of the hall. Griffin had earned his private space through over three decades with the FBI. He barely glanced up from his computer as I entered with a soft knock.

Griffin nodded toward the open window, which was almost as large as a door. A cool breeze flowed through it.

I returned the nod and clambered onto the fire escape balcony through the window, then entered the hidden "break room" that the smokers and vapers used.

Cowboy's eyes met mine. They were filled with a sorry excuse for an apology as he puffed out a cloud of vape. Behind him, agents from Cyber Crime and Organized Crime were chatting, all blowing vape clouds like chimneys.

"How the hell did you get down here so quickly?" I grumbled, pissed that my few quiet minutes were about to be ambushed with bullshit. Still, it beat getting my ass chewed out by McCourt.

"My uncle texted me he was on his way down." Cowboy shrugged.

I shot him a scolding look.

He shifted uneasily, a frown tugging at his lips. "You guys understand that I have to spend time with him outside of work too, right? It's bad right now. Really bad. My little sister's birthday last Sunday was a total shitshow. My uncle pissed off the moms there talking about attachment parenting. Said he's glad he'll be dead when this yoga-app, breastfed-until-college generation is asked to defend our nation. Said they'll all be pointing their guns backward."

"Jesus."

"Yup. Jen told my mom her only wish for Santa this year is to make Uncle Cliffy go away. Jen's five."

Yanking out my crumpled pack of cigarettes, I sparked one up only for Rose to stick her head through the window. "This is the twenty-first century. Who the hell still smokes cigarettes?"

I inhaled deeply. "I'm almost forty. I refuse to leave cotton candy-scented vape clouds behind at serial killer crime scenes. I'm shooting for a Detective Rust vibe here."

Rose emerged onto the balcony, her expression deadpan. "Well, *detective*, McCourt's looking for you."

Fuck.

Cowboy gave her a wry smile. "Ah, Sauron's unleashed his Nazgul, has he?"

Unfazed, Rose marched up to him and snatched his vape pen. "Is this original Cowboy wit, or is ChatGPT scripting for you again?" She inhaled deeply, blowing a cloud of vape in his face, and then coolly returned the pen.

I took another drag of my cig, grimacing at the nasty smell. Fifteen years smoke-free, yet here I was, back at it. The pressure was ripping me apart, and these brief nicotine hits gave me a fleeting illusion of calm and pleasure.

With a frown, I stubbed out the cigarette and then crammed it back into the pack.

"Sir," Agent Rose called out.

I turned.

"We got some calls from residents along the Neponset River. Complaints about a boat and lights in the marshes at night. It's unusual, they say. Never happened before. Thought it might be worth mentioning."

I stroked my chin thoughtfully. "Neponset is right here in Boston. Doesn't fit our search grid. We've been focusing north, Merrimack way, expecting Kirby's holed up in that vast forest."

Rose nodded, but then Cowboy chimed in. "What if the crazy bastard took his boat to the ocean at Newburyport and came back down?"

"On a RIB, in those ocean currents?" I scoffed.

"RIB?" Cowboy looked puzzled.

"Rigid inflatable boat. It would be crazy," Rose explained, rolling her eyes.

Cowboy's face lit up with understanding, then turned to defiance. "So?" he pushed, glancing at the Cyber team like a kid challenging an adult.

The Cyber agents grinned at his antics.

"This son of a bitch is skulking around in a skull mask, stabbing people, luring us with lemon law tricks, and setting up Vietnam-era booby traps. What's wrong with 'crazy' here?"

I locked eyes with Agent Rose, who shrugged in a "sounds far-fetched, but why not" kind of way.

I sighed. Of course, I'd be the one wading through tick-infested marshes to check this out. "I'll go take a look."

Cowboy's grin widened, victory written all over his face.

"I'm coming with you," Rose said.

"Meet me downstairs. If I'm not there in thirty, you might wanna fish my corpse out of McCourt's office."

No one cracked a smile. That joke was a little too close to reality.

"Good luck," Rose replied.

CHAPTER TWENTY-FOUR

Leah

The gloomy sky cast a somber hue, creating a bleak backdrop as I stepped into The Stance, one of the nation's most acclaimed restaurants. It was a typical gray fall day in Boston, with heavy clouds brooding low, diffusing light through the establishment's towering windows.

Inside, it was a world apart. Softly glowing golden light fixtures illuminated the space, while the air was perfumed with the aroma of exquisite French cuisine.

At a prime corner table away from the buzz sat Derek Beckett, the Massachusetts Attorney General. Apart from his pricey suit, there was nothing particularly remarkable about him. His hair, a mix of salt and pepper, was overly styled with gel, which did little to enhance his sharp features or the icy blue of his eyes. He surveyed the room with an unmistakable blend of arrogance and authority. Finally, his gaze settled on me.

His face lit up with an excited smile as he rose to greet me.

I moved toward our table with confident strides. My cream-colored cashmere dress, white coat, and leather gloves mirrored the restaurant's elegance. As I neared, Beckett reached out to help me with my chair and coat—a gesture meant to be chivalrous but one that ended up clumsy as his fingers grazed my skin.

Settling into my seat, I was again struck by how much I loathed lunches like this. I typically avoided these plays of wealth and power.

However, today, I was on a mission, and despite the unappealing company, I was determined to leave satisfied.

"I can't tell you how honored I am to receive this rare invitation," Derek said, smiling widely. "The world-famous Leah Nachtnebel."

I mirrored his smile. "A bottle of your Château Lafite Rothschild and your lunch special, please," I said to the waiter after he approached and welcomed us.

Derek's expression betrayed his concern—understandable, given the wine's eighteen-thousand-dollar price tag.

"It's my treat," I declared swiftly, watching his concern morph into delight.

He shifted impatiently in his seat as the waiter uncorked the bottle and poured our glasses. Of course, Derek didn't wait for me, taking a sip and shaking his head in amazement. "Incredible. I've never tasted wine quite like this."

I maintained my smile, though it was becoming more difficult. "I hope you don't mind if I'm direct and address something upfront so we can then fully enjoy our lunch."

"No, not at all," he replied, seemingly astounded at the thought that anything I could say might disturb him.

"Great. Then let me get straight to the point."

He took another sip of wine, more interested in the taste than in whatever I had to say.

"I must confess my invitation to this lunch came with an agenda. I own a property in Hillson County, right in a wetland buffer zone, and I'm planning to build a summer home by the water."

"That sounds delightful," he said. "I've considered something similar near Big Island Pond. I inherited some land from my late aunt up there."

"There's just something about entertaining by the water, isn't there? It appeals particularly to those accustomed to places like the Hamptons."

"Our state will hold its own against such locales," Derek quipped.

"Well," I leaned in to lay on some charm. "I must confess, I've encountered some obstacles with the local judge."

Derek furrowed his brow. "Hillson . . . isn't that Albert's jurisdiction? Albert White?"

"Possibly. But it's also Ethel Dunbar's."

The frown etched deeper into his forehead. "Never heard of her."

"Great. That will simplify matters. The city rejected my conditional-use application, and she's poised to back that decision in court, as she's done repeatedly, favoring an inept village council over the hardworking citizens footing the bill. I don't have the patience for such nonsense."

Derek set his glass down, visibly puzzled. "You want her off your case, or—"

"No, I want her out of the Hillson District Court entirely."

For a moment, Derek's expression was hard to read. "Ousting a judge isn't easy," he said, leaning back just as the waiter served the truffle and wild mushroom consommé. His tone left no room for doubt; he was curious about what I had up my sleeve in exchange.

"I can only imagine. Fortunately, this judge has quite a few complaints lodged against her."

"Maybe so, but complaints are common for judges. Every alcoholic in the state tries to whine over his DUI. Anything of substance?"

"I couldn't say," I replied, poised with my spoon, my gaze fixed on Derek as he indulged in his soup. "But I'm quite sure the vice president would appreciate your commitment to upholding justice, especially in an election year."

The spoon paused in midair as astonishment flooded Derek's face. "The . . . vice president?"

I picked up my wine, twirled the glass, and examined the deep red liquid. "Yes, he'll be attending my concert next month—for the fifth time, I believe. It's a challenge to keep track of all the politicians who attend. But I've reserved two tickets for you and your wife, should you be interested in meeting him."

"The vice president," he said again. It wasn't a question this time as much as a statement of awe.

I gave a nod, gracefully sipping my wine as he burst out with excitement.

"Yes!" His face lit up with anticipation, mirroring the eager excitement of a puppy awaiting the throw of a ball. "That . . . that would be amazing."

I offered another smile; it was almost genuine this time.

"And about your property issue," he said, topping off his glass, "sounds like we've got some digging to do in Hillsboro. We can't let corruption or shady dealings threaten our system. It's supposed to protect everyday folks, not power-hungry judges." After a hearty swig of wine, he added, "Consider it handled."

I'd figured as much, but having him confirm it was part of the game.

Switching gears, I asked, "So, how was Rome? Did you check out the Colosseum?"

As Derek started to babble, I tuned out, my mind wandering to Agent Richter and his Bay Reaper. Was he patrolling the Merrimack River by boat right now? The thought of Robert Kirby stirring up trouble only to vanish into some backwoods seemed off. A mass shooting at a local store? It didn't fit the cunning work he had come up with so far. His actions pointed to something grander.

But piecing that puzzle together was Richter's job. My only hope was that he'd wrap it up fast so we could return to our real work: killing monsters.

CHAPTER TWENTY-FIVE

Liam

"It sounded like the noise came from over there." Mrs. Waver, an elderly resident who had reported loud boat noises to the local police, gestured toward the direction she mentioned. We stood at the edge of the waist-high marsh grasses in Joseph Finnegan Park. This side of the Neponset River was crammed with single-family homes and urban development, all squeezed into thin stretches of parks and walkways along the riverbank. The rain had ceased, but the skies remained a somber gray, continuing the theme of what was shaping up to be one of the gloomiest falls on record.

Mrs. Waver likely noticed my hesitation to venture into the high grasses. So did Rose, who seemed happy to stall alongside me.

"Right out there, near the shore," Mrs. Waver repeated, pointing decisively. The short, stout woman was clad in a wool sweater and a skirt. Her feet were shoved into tiny ballerina flats that looked like they would explode any second. Her voice carried the weight of conviction, as if she'd just unearthed the key piece of evidence in a long-cold case. Her appearance suggested she came from modest means—a local Seacoast family clinging to her parents' home out of pride for her heritage, ignoring the cash its sale would bring in today's market.

She gestured toward the water beyond the endless expanse of marsh grass. Agent Rose gave me a look that silently pleaded for me to challenge the woman, but ultimately, I exhaled deeply and trudged into the grass.

"Damn it," Agent Rose muttered behind me. I turned and watched her pluck a tick from her white business shirt. "I swear, if there's a co-pay for doxycycline . . ." she grumbled.

By the time we reached the edge of the damn marsh grasses, my dress shoes were caked with mud. One sock was now thoroughly soaked.

The river's water was calm and wide. A group of ducks floated under the weight of the sheet metal sky.

"So, what are we expecting to find here besides Lyme disease?" Agent Rose asked.

"You mentioned you saw the boat's lights briefly here at the shore?" I called back to Mrs. Waver. There was nothing. No tracks, no trash—just grass, mud, and ticks.

"Wait a minute," Mrs. Waver said, scratching her curly white hair. "I think it was about a hundred feet to your left."

Agent Rose's glare was lethal. She sighed, hands on her hips. "Mrs. Waver," she called out, her voice strained with forced kindness. "Are you sure it was to our left?"

Mrs. Waver paused, scratching her head again. "No."

"Jesus Christ." Rose extracted her foot from the mud. Her shoes were now soaked and covered in dirt. "We're wasting our time. We should be focusing on the Merrimack River."

My gaze followed the ducks and settled on a larger wooded area in the distance across the river. "Most likely so. And if you think about it, it makes perfect sense to flee up north into one of the least populated parts of the US. But then, why go through all the trouble down here? The stabbings, the dead fisherman, the lemon law. All of that to flee without a big bang? I doubt he's doing all this just to shoot up some tiny gas station near the Canadian border."

Agent Rose paused, her gaze distant as she mulled over the situation.

My phone rang. It was Dan, my lawyer.

"Hello?" I answered.

"Liam," Dan said, sounding almost out of breath. "You're not going to believe this, but Judge Dunbar has been removed from the Hillsboro court."

"What?" I practically yelled.

Agent Rose turned to me. "What happened?"

"They haven't provided any specifics, which is typical when a judge is being investigated for something," Dan explained.

"Holy shit." Despite the cold seeping into my wet feet, the news ignited a fire within me.

"Holy shit, indeed. This is like Christmas, Hanukkah, and Ramadan rolled into one, my friend. Our new judge is Alex White. Tough but fair as hell. Can you come to my office right now? There are documents you need to sign. We have to move fast in case she gets reinstated."

"I'm on my way."

After hanging up, I turned to face Rose. "I need to leave, but let's catch up later at the office. Or you could head home and rest."

"At the office," Rose decided. "But it'll be a few hours."

"Same here," I said, glancing down at my soaked shoes and pants.

"Keep me updated if Mrs. Waver comes up with anything . . . substantial," I said with a grin. "I'm counting on you to keep scouting the marshes."

Rose flipped me the bird as I took my leave.

Was I joking again? How long had it been since I'd done that?

The excitement coursing through me was unmatched. Dan was spot on—this opportunity was a rare gift. And the thought of having Josie back was indescribable. It had been torture without her. I'd felt like I was running on a beach, kite in hand, trying to make it fly high without the slightest bit of wind.

But the shitshow of a man I had become was dead. I was reborn. Nothing could stand in my way now. Not Sarah, not the Bay Reaper, not the Train Track Killer. Nothing.

CHAPTER TWENTY-SIX

Agent Vallery Rose

Rose was determined to head straight home for a shower. Mrs. Waver had sent her traipsing along the damn river shore for nearly another hour, each time "remembering" where the elusive boat had supposedly anchored at night only to change her mind again and again.

Her legs and feet were a soggy, mud-caked mess, and Rose had already picked off eight ticks from her skin. Another one was audaciously exploring her steering wheel. She itched everywhere, constantly checking another prickling spot for one of those little bloodsuckers. And then there was the stench in her car—the murky, sulfurous scent that evoked wet soil and rampant algae growth. She had to drive all the way back to Roxbury with the windows down despite the rain that now drenched her torso as well. Her hair was a mess too, which irked her since she had just gotten a touch-up relaxer yesterday at Lanette's.

It was dark by the time she made it home. She was turning into her street when she suddenly remembered what Richter had said about the Bay Reaper's strange escape northward—without the "big bang," as he had put it. As much as she loathed to admit it, his words bore some truth.

Why the hell would he go through all the trouble and planning, including an IED booby trap at his home, just to vanish in the woods?

No.

Something was fishy here, beyond her own smelly self and her car.

This truth made her skip her driveway and head all the way up to the old, unrestored historic mansion at the corner of the park.

The paint was peeling from the wooden siding, and dry rot marred its surface, visible even in the dim light cast by the street lantern.

Rose stepped out of her car and navigated the uneven brick walkway up to the sprawling front porch. Inside, music throbbed through the walls as she knocked loudly. She peered through the window, her gaze cutting through the throng of Black, Latino, and White individuals directly to Vito.

He caught her eye and wove through the crowd of gang members to the door.

As he opened it, a blast of loud hip-hop bass surged forth. He gave her a once-over, his eyebrow arching in question.

"Can I come in for a minute?" Rose asked.

Vito gave her another scrutinizing look. The lines on his face deepened. "Nope," he responded, the gold in his necklace glinting under the porch light.

Rose arched an eyebrow. "Afraid I might stumble upon something I shouldn't?" She crossed her arms and craned her neck to glimpse the party through the window.

"No," Vito shot back. "Because you stink, and you'd drag mud all over my new carpet."

"Fair enough," Rose conceded. "Can you step outside for a minute, then? I really need to talk to you."

The unflinching shift in Vito's expression made it clear he was anything but eager for this conversation.

"Please?" Rose added, her tone softening.

Vito paused, considering for a moment, then stepped outside, shutting the door behind him. The clamor from inside was immediately muffled.

He walked over to the porch railing and leaned against it.

"I need some information," Rose said cautiously, leaning beside him against the railing.

"Of course you do, but that doesn't mean I'm gonna give it."

She nodded. "Nothing about you or any other gangs in the neighborhood."

This piqued his curiosity.

"Have you heard about the Bay Reaper?"

A subtle shift in his demeanor betrayed his surprise at her question. "The sick fuck stabbing people while wearing a Halloween mask?"

"Yeah. He blew up his house during a search warrant and is on the run."

Vito smirked. "I guess he don't like you much."

Rose leaned over the railing. "We think he's about to do something big. Really big."

"Like a mass shooting?"

Rose nodded.

"Sounds like typical white people shit. What the hell do you want from me? He ain't gonna find a place to squat in my hood, that's for sure."

"I know. But this one is smart enough to go about it the right way. Tricking people. I was just wondering if you heard anything."

"Such as?"

"Military-grade sales. Stuff to build large bombs or generally just fuck shit up."

Vito fell silent.

"You heard something?" Rose asked, encouraged.

He scowled at the ground.

"Vito," Rose pressed.

"Maybe, but I ain't gonna snitch."

"Well, in that case, maybe I should finally take a closer look at what happens in your shed every other Saturday, which, wait, would be today. You really gonna make me call the cops to search it?"

His anger flared. "You threatening me?"

"Do I have to, Vito? Threaten you to get your help to prevent an attack that could be bigger than the Oklahoma bombing? Do you remember how many people died? One hundred sixty-seven, Vito. One, six, seven. Including kids."

Vito pushed off from the railing. "Damn it, Rose, I knew you were trouble."

"What have you heard?" Rose pressed.

He was still hesitant, the internal struggle etched clearly across his face.

Rose understood his dilemma all too well. In the hood, being labeled a snitch was a fate worse than death. Her own brother had paid dearly for it.

Rose threw her hands up in frustration. "Do I need to remind you—"

"Some white guy was asking about buying Tovex," Vito said.

"The explosive that IEDs are made of? Did you sell it to him?"

"No!" Vito looked offended. "What the fuck, Rose. You hang with the pigs too much if you think your own would sell that kind of shit to psychos!"

Rose took a step forward, her voice softer. "Who would deal with it around here?"

He shrugged nonchalantly, lighting a cigarette. "The Russian cartel, if the price is right. Nobody, if it's obvious the buyer is some FBI-wanted white boy planning to blow shit up."

"Let's say the price was right, that the Russians were willing to sell. Where would they do it?"

Vito met Rose's gaze. "Can't say for sure, but a handoff like that would need time. That stuff isn't easy to get. It's heavily regulated, more dangerous to deal with than drugs. But if your ifs are really happening . . . might wanna start looking south."

"South?" Rose echoed, taken aback. "How far south? As far as the Neponset River?"

Vito remained silent, drawing deeply on his cigarette and exhaling a thick cloud of smoke.

"Fuck," Rose muttered, hurrying down the porch steps, her body radiating with urgency. Nothing was a given, but maybe Mrs. Waver was onto something after all.

She reached for her phone and dialed Richter only to be met with the incessant ring of an unanswered call.

"Rose!"

Rose turned.

"I didn't help you because you played bad cop. I . . ." Vito paused, the emotions evident in his face. "I did it for Nario."

An overwhelming coldness enveloped Rose, that all-too-familiar ache that surfaced whenever someone mentioned her brother's name.

"I still wake up at night when he visits me in my nightmares. But what happened back then . . ." Vito said. "It happened because he was protecting his brothers."

No matter how many years passed, grappling with that truth offered no solace. "Maybe he should have protected his family instead," Rose retorted.

"He did," Vito insisted, his gaze softening. "Just maybe not the right one."

Her expression twisted into a blend of pain and sarcasm. Rose acknowledged his words with a half nod, then walked back to her car to call Cowboy.

"Where the hell are you?" he barked through the phone as she slid into her car.

"Following up on a lead on the Neponset River."

"That old lady seeing a boat at night?"

"Kinda. But there could be more to it. Some guy trying to buy—"

"We have a possible sighting of Kirby near a small town by the Merrimack River," Cowboy interrupted. "I'll text you the location."

"Who's on it?"

"Everybody except Richter. Just called him, and he didn't answer his phone."

"Do you need me? I want to check on this lead."

"All right. You won't make it up in time anyway. Chase your lead. I'll keep you posted."

"Thanks."

The car's engine roared to life as Rose weighed her options: drive north to join Cowboy or follow her gut. Something felt off. She thought about Kirby's madness, his potential route back to Boston via the ocean. Then Mrs. Waver's words echoed in her mind, hinting that the boat might have anchored on the opposite side near a large patch of woods.

She set the car in motion and headed toward the Neponset River.

What if everything hinged on this one tip? She had to pursue it.

Her mood sank as she thought about the daunting marsh grass and the encroaching high tide.

She dialed Richter again. No answer.

Common sense urged her to wait, to let Richter know and join her in pursuing this lead. But deep down, she thought it was likely nothing. And if there was even a hint of suspicion once she reached the river, she could always call Richter or for backup.

CHAPTER TWENTY-SEVEN

Leah

Every seat in the symphony hall was about to be filled. Adjusting the short train of my black evening dress for the night's performance, I entered Luca's box on the first balcony, which boasted some of the best views in the concert hall except for the one opposite us. It was now occupied by the Prince of Qatar and the Vice President of the United States. A nervously rambling Derek Beckett was clearly getting on their nerves.

As always, Luca was the personification of sophistication. His long legs were crossed elegantly. White tux. Hand-tailored.

"What a great honor for you to visit me here, especially with such distinguished company in tow. Aren't you expected over there?" he asked, gazing intently at the box across from his, then at the gradually filling seats below.

"By now, you should know that I am where I desire to be, not where others expect me to be. Usually." I offered a polite smile and nod to the vice president, who reciprocated with a wave.

"To what do I owe this pleasure?" he asked.

"Do I need a reason to enjoy the company of an old friend?"

Luca smiled. "I came to understand that La Imperatrice navigates the intricate games of life at all times."

I settled into one of the gilded chairs beside him. "Who doesn't?"

"That's fair enough," he conceded.

Our eyes locked.

"Are you still angry with me?" I asked.

After a pause, Luca responded, "Disappointed."

"Is that worse than angry?" I didn't know the answer to that. The subtle differences in these emotions were alien to me.

"In my case, no. My anger is far more feared than my disappointment."

I nodded. "Will you join me for dinner? Whenever it's convenient for you."

Luca's gaze shifted forward, deliberately avoiding mine and meeting that of the vice president, who clearly recognized Luca but chose not to publicly acknowledge him.

"Unless you withdraw your last request, I'd prefer not to."

"I'm afraid I can't do that."

Silence.

"Would you still . . ." I asked hesitantly, "look into something for me?"

Luca scoffed. "Ah, there it is. I knew there was a reason for your visit."

Gently, I placed a hand on his forearm. He recoiled slightly from the contact but didn't withdraw. "I did come to invite you to dinner . . . and to ask you about Jan Novak."

Luca still avoided eye contact, but he softened his tone. "What makes you think I've looked into him? You asked me not to."

I withdrew my hand and rose. "For old time's sake. Please let me know what you discover. It's very important to me. Goodbye, old friend."

As I rose and turned to leave, Luca gently caught my arm, his hold as delicate as if he were cradling the neck of a fragile bird. "Stay away from him," he advised, his gaze piercing.

My eyebrows furrowed. "So, you did look into him. What did you find?"

He leaned in. "Absolutely nothing."

I remained silent, prompting him to elaborate as he released my arm. "And that's very unsettling as I always find something, no matter the subject," he continued. "There's been only one other instance where I failed."

"And who was that?" I knew the answer but asked anyway.

His gaze swept over me from head to toe, then returned to the crowd ahead as he turned his back to me.

"You."

Chapter Twenty-Eight

Agent Vallery Rose

Rose had been navigating the marshes along the Neponset River for nearly half an hour, her shoes wet and soaked once again. On this side of the river, there was an eerie solitude in the darkness. The sky above was obscured by clouds, eliminating any light from the stars or moon. Her phone was fully charged, yet she was aware that using the flashlight would drain it quickly, so she picked up her pace.

Another mosquito buzzed by her ear. She couldn't stop herself from slapping a palm against the side of her head.

"Damn it."

It was then that she noticed a patch in the marsh grass flattened into a small circle.

As she hurried over, her flashlight revealed patterns of boot prints at the water's edge: a possible sign of someone repeatedly entering or exiting a boat at this spot.

Turning, she aimed her flashlight along a path carved through the grass from the riverbank. It led into a densely wooded area seemingly untouched by human hands. This was likely private property, maybe owned by a business or by wealthy individuals desiring solitude around their mansions—characteristic of the nearby area known for its rich residents and expansive estates.

Instantly, Rose turned off her flashlight and dialed Richter.

Voicemail again. Then the beep.

"SAC," she whispered, "I think I've found something on the Neponset. Kirby might still be here, waiting for a Tovex order from the Russians. I'll call for backup near the—"

Suddenly, a heron burst from the grass in a flurry. One of its massive wings struck Rose in the head. Reflexively, she drew her gun with her right hand while still clutching the phone, which slipped from her grasp. The phone made a sharp *blop* as it hit the water. Then everything was silent again.

"Fuck," she cursed quietly, kneeling at the water's edge to retrieve the device, but her hands found only water. It was deeper than she had anticipated, which aligned with the theory that this could be an ideal location for a small boat like a RIB.

Gradually, Rose's eyes adjusted to the surrounding darkness. It was remarkable how she could be so close to the city and yet so alone.

She considered the distant lights on the opposite side of the river, then the dark woods looming behind her. The sensible decision would be to return and contact Richter and backup using the radio in her car. That was the safer option. But if Kirby was indeed nearby and the transfer of Tovex had already occurred, every minute was vital.

Facing the woods, Rose made her way as quietly as possible down the path left by someone else, leading into the expansive, shadowy forest—a path that could tip the scales of life and death not just for herself but for many others.

CHAPTER TWENTY-NINE

Liam

Dan was an older, short man who resembled a car salesman in an ill-fitting suit. He lacked the aggression of younger attorneys but had a deep understanding of the law, treating it with the familiarity and consideration of a mother caring for her child. He'd worked for my family for decades. Starting as my dad's lawyer, he now represented me.

He organized the papers I'd signed and looked up at me with a smile. "I'll file these first thing in the morning. And call your mom back, will you? She's called me eight times, complaining." He stood up but quickly noticed that I'd remained seated, which prompted him to sit back down.

"Did . . . you know?" I asked, my voice packed with disappointment. "About my half-sister," I pressed, sidestepping any potential evasion.

Dan's expression was a mix of discomfort and regret. "I did."

"Goddamn it, Dan! Did you ever consider telling us?"

"Well, first, there was client-attorney privilege between your dad and me, and I'm bound by that. Your father insisted this remain secret until after his passing. What your mother did with the information afterward isn't my responsibility, Liam."

I straightened in my chair. "Wait. My mom knew about this second family since my dad passed?"

Dan's mouth hung open as if he'd inadvertently revealed the secret ingredient to Betty Crocker's world-famous pumpkin pie. "Your father," he started, his voice softening, "came to me just before he passed, asking that a portion of the inheritance intended for your mom be allocated to his other family. For the children, you understand. Your sister and, I believe, a now-deceased brother."

The revelation was overwhelming. I'd been dodging this reality, burying myself in work, avoiding reflection. But facing Dan, my father's longtime lawyer and friend, brought everything rushing back like acid reflux.

"Your dad was a good man," Dan said.

"That's what I spent my whole life believing, Dan." My voice dripped with malice. "But 'good man' doesn't describe someone who cheats on his wife and creates an entire second family. Actually," I said, rising and pulling out my phone, "'asshole' seems more fitting. Big. Fucking. Asshole. Piece. Of. Shit. To be exact."

Memories of my first conversation with Leah, when she'd probed the clear roles of my parents as if she'd known their secrets, flooded my mind. She'd been right all along.

Dan sighed. "Liam, life isn't always black and white."

"In this instance, it's quite black and white, Dan." I glanced at my phone, noticing the absence of the "5G" signal next to the battery indicator. "I need to go. There's no reception here, and the Kirby case is heating up."

Dan walked me out in silence, not mentioning my father again, which I appreciated. Once the fresh air hit me in the parking lot, my phone lit up with several missed calls, including a voicemail from Rose.

"SAC," her voice played quietly from the voicemail. "I think I found something on the Neponset. Kirby might still be here, waiting for a Tovex order from the Russians. I'll call backup near the—"

Then the voicemail cut off.

A wave of adrenaline rushed through me. I called Rose repeatedly, but the calls went straight to voicemail.

"Shit."

Without a second to waste, I dialed the FBI's internal communication system.

"Special Agent in Charge Liam Richter speaking. I need immediate backup for a potential encounter with Robert Kirby in the Neponset River Reservation Park area. The exact location is unknown. Agent Valerie Rose may be engaging him at this moment and is unresponsive to communication."

"Did you say Neponset River Reservation Park?" came the operator's voice.

"Yes."

"We just received calls from residents about possible gunfire. Local law enforcement was dispatched to the area around five minutes ago, but they're still searching the area. It's quite large."

Fuck. Fuck. Fuck!

"Deploy every available unit and search the park now!" I ordered. "We might have an active shooter."

"Understood, sir!"

I ended the call and leaped into my SUV. The engine roared to life as I sped off with sirens blaring and lights flashing, parting traffic like Moses parting the Red Sea.

I dialed Cowboy. "Cowboy, where are you?"

"Heading back. We followed a false lead on Kirby up north. I tried to call—"

"He's here! In Boston. Near the Neponset River," I said. "Kirby. He never left."

"Fuck," Cowboy blurted. "Rose called earlier about a lead there."

"Where exactly did she say she was going?"

"Just mentioned a potential lead near the river."

"Damn it!" Why didn't she wait for backup?

"We're en route, but it'll be about fifty minutes."

"Coordinate the search location with local law enforcement. I'll meet you there."

I hung up, frustration mounting. This was bad, bad, bad. Kirby, that bastard, had taken his flimsy-ass boat from the Merrimack River down over the dangerous ocean to the Boston area for his final move.

At least I was nearby, as Dan's office was south of Boston. But nearby to where exactly? The Neponset River covered a vast area with miles of nature trails and neighborhoods.

No one but Rose knew exactly where he might be hiding.

Except for Leah.

I told her that I'd never ask her to play Sherlock Homes with me again. But this wasn't only about the life of an agent. It was about countless others as well.

I dialed her.

My dark thoughts filled with hope.

The phone rang a few times, and then she answered.

CHAPTER THIRTY

Leah

My reflection in the mirror appeared unusually fatigued. Seated at the golden makeup table in my personal backstage quarters, I was interrupted by Crystal's knock, which indicated the start of my concert was imminent.

I couldn't get the Train Track Killer out of my mind. The thought of him overshadowed my collaboration with Agent Richter. My focus had been solely on this case. I'd broadened my search from suicides on tracks to all manner of tragedies across the city. Yet the sheer volume of cases was overwhelming. I'd need an entire team just to cover Boston.

Feeling disheartened, I reached for my flip phone, a habit that had become all too common.

No new messages.

Richter hadn't provided any updates on the Train Track Killer.

"Leah?" Crystal's voice echoed in the hallway. It was accompanied by a knock. "Everyone is seated. We're ready."

I stored the phone away and stepped into the corridor.

"A few people didn't show, but we've filled those seats with those waiting for cancellations outside the symphony hall," she said.

I nodded, securing the door behind me. We had taken only a few steps when the distinct ringtone of my flip phone halted me.

I paused, sensing Crystal's concern.

"Is everything all right?" she asked.

I turned, staring at my door. Did he have new information on the Train Track Killer? My gaze jerked down the hallway toward the stage.

I hesitated, torn between my performance and the potential call. Could it wait? But why would he call unless it was urgent?

"Wait here, please," I instructed Crystal as she glanced nervously toward the stage.

Quickly, I returned and shut the door. The ringing continued without pause.

"Hello?" I answered quietly, ensuring my voice wouldn't carry to the hallway.

Richter's voice came through, desperation clear amid the backdrop of sirens. "I need your help."

"Go on," I urged.

"Kirby is here, in Boston. Agent Rose is engaging him in a shootout somewhere along the Neponset River, but her location is unknown."

Using my photographic memory, I visualized the map of Boston, including the Neponset River. My eyes closed momentarily.

"The Neponset River stretches for twenty-nine miles. Provide any details you have."

"Shit . . . um . . . Rose mentioned a potential Tovex deal with the Russians."

"The Russians typically utilize waterways for their illegal transactions. Does Kirby have a boat?"

"We believe so."

I conjured the image of the Neponset River, pinpointing it instantly.

"If the deal occurred along the Neponset, it would likely be near the Baker Dam in Lower Mills. Beyond that point, they'd encounter low water levels."

"Lower Mills area? But where could someone hide out there?"

I concentrated, searching my memory.

"Think, Leah! Please!"

The untouched acres of forest behind the grand mansions near St. Luke Church flashed before me like a vivid photograph.

"There's a large expanse of private woodland behind some mansions right on the river, not far from Baker Dam. Someone could easily navigate through the marshes by boat and remain hidden there."

"St. Luke Church?" Richter echoed, the sound of screeching wheels audible on his end.

"Roger's Lane is a narrow road that leads deep into the woodland at the rear of the villas. From there, it's entirely on foot. You need to wait for backup. Vehicles can't navigate those woods efficiently, and facing Kirby alone on foot is far too dangerous."

"I can't do that, Leah." Richter's voice was urgent.

"Richter, listen to me. On foot, you'll be a needle in a haystack. If you run into Kirby alone, it might take backup too long to find you."

Richter was silent.

"Do not engage alone, Richter," I demanded. "Kirby is likely well-armed."

Another pause, broken only by distant sirens.

"I'm . . . sorry, Leah."

"Liam. Listen to—"

"Kill as many as you can—" he said before hanging up.

I stood there, overwhelmed with shock. But why? Richter's altruistic nature was precisely why I had chosen him. I should have known it might turn against me. I had exchanged a monster for a human, and humans trusted their hearts over logic.

Exiting into the hallway, I found Crystal waiting anxiously. I looked at her, then at the stage. Then I looked the other direction, down the corridor leading to my car, which would transport me to a storage unit in South Boston near the Neponset River. There, I kept a dirt bike, among other escape essentials: cash, a gun, and fake passports.

The mere thought was absurd.

Reckless.

Impulsive.

Unplanned.

Potentially fatal.

If Richter met his end, it would be due to his own heroic foolishness.

And yet . . .

I turned to see Crystal approaching, her face etched with deep concern.

Moments had passed, critical moments that could determine life or death for either me or Richter.

"Cancel the concert," I declared abruptly.

"What?" Crystal's eyes went saucer-wide. "But—"

"I'm not feeling good. Cancel it," I insisted, my tone brooking no argument.

Richter's recklessness astounded me. Agent Rose might already be beyond help. Why would he risk everything without waiting for backup?

Dressed for the evening, I rushed down the hallway and darted through the employees-only passages, then slipped out into the secluded alley where my car was parked.

I ignited my Audi's engine, urgency propelling each movement. Every second was precious. I ignored traffic signals as I sped toward my storage unit on the outskirts of Boston, near the Neponset River.

After bursting through the rundown storage unit's door, I ditched my heels, seized the handgun from the duffel bag, which also contained cash and a passport, and secured the gun inside my pantyhose, ensuring it stayed put below the waistband.

There wasn't time to put on the protective leather suit, so I strapped on the helmet and mounted the dirt bike. Accelerating briskly, I launched out the rear end of the storage facility, which I'd strategically chosen for its protection from surveillance and streetlights. My dress's train billowed behind me like a cape, while the cold wind and light drizzle chilled my bare arms, legs, and feet.

Before long, I encountered a procession of police cars heading for the bridge over the Neponset River, leading toward the wooded areas near the mansions. Despite the imminent arrival of backup, Richter might have already initiated contact with Kirby.

One police car seemed to notice me tailing them and slowed as we crossed the bridge. The rest of the convoy pressed forward. I decelerated and took a side road that led to the eastern edge of the woods.

My bike's light was the sole beacon illuminating the challenging deer paths littered with rocks and fallen branches. Despite the obstacles, I was faster than any on-foot backup approaching from the south. Only a few minutes ahead, but in situations like this, a bullet needed only the blink of an eye to find its target.

CHAPTER THIRTY-ONE

Liam

The muffled sounds of sirens sliced through the darkness of the woods from the south—the direction from which I had entered the densely overgrown area. Gun drawn and pointing ahead, I resisted the urge to call out for Rose, as I feared Kirby might hear me and either shoot or detonate a bomb, endangering us all.

It was almost pitch black as I ventured deeper into the patch of untouched forest on the outskirts of Boston. It felt as if I had stumbled into a hidden, otherworldly realm. The drizzle intensified, with thick clouds obliterating any traces of moonlight.

A branch snapped under my foot, startling birds above and sending shivers down my spine. I quickly refocused on the narrow deer path below—one of countless intertwining trails in this wilderness. Leah was right. With all these paths, there was a real risk that any backup might not arrive in time.

I had hiked the path for a few minutes when I spotted what appeared to be a large rock partially concealed by bushes and nearly crushed by a massive fallen tree.

As I approached cautiously, the silhouette of a black tent began to materialize before me, not far from the rock. It was ingeniously blended with the underbrush as if nature itself had built it.

Holding my breath, I listened intently for any surrounding sounds. With the woods seemingly silent except for my pounding heart, I risked a brief flash of light from my phone.

"Holy fuck," I whispered as the light reflected off the largest IED bomb I had ever seen. It was protruding from a military-grade backpack alongside an M249 Squad Automatic Weapon and a huge pile of ammo. Scattered around were empty food cans, water bottles, ammunition, and IED assembly equipment.

My shock was shattered by a faint, guttural sound—something I might have missed earlier. I swung the flashlight toward the noise and nearly dropped it when the beam highlighted Agent Rose lying on the leaf-strewn ground. Her eyes were wide with terror as she clutched her stomach, her hands trembling over her blood-soaked shirt. She struggled to speak, a gurgling sound mingling with blood.

"Rose!" I exclaimed, rushing to her side and kneeling on the muddy ground.

"Armor . . ." she managed just as the first rounds of gunfire erupted. I launched myself behind the rock as bullets ejected sparks and rock chips under a high-pitched ping.

Then an eerie silence swallowed us.

A whirlwind of sensations overcame me—I was hot, cold, nauseous—as I cautiously peered around the rock. My phone, the flashlight still on, lay on the ground. The dim silver light revealed the figure of a man standing near the tent.

Fucking Kirby.

Without hesitation, I fired.

One, two, three, four, five shots, each striking him squarely in the chest. Picture-perfect, just as I was taught in the academy.

But the anticipated thud of a body never came. Instead, Kirby remained upright, unfazed.

I fired again, three more rounds aimed closer to his upper chest, one possibly near the head. But in the darkness and from this distance, my supposed headshot was ineffective. I was immediately met with a return avalanche from his automatic rifle.

I took cover behind the rock. Rose's word came back to me. "Armor"

The North Hollywood shootout between heavily armored criminals Larry Phillips Jr. and Emil Mătăsăreanu flashed in my mind. I recalled the intense gunfight they unleashed against the LAPD. And now, here we were, in a forest at night. Kirby could shoot us all and then rampage through the nearest neighborhood.

Suddenly, silence again.

Time slowed as I heard the rustle of leaves and snapping branches, the sounds inching closer to my hiding spot. What could I possibly do now? He was armored, armed with an automatic rifle, and likely equipped with night vision. Running for it was a death sentence, as was remaining here.

"Kirby!" I called out, pressed tightly against the cold rock. "The man you stabbed at the docks had a history of rape and domestic violence, so no real loss there. We can get you help. Real help. I promise you, I'll make sure of it."

The snapping of twigs continued.

"Let me get my agent out of here. We can still save her. She's just doing her job like you once did to protect us."

He kept advancing.

A wave of horror washed over me. Would this be it?

"I met your parents," I said. "Your mother . . . she just wants you to know everything will be okay and that she's here for you no matter what."

Silence, then another branch snapped, now alarmingly close to my cover.

"Nothing is okay in this shithole we call America," retorted an empty voice from mere feet away on the other side of the rock.

"Tell me about it," I said quickly. "You're not the only one getting screwed over. My life's pretty shitty as well right now. But we have to keep fighting. If not for ourselves, then for the people who love us."

The sounds halted, presumably from just behind the rock. Had I gotten through to him?

"And you have people who love you, Kirby," I quickly continued.

Silence.

"Your family wants to work with us to get you the help you need. Real help, not just a quick prescription that won't stop the nightmares and pain."

"It's . . . too late," Kirby said, his voice weak and filled with pain. "He's too powerful."

"Who?" I pressed. "Who are you talking about?"

After a brief silence, the dark figure of Robert Kirby emerged from the right side of the rock, maintaining a distance that allowed for effective use of his M249 Squad Automatic. He was armored from head to toe, his eyes deadly, piercing the night like a nocturnal demon.

"You're just as blind as the rest of them," he concluded firmly. "Someone needs to open your eyes. And that burden falls on me."

He aimed the weapon at me.

Fuck.

My gaze shifted to Rose, whose wide eyes were filled with pain and fear, grasping at the last seconds of life.

I attempted a comforting smile as if to reassure her everything would be all right, either in this life or the next. Then I braced myself for Kirby's final act, wondering if this old dog was worthy of heaven.

CHAPTER THIRTY-TWO

Leah

I navigated my dirt bike along narrow deer trails, veering close to the riverbed, the most logical place for a campsite accessible by boat. Branches lashed against my exposed arms as if the trees themselves were trying to thwart my advance, branding me an enemy. My feet were in agony from several barefoot stops on the forest floor as I negotiated sharp rocks and branches—a necessary evil to avoid slipping off the throttle with high heels and losing control.

Soon, a faint light pierced through the trees. I burst into a clearing, instantly assessing the scene: Kirby aiming at Richter, a wounded agent on the ground.

Without hesitation, I emptied my Glock 19's magazine into Kirby. Fifteen rounds fired into his chest with precision and speed.

Yet Kirby remained upright and turned his weapon toward me.

"He's—" Richter attempted to warn, but I was already in motion.

I slammed the bike into first gear, twisted the throttle to its limit, and released the clutch, charging at Kirby with the bike rearing up in full, reckless abandon.

Rat-tat-tat! His shots barely missed me and hit the undercarriage as we collided with brutal force. I was flung from the bike, tumbling over rocks and scraping my skin before coming to a halt. The instant sharp pain in my chest and back left no doubt that I had broken a few ribs.

Kirby was knocked back, his weapon sliding away into the darkness. The bike, now without its rider, skidded to a stop, its engine still rumbling defiantly.

Kirby staggered to his feet and quickly recovered, jumping on top of me to pin me down, his armored weight pressing me into the mud. The silver blade of his knife glinted dangerously close to my neck. It was halted by the edge of my helmet, then cut into my flesh just as Richter slammed into Kirby with the same momentum as the bike, dislodging Kirby's armored helmet.

I staggered to my feet, panting. Kirby, now helmetless and pinned underneath Richter, struck Richter on the head with a rock, momentarily stunning him before pushing him off.

But Richter, who'd found his own rock, rose again.

The two exchanged clumsy swings, dodging blows with difficulty. Kirby, with superior hand-to-hand combat skills, struck Richter across the jaw. He staggered.

As Kirby raised his rock for a decisive blow, I launched in excruciating pain and struck him from behind with my own rock.

My feet felt lacerated, probably embedded with small stones and debris. I was concussed as well, as evidenced by my overwhelming nausea.

Kirby was quick to turn and swing at me, landing a heavy blow on my helmet that sent me tumbling backward. The world spun around me even after I'd landed. But Richter was right behind him, slamming his rock onto the side of Kirby's head. Kirby stumbled but managed to stay upright. With a blank face, he turned to Richter. Clearly, he'd endured pain or been taught to endure it during his time in the military.

It was my turn to dive back in. Richter and I swung at Kirby in a brutal, bloody dance.

246

Finally, Richter landed the heavy blow that took Kirby down, then leaped on top of him, relentless. Again and again, he unleashed a never-ending avalanche of strikes. Each time, he raised the rock high above his head before bringing it down with savage force.

"Richter," I said, stepping up beside him.

But he persisted, an animalistic scream of raw frustration escaping his lungs.

"Richter, stop!" I demanded, staring into Kirby's face, now awash in a flood of blood. His eyes were wide open, a silent testament to his tragic death.

Richter raised his arm for another blow, so I grabbed his wrist to stop him.

That seemed to snap him out of his frenzied trance. He looked at me in utter shock, then at Kirby's blood-soaked face and gaping head wound.

"Fuck," he muttered, climbing off Kirby, letting the rock slip from his grasp.

He turned away, his face a mask of pain, agony, and disgust, while I stared emotionlessly at Kirby.

"Spare yourself the guilt. This was mercy," I said, words that Richter acknowledged before he rushed over to the critically wounded agent. Her breathing was now shallow and rapid, her vacant eyes staring into oblivion.

She was in shock; her time was running out.

"Rose!" Richter cried out, his eyes scanning her bloodied torso.

I turned to limp toward my bike; I had to escape. The first helicopters hovered anxiously over the woods, their lights scouring the darkness, every visible inch. The barking dogs were closing in. We had a minute, tops, before this place swarmed with them.

"Wait!" Richter called after me.

I knew better than to stop; I had to keep moving.

"Please, help her!" Richter's voice halted me, his desperation anchoring my feet as if they weren't my own.

I turned to face his pain-streaked visage.

"Please save her, please," he pleaded.

I glanced at my bike, then back at him, caught by the raw desperation in his eyes—an emotion that unexpectedly stirred something within me.

"Damn . . . "

With a quick limp, I approached the agent, lifting my visor to see her more clearly. Our eyes locked. Hers were filled with a haunting resignation, as if she saw me as the angel of death come to take her away.

"There's a chance she's still conscious enough to remember all of this," I said, standing motionless as the barking grew closer. "She'll come after me, this one . . . after us. I can see it in her eyes."

Richter focused on Rose, now holding her hand.

"You didn't kill her," I said. "Is this worth losing everything for, including your daughter?"

He stared at her, perhaps envisioning the smiling face of his daughter, a face he would never see again should our secret come to light. But then that moment passed, and he looked back at me. "Save her."

I gazed at Richter, the man I once considered an ally, now potentially the one who could cause my downfall. But then, wasn't this the very reason I had sought him out? To save me from my true self and the dark deeds I might commit in moments like these? If I walked away now, it would be a "real" murder weighing on my conscience, as the monsters never counted.

Quickly, I removed my helmet and kneeled next to her, opposite Richter. "Sit her up," I instructed, pressing my ear against her back to listen to her lungs. "Collapsed lung. Air is trapped in her pleural space, putting pressure on the lung, impairing her breathing."

I held a hand over her shoulders to prevent her from slumping as she desperately attempted to breathe.

"Do you have a pen?" I asked, maintaining my usual calm despite my own pain.

"What?" Richter looked confused, panicked.

"A pen," I repeated firmly.

He frantically searched his jacket pockets, then the front of his suit shirt, and finally pulled out a pen.

I took it and unscrewed it in the middle. Then I tossed aside the upper part, keeping only the chamber of the lower part, which would now function like a short straw.

Rose flinched as I used my fingers to locate the exact spot at the second intercostal space between the second and third ribs along the midclavicular line.

"Go behind her and hold her tight."

Richter positioned himself behind her, stretching his legs out next to hers, with her in the middle.

I used the train of my dress to wipe down and hold the pen, ensuring that I left no prints.

Quickly, I took a rock, placed the empty pen chamber at the precise spot of her upper ribs, and, with one strong swing, drove the pen into her flesh. She mustered a final burst of strength to resist me. If this were a movie, that single blow would have sufficed, allowing the pen to pierce her lungs and miraculously save her life. But reality is no film, and I found myself having to strike the pen multiple times with the rock to embed it fully into her lungs, sunk deep into her flesh like a nail driven into a wall.

Instantly, air and blood escaped through the pen, alleviating the pressure and, more importantly, allowing the lung to partially re-expand.

Rose gasped as the sudden influx of air revived her. She drew long, haggard breaths like she'd just broken the surface after being submerged for too long.

I didn't wait a second longer. I jumped to my feet, rock still in hand, and ran to retrieve my bike. Despite my pain and a broken rib, I lifted it with adrenaline fueled by the barking dogs only moments away.

I mounted the bike and sped into the darkness along the small path I had come from. There was a decent chance that law enforcement hadn't yet encircled the entire woods to focus manpower on the site Richter had sent them to. That would leave my escape route open, especially now that they would find Richter with Kirby dead and wouldn't be looking for another suspect.

Relief greeted me as I emerged onto the bridge where I had entered the woods earlier and found no law enforcement blocking the road. I saw cars with sirens passing, but none seemed to be looking for me.

I drove past them over the bridge, briefly slowing to throw the rock with my prints into the river. Then I increased my speed again.

I was tempted to head straight home on the bike, but this was unadvisable despite the intense pain. I had to return to my own car and then drive home, ensuring my outdoor security camera captured my return in the vehicle I had left in.

I would call Ida to assist me in the basement where I kept all my medical equipment. Then I would heal at home, informing Crystal that personal matters had arisen, and I needed some time to myself.

This wasn't the first time Ida would assist me in the basement. My hobby came with physical dangers, though this was the most severe I'd suffered so far. She never asked for details. I paid her too well, and the money meant a lot to her family. My demise would be hers as well. Her children and grandchildren. Ida would never talk. She was a mother, and silence was a matter of survival for what she loved.

For a brief moment, my mind drifted away from the pain as I contemplated the aftermath of all this.

There was a slight chance that Agent Rose had seen me, maybe even witnessed the entire fight, and would remember it. Of course, there was also the chance that she had been battling for her own life so fiercely that she hadn't focused on the fight with Kirby. Maybe it would all seem like a dream to her.

But there was a real possibility I could soon face legal trouble. Although I could likely navigate any scandal, given that the law often sided with money, predicting the outcome without all the facts was difficult.

No, Agent Rose had now become a liability. A threat to my life and Richter's. One I could have eliminated by simply letting her die.

And yet . . . I felt calm.

The monster deep within me was locked away tonight. Richter had awakened my humanity. He had saved me from myself.

As I huffed my way back to my car at the storage unit, breathing heavily and grunting with immense pain, calmness washed over me.

If I went down because I'd saved a life and not because I'd taken one, I was okay with that.

I was, for once, at peace.

CHAPTER THIRTY-THREE

Liam

The hospital ICU floor was in a frenzy, with journalists, FBI agents, and police officers milling about. The flash of cameras illuminated Agent Rose's room, casting light into the hallway where I was waiting. I didn't need to see it to know the picture being taken: McCourt shaking Rose's hand, handing her an award, his smile fake and slimy.

They made their way out, with Rose being wheeled in a wheelchair by nurses. Machines and a saline drip were attached to her arm. As they emerged into the hallway, loud clapping erupted around her.

Rose was being transferred to a lower-intensity unit. She was still in pretty bad shape but was out of the woods now. Her eyes caught mine as the nurses pushed her down the hallway past me, a small train of doctors and staff following her—all for the cameras, of course.

The story was simple. Rose had saved the day by finding Kirby and helping bring him down, taking a bullet in the process. The buzz was all about her, which she deserved. It was she who had found Kirby before he could take more lives.

"I need to talk to you," I said, trying to stop her briefly as she was pushed past me. However, all she did was throw me a weary look that I couldn't decipher. Of course, she was tired; she'd almost died. But was there something else in that look. Would she talk to McCourt, tell him about the woman who had saved her and helped kill Kirby? Or had she already spoken to him?

Anxious worry formed in my chest as McCourt stepped next to me. We both watched Rose roll past a small group of cops, none of them clapping but smiling dismissively. Typical macho pricks.

"Has she said anything?" I carefully asked McCourt. We watched her all the way to the elevator, waiting for it to open.

"Not much, but I doubt she remembers much anyway. I can't believe you saved her life with a pen. When the hell did you turn into MacGyver?" His gray eyes gave me a cunning, questioning look.

"CPR training. Some guy in the class asked about a trick with a pen he'd seen on TV. The trainer walked us through it, telling us how real it actually was."

McCourt scratched his jaw, shaking his head. To him, this was all wonderful: No bomb went off, nobody was killed but Kirby, and McCourt looked like he knew how to run the show.

"Maybe Jesus is real after all," he said as we continued to look at Rose in the distance.

"Maybe," I countered, discouraged, worried Rose might remember too much, though it didn't seem as if she had snitched on me yet. But why hadn't she? She was McCourt's top dog. This unnerved me almost as much as if she had.

McCourt's eyes fell on the group of male cops and agents. "That's what happens when you let a woman hold a badge," joked one of them, a middle-aged cop. The others laughed right under the nose of a journalist who was walking by them, stopping and noting every word in his notepad.

"Ah, for Christ's sake," McCourt cursed under his breath, "the children are pissing on my moment again." Then he strode over, and I followed. He stopped in front of the cop who had made the misogynistic joke. "What's your name?" he asked with a fake smile that seemed to make the officer think McCourt found his sexist joke funny.

The blond officer smiled wide in response. "I'm Officer—"

"Don't bother, I already know who you are," McCourt said loudly.

Every cop and agent on the floor turned quiet, avoiding eye contact—except for the sexist asshole, who now looked like he was about to piss himself.

"You're the kind of guy who thinks he's a main character," McCourt said loudly. "But the truth is, you're just a child whose Mommy makes you call a fart a 'fluffy,' and now you walk around thinking that being a fluffer is a good thing."

McCourt turned to me as I stood in shock. I was Team McCourt on this one. But damn...

Then McCourt took the badge off the officer's chest. "You can go now. You're suspended without pay." McCourt briefly looked over at the journalist to make sure the man got it all. Then he nodded at me to follow him to the stairs.

When we made it into the quiet of the stairs, McCourt asked, "You think the media overhead me?"

"I'm pretty sure they did."

"Good," he said. "This will go well with the whole 'woke' thing that's going on now. Red hats and tree huggers will love this alike. Gotta be on good terms with both sides of the swamp."

"If you say so, sir," I mumbled.

We walked down the stairs all the way to the first floor.

"Good work," McCourt said. "Killing Kirby saved all of us."

"It was all Agent Rose," I said. "She found him and stopped him. I only helped toward the end, and even that was almost too late."

He faintly smirked. "She's a hell of an agent, that's for sure. I saw that certain something in her the moment I first looked into her eyes. Kids just aren't made like that anymore. It's fucking depressing."

"I think the kids will be alright," I politely disagreed.

"We have a mandatory debrief at four today," McCourt said, changing the topic.

I froze. McCourt turned to look at me. "I have court today. The custody battle," I said.

He stared at me for a moment, then nodded. "I'll see you tomorrow then."

Shit, he was in the best mood I'd ever seen him in.

"Yes, sir. Thank you."

I watched for a moment as he disappeared behind the door into the foyer. There was no way he knew anything. Rose must have stayed quiet, which made my story about killing Kirby by myself when I found Rose the only story there was. Forensics suspected the dirt bike tracks from Leah were Kirby's from when he hauled supplies to the scene. By boat and, occasionally, on a dirt bike.

Nobody questioned anything.

Nobody but, maybe, Rose.

I had no doubt that saving her was the right thing to do, no matter what would happen, but I had a hard time accepting the possible outcome with grace. The mere thought of Rose hunting down Leah and ultimately finding out about us tore me apart. It could ruin my chances of getting Josie back.

If there was one agent in the FBI who could uncover the truth, it was Rose.

CHAPTER THIRTY-FOUR

Liam

It was dead silent in the courtroom. Sarah, her boy toy, and her older lawyer sat at their table next to Dan and me, both of us facing the judge's empty bench. Judge Albert White was in his chambers, talking privately to Josie. My mom and sister sat on the benches behind me, their tension and worry clutching at me like an invisible hand.

Sarah and her lawyer were glancing around the room, their feet tapping in unison. I couldn't blame them. Hell, I was nervous too. The room seemed to be closing in, the walls encircling me. Breathing became a chore. I kept tugging at the tie around my neck, loosening and then tightening it to appear immaculate for the judge.

I checked my phone again.

Still no answer from Leah.

This was a brand-new phone that I'd received via courier at my apartment. As always, it had only one number saved in it—hers. But none of my texts had been answered since the one I'd received over two weeks ago, which only said *Talk soon*.

What the hell did that mean? *Talk soon* as in, *I'm not well, but we'll talk when I'm better*?

Or *Talk soon* as in, *All is great, see you soon*? I had asked this in brief texts, but no response ever came. The fact that her concerts had been canceled until further notice only made things worse. Depending on the moment, I pictured Leah either in her bed in some private hospital setting with a million-dollar concierge doctor team tending to her or in a ditch somewhere, bleeding to death.

Worry and guilt pressed down on me so hard that even the thought of holding Josie again eased it only a little.

"Goddamn it," I mumbled under my breath.

"All rise," the court clerk announced as Judge White stepped back into the courtroom and took his seat. He was an older, bald man dressed in a black judicial robe. Despite his authoritative presence, he seemed approachable and fair.

"Your honor, we would like to petition the court to add additional evidence regarding Liam Richter's deeply disturbing father who—" Sarah's lawyer began, rising quickly to his feet, but Judge White waved him off.

"That's not necessary."

"But your honor—" Sarah's lawyer interjected only to be met with a forceful "I said that's not necessary" from Judge White.

The judge continued. "I have reviewed the entire case and spoken to Josie, who is, quite frankly, one of the most reasonable individuals I've ever encountered in my courtroom. She made it very clear what she wanted, and I can support her wish wholeheartedly as the best for the child."

"Your honor," Sarah tried anxiously, "my daughter is just a child. She doesn't know what's best for her."

Judge White raised an eyebrow at Sarah as if he'd just caught her with her hand in a cookie jar. "Mrs. Richter, considering everything at hand, I would kindly ask you to refrain from speaking. I've heard enough."

"But your honor—"

"I said I've heard enough!" Judge White lashed out at her. "I wanted this to be graceful, for your sake and the child's, but if you want my honest opinion, I find this whole smear campaign you've started against your ex-husband—who has done nothing but try to make this easy for you and your daughter—despicable. First, you cheat on him, then you financially destroy him with your unreasonable demands, which he agreed to—an act of compliance I have never seen in this court before—all for the love of his child. And now, you have the audacity to question your own child's wish to be with her loving father? If I hear one more word from you, I will hold you in contempt of court and sentence you to a fine and a week in jail to think things over."

After staring down a whimpering Sarah for a few moments, the judge turned to me.

"Special Agent in Charge Richter, I hereby grant you joint custody with your ex-wife. I will personally appoint a court social worker as a mediator to ensure the custody schedule is fifty-fifty and without issues. Thank you for the hard work you do to keep us all safe. Your daughter is waiting outside. She wants to spend the weekend with you if your schedule allows—"

I was already on my feet, running out of the courtroom. Thank God, Josie was right there, holding hands with a woman who was most likely a social worker.

"Dad!" Josie yelled, jumping into my arms, tears streaming down her face.

I felt a burning in my eyes. Fuck, was I crying too?

I squeezed her and reassured her that all was good now. Moments later, I felt my mom and sister join our embrace. Both were shedding tears.

"I made chocolate chip cookies," my sister announced, her long, loose hair partially covering Josie's face in our group hug.

"Good God, that vegan horror," my mom remarked dismissively. Josie laughed, and even my sister chuckled.

"Let's go," my sister said, taking Josie by the hand. As the doors swung open again, Sarah, her boy toy, and her lawyer emerged. Josie froze, looking guilty, the weight of her conversation with Judge White apparent in her tear-streaked face.

Sarah's eyes met mine. They were filled with venom. For a moment, I wondered if she'd pull a knife from the fancy designer bag I'd bought her for our fifth anniversary.

"Wait here, sweetie," I told Josie, then approached Sarah. I leaned in, my next words meant only for her. "Do the right thing for once and smile for our daughter, or I'll file for full custody and make you work for your money again."

Sarah's shock was apparent, but then, as if under duress, she smiled widely for Josie.

The relief on my little girl's face, seeing her mother's approving smile, felt like the gates of heaven opening to bless her with peace and happiness.

"Vanilla is the most popular flavor in the world, honey," I said to Sarah. "Don't ever fuck with me again."

I returned to Josie.

What a win.

What a day.

My girl was back.

I was back.

Kirby was taken care of. No more lives were lost this time. And with a bit more luck, Rose might not remember anything at all.

I held one of Josie's hands, and my sister held the other as we made our way to the parking lot. My mother and sister argued about the vegan cookies, which made Josie and me smile. That was when my work phone rang.

"Richter here," I answered.

"Wow. You sound happy. I take it things went well?" Heather asked.

"They did."

"God, I'm so happy for you," she said, her voice trailing off.

"Why?" I asked, slowing my pace.

The silence that followed made me let go of Josie's hand. I gestured to my mom to take her to the car. She nodded, and they walked ahead.

"Heather?" I urged. "What's wrong?"

Heather sighed through the phone. "Fuck. It's . . . it's Anna."

A chill colder than an Arctic storm seized me from within as I braced for her next words.

"She was found dead in the woods."

CHAPTER THIRTY-FIVE

Anna

Ah, so you've come at last. Thank you for caring about me enough to stop by. In a world full of sorrow and horror, your attention to my tragedy means a lot to me. I feel so lonely and scared, it could kill me all over again.

You wouldn't notice me at first, lying where the woods meet the river, at the foot of the cliff. It's cold. Both of my legs are soaked with crystal-clear water that sounds soothing at night but restless during the day. Days have passed, weeks maybe, and the trees have been both a silent witness and an active participant in my slow mission to merge their falling leaves with the dirt beneath me.

Day and night have danced their endless cycle. So have rain and moonshine, washing over me in powerful, cleansing torrents, both leaving their marks on my body, soul, and heart . . . whatever might be left of it.

I've felt the curious nudges of small creatures and a more serious bite by a bear. The cautious steps of rabbits and deer have entertained me. Even the stars have cast their eternal gaze upon me—some of them judging the sins of my past, others sharing my pain, but all of them constant.

Will you shed a tear for me?

You can't say?

Then you have shed too many in this cold world already, and I'll shed one for you.

But if you shed one for me after all, I shall be forever in your debt.

The occasional hikers have wandered close, their voices a distant murmur. They linger for selfies on the cliff, eyes scanning the distant horizon one last time before continuing on their path, oblivious to my tragic story lying mere steps away. They move on, leaving me to the embrace of my utter loneliness.

But today, there's a different sound, a persistent bark breaking the serene quiet. A dog with senses sharper than its human companion has found me. I hear the owner's approach, a mix of anger and urgency in their footsteps.

Ah, there you are, I think the moment he stops and his wide eyes stare at me in horror. I don't know you, but I'm sorry it was you who found me. I'm sorry your day filled with nature's calming peace has turned to darkness.

Forgive me that a sense of relief is washing over me as your shaking hands dial 911. Forgive me that I might visit you in your dreams. But maybe now, thanks to your discovery, I can finally find peace.

Suddenly, the scene around me shifts. Do you see it? The police crew invades, blue and red lights slicing through the calm I've found here. You see, the EMTs don't even pretend to save me. I'm already long dead. My body left to rot in this world, my soul in another, watching.

The officers stand around, their eyes reflecting the weight of a world where darkness like this happens. "Look harder, he left a mark," I wish I could tell them as one silently prays for me, for the soul speaking to you right now.

See how the investigators swarm, collecting evidence, cameras flashing, intruding on the peace of this lonely spot I'd come to accept. But they're missing it, aren't they?

The ankh symbol.

His signature, hidden under a rock.

Suddenly, an officer stumbles across it by accident, his foot slipping on the rock where the mark was left. However, there's no shock, no realization. Just a quick photo of the symbol, and then they move on, stepping all over the very clue they need.

They leave, making all this noise, blind to what they should be seeing. They take what's left of me, but here I am, still with you, still by this creek.

Days pass.

Then I sense her before I can hear her steps.

My angel of darkness.

Have you come to save my immortal soul? Will you get the revenge I crave and deserve?

I see *he* has brought you here.

The two of you like predator and prey, trapped in a violent storm.

So, he joined us after all? But does he truly accept his part in this heartless world?

As my spirit is pulled away, I'm filled with an aching need. I haven't seen how it all ends. Will you watch for me to see what happens?

Please tell me in a prayer once it's done so I can rest for all eternity.

CHAPTER THIRTY-SIX

Leah

Wet twigs snapped under my feet as I followed the hiking trail in Bigelow Hollow State Park toward the creek where Anna's body had been discovered about a week prior. It was yet another gloomy day; the wet canopy teemed with ravens and their ominous caws—a fitting soundtrack for the grim scene that awaited me. The familiar yellow "do not cross" crime scene tape still sectioned off the last part of the trail to the creek and the small rocky cliff from whose base her body had been recovered after several weeks.

This would be the first time I'd seen Richter since the Kirby incident. He had been hounding me over the phone, requesting meetings. However, as I was still recovering from two broken ribs, stitches on my cut feet, and two on my neck—the spot where Kirby had pressed his knife—I wasn't up for it.

When I emerged into the clearing, he was standing by the edge of the creek, lost in thought. I had no doubt he would blame himself for Anna's death, though he had done everything within his power to prevent it. That was just the kind of man he was.

He turned the moment I stepped closer, his intense gaze meeting mine.

"I see you're well," he said, sizing me up, his eyes briefly lingering on the small, visible wound on my neck.

"Well enough," I replied.

He nodded. "I'd be mad about you forbidding me to check in on you, but I'm just too freaking grateful to you."

I tilted my head.

"Josie . . . that was you, wasn't it? The miracle of having Judge White take over my case."

"No gratitude necessary. It was in my own best interest to alleviate some of your stressors."

He smiled, but the smile vanished as he walked over to where Anna's body had been discovered. "Forensics found no sign of struggle," Liam said, his voice laced with guilt and sadness. "They detected benzos in a hair sample that corresponded with the time of death. No weapons, no witnesses. Anna was ruled a tragic accident."

Of course, she was.

"It seems he has moved his operations from the tracks to the rivers, which gives him a hell of a lot larger canvas than before," I concluded. "We're talking thousands of miles of rivers and creeks on the East Coast." It was a hard truth to digest. "If the body wasn't Anna's, who knows if we would have realized it was him behind this."

Richter shook his head, unable to fathom the enormity of the enemy we faced.

But something seemed different about Anna's murder. It was as if the shift in scenery from rail to river made it less significant for him. Less personal.

"I went over the college security cam. We can see Anna leave the campus by herself in the opposite direction of where the patrol officer watching her was parked. As if she knew the risk and didn't care."

I was about to speak when a branch snapped behind us. Agent Vallery Rose stepped into the clearing. The moment she saw me, her hand moved to the gun in her chest holster. In reflex, Richter threw himself into harm's way, drawing his own weapon.

Rose paused, looking at him and his hand on his gun. Then her gaze snapped back to me. "You . . ." she said. "You're the woman who helped kill Kirby that night!" Her grip on her gun tightened. Confusion and fear flared in her eyes as if she were a cornered deer.

"Rose!" Richter said firmly. "Remove your hand from the gun."

"What?" she asked, betrayal washing over her. "What's going on here?" Her hand was still lingering on her gun. Richter's hand remained on his own.

Slowly, I stepped closer to her, relieved that she still hadn't drawn her gun as the distance between us closed.

"Rose," Richter said, his voice cautious. "Let's talk, but lower—"

"If I wanted you dead, I wouldn't have risked getting caught to save you," I said, stepping in front of her. "Now let go of the gun. You already know that you don't have the upper hand here." I pointed to the yellow pus mark on her white shirt. "They put you on the wrong antibiotics. May I?"

Her head twitched back as I reached for her collar, pausing for her nod of consent. Gently pulling it down, I exposed the bandaged bullet wound on her upper chest and lifted the dressing. The wound was stitched but swollen and oozing with pus.

"Did they give you Azithromycin?"

She looked at me as if all of this were a dream, then nodded.

"Call your doctor and ask for Cephalexin. Otherwise, you'll need to start wound care treatment soon." I let go of her shirt and moved to stand beside Richter near where Anna was found.

Rose slowly removed her hand from her gun and straightened her shirt before joining us at the crime scene, maintaining a healthy distance. "Who the hell are you?" she demanded. "And why did you ask me to come here?"

Richter, too, removed his hand from his gun, slightly easing the tension. "That's a question I'd also like answered," he said, his tone marked by frustration.

I circled the scene under their vigilant watch, then halted where the small ankh sign was etched into the rock near the river. One had to consider it carefully to associate it with the ancient symbol, as its carving had a certain natural rawness. However, upon direct inspection, there was no doubt.

"Do you recognize this?" I asked Rose, gesturing toward the symbol on the ground. She approached slowly, then shook her head.

"It's the Train Track Killer's signature, the Egyptian ankh symbol," I clarified. "He leaves it at all his crime scenes."

Rose recoiled slightly, her eyes examining the ground. "But that's impossible. Patel is dead."

Richter cursed under his breath as he threw me a "what the fuck are you doing?" look as sharp as an arrow. He took a step closer. "Patel wasn't the Train Track Killer," he said. "He was just some guy who we suspect worked with him. Or, more likely, was used by the Train Track Killer as some sort of footman."

Rose scoffed. "That's ridiculous. Are you guys smoking peyote or something? The Train Track Killer is dead. And the only real question here is, who is this woman and why the hell did she kill Kirby?" She turned to me. "You CIA or something?"

An intense silence settled over us. Once again, Liam used that moment to throw me another gaze, this one even more threatening than the last. "Leah, no," he said.

"I'm . . . not part of the Central Intelligence Agency," I said.

Richter stepped closer. "Leah." His tone was low and filled with warning.

"Nor am I part of any other law enforcement or government agency."

"Leah, don't!" His voice grew even louder.

I briefly looked at him, then faced Agent Rose. "I kill people, if you want me to be honest and precise."

"Leah, goddamn it!" Richter cursed. "Stop!"

"I kill serial killers," I clarified, ignoring Richter. "Harvey Grant was one of my more recent works."

Rose laughed, but the moment she looked at Richter, the way he ran his hand through his hair, every muscle tense and anxious, the laugh was smacked right off her face.

"Leah, what the fuck!" he cursed at me. "Have you lost your mind?"

I took a step closer to Rose, who was now backing up slowly. "I'm quite busy and not good with emotional encounters. So, let's skip straight to the point. The man who killed Anna and countless other people is still out there. He's a genius mastermind who not only has played law enforcement for years but won't stop killing until he's taken out. I take you for a woman of facts and logic, so instead of going back and forth trying to convince you of something so outrageous it would top the JFK assassination theories, I propose you go back to the office and do your own research."

Rose, who looked as if she was ready to call in for support any moment, now seemed curious.

Slowly, I pulled a paper out of the pocket of my cashmere coat and held it up to her. "You'll find the ankh symbol I showed you here today at every single one of these murder scenes. Carved into the tracks close to where the bodies were found. He stages his murders to look like suicides. Just like Anna." I nodded toward where her body was found. "He won't stop killing until someone makes him. An arrest is out of the question. He's too genius to get convicted in our useless courts. Especially since I believe he might have extreme wealth and power."

Rose stood still for a moment before her amber eyes shot to the paper in my hand. She suddenly grabbed it from me and looked at the names and locations of deaths written on it. "You're the pianist, aren't you? I saw you on TV," she said.

This threw me off. The question seemed out of place, given everything I'd just said. I nodded as I held her gaze.

She responded with a sarcastic smile, then peeked at Richter, who stood frozen in shock. "Is it true?" Rose asked him. "What she says?"

His gaze dropped to the ground before returning to hers. For a moment, they stared at one another. Then he nodded, brief and quick.

"Mm-hmm. So, let's say all of this crazy shit is true," she said. "Why are you telling me?"

"I thought that was evident," I countered.

She thought about this for a moment, then frowned. "You're worried I saw you at the Kirby crime scene and will tell McCourt about it." She sounded disappointed, as if she'd hoped to have been called here today for a different reason. Which there was.

"There are other benefits for you to know," I said. "The Train Track Killer is one of the most genius humans who has ever walked this earth. An extra pair of hands and eyes could be beneficial in the task of killing—"

"Stop!" Rose cut me off. "This is insane! Even if all of this is true, what makes you think I won't arrest you? If you really kill people, bad or not, you belong behind bars just like them!"

Richter ran a hand through his hair, his complexion pale.

"You can certainly try to bring me to justice," I offered. "But what evidence do you have? I'm the world's most famous virtuoso. Besides resources for a legal team that will greatly surpass the skillset of the government's lawyers, I have friends in powerful positions. You, on the other hand, have nothing. The scandal could destroy my career and cause enormous problems within the FBI and its reputation. The situation with Larsen would be nothing compared to this. But you strike me as a woman of logic. Would that be an outcome you deem worth the short-term gratification of arresting me? The FBI in shambles. The Train Track Killer still out there, killing and killing until the day he dies."

Rose's gaze fell onto the paper in her hands again, the names.

"Rose, listen to me," Richter said, throwing me an angry look. "Leah is the only chance we have to get rid of this monster. I know how you feel. I was where you are right now. Torn between black and white, right and wrong. Good and evil."

"So, what happened?" she asked, her tone accusing. "I mean, to the man I thought you were. The one fighting for the people of this country against the bad guys."

For a moment, I thought Richter would cave at that—he'd probably asked himself the same question. But, instead, he looked her in the eyes and said, "He's standing right here doing just that."

This threw Rose off. Her eyes blinked rapidly, but then she shook her head. "This is crazy, Richter. If this woman is telling the truth, what makes her so different from the Train Track Killer? She's just like them. A crazy killer. And killers can't be trusted!"

It was a good point. So, instead of arguing her logic, I decided to give her the one thing she needed to even consider the offer I was about to give her.

"I don't need your trust, nor do you need mine," I said. "I have arranged a safety net for Agent Richter in case he ever needs to end our partnership."

Richter's eyebrows rose. "What are you talking about?"

I glanced at Rose, then back at Richter. "There's an associate of mine, Luca Domizio, a former mob boss. He's agreed to kill me if the FBI approaches him for that purpose. Nobody knows about this. Nobody but you two."

"What!" Richter's disbelief was palpable. "Luca Domizio? Kill you?"

Ignoring his astonishment, I moved past them, positioning myself at the edge of the creek. "Time is running out," I said. "I suggest you take action, Agent Rose. But consider the innocent victims before you do. You might regret the bed you've made for yourself when you have to keep adding names to the list. I assume you're the type of person who might go mad over the fact that you missed the chance to stop one monster by leveraging another. It will eat you up from the inside. Just like your brother's death did."

Rose remained silent, grappling with the line I had crossed, before throwing her hands up in frustration. "Fuck this, I'm going to McCourt," she announced and stormed off.

"Rose!" Richter's voice was full of desperation. "Rose, wait!" he continued as she disappeared, leaving the tranquil silence of the woods behind.

But that tranquility was short-lived.

"What the fuck, Leah!" Richter exploded. "You're jeopardizing everything. Destroying us both!"

"Quite the opposite," I countered calmly. "The risk of her spotting me at the Kirby scene was too significant. She's persistent and cunning enough to eventually connect the dots. We needed to act before she convinced herself that pursuing me was the right thing to do."

Liam gazed into the distance, his head shaking in disbelief. "This is bad, Leah. A complete disaster. I just got Josie back. Now this. Rose is going to tell McCourt."

"Not if we can demonstrate the immense necessity of eliminating the Train Track Killer. A woman of her integrity will logically examine the facts I've provided. If she reaches the conclusion that everything I've said is true—"

"She might come around?"

"Or at least remain silent until the Train Track Killer is dealt with."

"And then what?" Richter pressed.

"We'll see. You've put us in this position by saving her life."

The words caused Richter to recoil.

"Maybe she'll come to appreciate that before she goes to McCourt," I said. "After all, I've never harmed a real human being."

"Is it true?" Richter said, his tone calmer, almost tender. His eyes locked with mine. "The thing with Luca?"

I remained silent.

"Goddamn it, Leah," he swore, his hands balling into fists. "Don't you think we need to discuss any assassination plans you're making?"

"No. Not if it's aimed at me. Or you," I replied, logical and detached.

I noticed a mix of emotions in his gaze—pity, sadness?

He dismissed it, looking in the direction Rose had vanished. "I don't like any of this."

"I know, but it's our only option. We must stop him, regardless of the cost. And we can't afford her flanking us when we're at full-blown war with him."

I took Liam's silence as a sign of agreement.

"She's not like me," he finally said. "Rose. She might betray us. Destroy us. Something's going on with her and McCourt."

"I know. But unless he has something that could threaten her life, there's a chance she might come to terms with the fact that our goals aren't so different. He's going to kill again soon. Every moment he's free, the threat of death lingers. She understands that. More so than any promotion McCourt might give her."

"How can you be so sure?" Richter asked.

"I can't. But in the woods, she chose to risk her life by chasing down Kirby before backup arrived. And just like you, she thought it was the right thing to do to save the lives of others." I smiled faintly. "Where is your trust, Agent Richter? She can't trust me. I agree with her. But you . . . you can. For now, at least."

He pinched his lips as we both looked toward the spot where Anna's body had been found. Unlike Liam, whose face was marred by sorrow and guilt, I had accepted her fate the moment Anna refused my offer to escape. Her death was sealed then and there. Also unlike Liam, I was able to interpret her end as a sacrifice for the greater good. We had another victim, another clue. He was now active along the rivers, and if Agent Rose was anything like Richter, Anna's death might have enlisted another ally for our cause. Sure, this new ally was more unpredictable than Liam and could turn on me at any moment, but as long as I maintained my strategy, she posed no threat to us.

With this new lead, I could practically taste the trail of blood in the air. Now all I had to do was follow it. No matter the cost.

CHAPTER THIRTY-SEVEN

Rose

On her drive to headquarters, Rose was more certain than ever that she would walk straight into McCourt's office and tell him everything. As crazy as it all sounded, she couldn't let this slide. With Ms. Nachtnebel's identity now known to her, she could establish some sort of connection to Kirby's crime scene. Or Harvey Grand. Maybe a lie detector test, maybe some blood at the Kirby scene that would reveal her DNA. Rose could turn over every rock that could have possibly touched that woman during the fight with Kirby.

She was a hell of a woman, this Nachtnebel. Rose had to give her that.

But the audacity to bring up her dead brother as a psychological tactic . . . like a looming threat of failure on her end.

It wasn't until Rose was already in the elevator that she felt the paper in her coat pocket—the paper that Leah had handed her.

Might be a good idea to check on those names. Better to have something concrete for McCourt when she talked to him about this.

So, she went straight to her desk instead of McCourt's office. What followed was absolute madness.

At first, there was nothing. No ankh sign was visible in the crime scene pictures, which were horrendous. Rose was pissed off that she had to look at them. However, once she examined a picture of Emma Mauser's body a second time, she found it.

The damn ankh symbol was right there, carved into the tracks! It was tiny, but once she knew what to look for, she had no doubt about it.

After that, she discovered the symbol at another crime scene. That meant Rose now had to drive to the other crime scenes to make sure this symbol was really there as well.

And it freaking was! At every single location on the list. It took a lot of her sick days, but she found each one.

Rose wasn't sure how long she sat in the woods on the tracks of the last crime scene. But she just sat there, in disbelief.

The Train Track Killer was real. And worst of all, not only was he still out there, but he was one of the most cunning and monstrous killers she had ever heard of. As much as Rose hated it, Leah Nachtnebel was right. Should Rose do something that would contribute in any shape or form to the killer's success in murdering more people, she would never forgive herself.

She had to stop this sick fuck, no matter the cost.

But how could she know what the right thing to do was? The FBI was a powerful force, surely more powerful than a pianist and Richter, no matter how genius the pianist might be. But then, why didn't the FBI know about the Train Track Killer in the first place? After all these murders?

Rose spent the rest of her day at the office looking into Leah Nachtnebel, the world-renowned pianist. She was rich, pretty, and—from every article Rose could find—a genius.

People compared her to Einstein and Tesla, to Mozart and Beethoven. Rose wasn't into classical music, so she'd never heard much about her, but now she had no doubt that what Leah had told her was the truth— including the fact that she would be a very hard person to bust.

So, just let her do her thing, then? Keep killing and hope she'd get rid of the Train Track Killer?

It was early evening. Rose was still hovering over her desk at the FBI headquarters when she noticed something strange in the file of Emma Mauser, a young woman killed after disappearing from a college party in Philly. As with all the other murders, the train track police had initially deemed the murder a suicide. However, closer inspection of the file's police report revealed that the word "homicide" was crossed out and "suicide" written above it, signed and dated by Officer Wagner from a station outside Philly where the body was found.

She pulled up the file on the computer. The forensic report clearly stated "suicide." Something was off here.

Quickly, she picked up the phone and called the Philly police station. "Agent Vallery Rose from the Boston FBI headquarters," she said to the secretary on the other end. "Is Officer Wagner on duty?"

"Hold on a minute," the secretary replied, putting Rose on hold. "He is," she said again after a minute. "Would you like me to connect you?"

"Yes, please."

After a brief wait, a low male voice answered. "Officer Wagner speaking."

"Yes, hi, this is Agent Rose from Boston FBI headquarters. I'm calling regarding the death of Emma Mauser. Does that ring a bell?"

"Phew," Wagner sighed. "That's one of those cases I'll carry with me until my last breath. Don't look at the crime scene pictures unless you have to. What trains can do to the human body . . . horrible. Truly horrible."

"Too late, I'm afraid," Rose said as she glanced over the picture of the dead woman's body on her desk. "But I was wondering if you could answer a question."

"I'll try my best."

"In your report, you initially wrote homicide as the cause of death but then crossed that out and marked it as a suicide. Could you tell me why?"

"Yes. When I wrote the report, I swore the coroner at Jenkins Hospital told me he suspected foul play. But then my chief called me in and told me it was a mistake on my end. He showed me the coroner's report on the computer, which clearly stated suicide. So, I corrected the original document. I had no clue you had a copy of that."

Rose pondered this for a moment. "I see. Well, we pulled the copies of the original files for a different investigation," she lied, assuming it was Richter who had pulled the original files' copies while hunting his killer in secret.

"Oh, okay. Not sure why you're looking into this case, but I usually don't make mistakes like that. I could have sworn the coroner told me he suspected foul play. I think he mentioned rope marks on her wrists or something. I'm not in some sort of trouble here, am I? Please tell me Netflix isn't making a documentary out of this, and I'm going to look like an idiot in front of the whole country."

"Nah, nothing like that. Just finishing up some paperwork on an old case and wasn't sure about the correction."

"I see."

"Why did you never double-check with the coroner?"

"Honestly, between us, we're understaffed and pulling double shifts all the time, so mistakes are very possible on our end."

"I hear you. Same here. Same, but different. Well, thanks, Officer. Stay safe out there."

"Thanks, you too."

Rose stared at the file on her desk, then at her computer. In no time, she was looking up the coroner's report, which clearly stated suicide. Then she dialed the number of his hospital.

Shit, she was already more invested in this case than she had wanted to be.

After a few back-and-forths, she was transferred to Dr. Clark Post.

"Dr. Post," he answered.

"Yes, um, hi, this is Agent Rose from the Boston FBI headquarters. I'm combing through some suicide cases in your area in search of a missing person."

Why the hell was she lying to him? Was she already working on the case with the "killer" squad?

"Do you remember the Emma Mauser case?" Rose asked.

"I do," Dr. Post confirmed. "Terrible tragedy. The body was horrific to work on. Very messy case. The family personally contacted me on that one."

"Really? Why is that?"

"Well, for some reason, they thought I had deemed the case a suicide—"

Rose straightened in her chair.

"But I told them that I didn't."

"You didn't?"

"No. I clearly stated in the paperwork that homicide was possible due to rope marks on her wrists. Also, the motive for the suicide didn't add up to me. She'd never used drugs before, but her system was full of opiates."

Drugs in the system of a non-user. Just like Anna.

Shit.

"Why? Is there still a problem with my report? I thought it was fixed."

Shit. He didn't know the death was still described as suicide? What was going on here?

"No, no," she lied. "I was just curious about the officer's original report and why corrections were made."

"Good luck," he laughed. "You can find discrepancies and corrections in every case out there."

"Very true."

Suddenly, horrific guilt overcame Rose. Did the family think their daughter did this to herself when it was actually murder? How could Rose keep such a painful secret to herself? It felt like deception.

"You said the family knows about this mistake?"

"Absolutely. They made quite a fuss about this. But as sad as it is, it doesn't really change much. No other evidence points to homicide. I'm afraid my findings were not enough to keep the case going one way or the other."

"Well, thank you. Hope you get to go home soon."

"Me too. Have a good evening."

"Thanks, you too."

Rose hung up, deep in thought. Why the hell did the computer files still deem the incident a suicide, contradicting Dr. Post's real opinion? The files were also missing the rope marks on the wrists that he mentioned.

He was right that discrepancies in files were common, but this was not a minor mistake. How had this been handled so poorly?

A quick search revealed why: because the file of Emma Mauser was labeled *Active investigation, not to be released.*

"God, please, fucking no," Rose cursed under her breath as she stared at the computer. Did Richter have a hand in this? This kind of shit was usually reserved for a handful of files of great political importance or of three-letter agency involvement to protect national interests. Not some murder on small-town train tracks.

Something was off here. Really, really off.

Rose had picked up the phone again to request the original copy of Dr. Post's report when her heart nearly stopped.

Straight ahead, by the elevator, was McCourt. He wasn't the problem, but who he was with certainly was.

Fucking Special Agent Jack Rice, that piece of shit.

The shock caused the handset to slip from her grip. It landed on her desk with a loud bang.

Jack Rice. Head instructor of interrogation tactics at the FBI academy.

The man who had nearly destroyed her life. And he was here, with McCourt.

It was a nightmare.

She was already on her feet, watching as if this were an out-of-body experience. Rice left using the stairs but not before turning and throwing her a hateful glare.

Then he was gone.

McCourt, on the other hand, stood by the elevator, staring straight at her. His face was like the calm before the storm.

Rose was by his side in moments, the air in her lungs deflating quickly. "S-sir," she stuttered, looking at the door Rice had just disappeared through. "May I ask—"

"Come with me," was all he said.

He led her back to his office. Rose stumbled after him like an idiot. She knew why he had paraded Rice in front of her like this. It was all part of his psychological warfare. Something bad had happened on McCourt's end. It might be the end of her FBI career. Maybe even jail time.

McCourt took a seat in the wide massage chair behind his mahogany desk. The Arab princes and presidents shaking his hand in photos behind McCourt stared at Rose as if they were his army.

"Sir, may I ask—" Her voice broke off. God, it was so freaking hot in here. She was sweating. "May I ask what's wrong?"

McCourt frowned. "Wrong? Why would anything be wrong? You risked your life to save this pathetic unit, which unfortunately includes me at its helm, so I wanted to do something for you in return."

Desperate, Rose tried to analyze what he'd just said. Was he being sarcastic? Sincere?

He pushed a manila folder toward her, then leaned back in his chair. "For you," he said.

Carefully, Rose pulled it closer, opening it as if a bomb might detonate inside. A sigh of shock escaped her lips when she saw the contents.

It was her lie detector exam from her application to the FBI. The one she'd spent weeks training for so she could successfully lie about her past—and pass.

"Sir?" Rose asked, confused.

"This is what Rice used to report you to me, wasn't it?"

Rose nodded.

"The one where you lied about that incident in your childhood. To be precise, the question of if you've ever killed before."

The horrific scene of the worst moment in Rose's life washed over her like a tsunami. She couldn't stop it from replaying in her mind. The shots came in through the downstairs window while she played in her room upstairs. The blood. The tears. The screams. Her dead mother and wounded brother in the living room. Nausea overcame her at the memory of the little girl—her—looking into the eyes of her dead mother. Bullets had riddled her mother's body and the wall behind her, causing the glass of the window to shatter into a million pieces.

"Run." Her brother coughed up blood, too badly shot to speak a full sentence. His eyes stared past Rose, knowing his fate. "Run, Boo-girl," he coughed over and over, using the nickname he'd given her. Her first word had been "boo" on Halloween.

But Rose did not run.

Instead, she grabbed the gun in his twitching hand. And when the man in the black ski mask entered the home, machine gun in hand, his eyes landing on her, she didn't run. She wanted to, having never been more scared in her life, but when the man ignored her, stepped over her dead mother, and pointed his machine gun at her brother's head, Rose did the only thing she could think of.

She emptied the gun into the man until there were no bullets left to shoot.

Now, many years later, she was sitting in front of the lie detector test she'd lied on. The one she'd passed to be chosen to attend the academy: one of the few chosen out of tens of thousands of applicants.

She had worked so hard for this. The terrible foster homes, high school, and college.

But the dream hadn't lasted long. Karma had pulled off the unthinkable: The same police officer who had processed Rose's statement after the shooting was the one leading the procedures training course at the academy.

He instantly recognized Rose and spoke about her to Rice, saying how happy he was to see her come so far after such tragedy in her childhood. It didn't take long before Rice uncovered Rose's lies in her application. As a seasoned son of a bitch, he interrogated her and found out the truth—every dirty little detail that the police never found. When the cops arrived that day, they concluded her brother had killed the intruder before he died. They asked Rose if she had taken the gun out of his hand when everybody was dead—hence the fingerprints. She wrongfully confirmed this with a simple nod.

Scared to death, and a child, she worried she might be sent to prison.

"It's the only copy of it," McCourt said, tearing her out of her thoughts. He was analyzing her every breath. "The one on the computer is already erased."

Rose stared at the file. The file that should have gotten her kicked out of the academy and charged with a felony for lying to a federal agency.

"I never understood men like Rice. Insecure little cunts," McCourt continued, steepling his fingers. "The day he approached me with your case, I could tell he was a slimeball. He left a trail like a poisonous snail. Any good mentor who scouts a flaw in one of the best trainees we've had in years would have looked the other way.

"I mean, look at the applicants we had in recent years. Gen Z. An overly sensitive and entitled bunch who are more interested in TikTok likes than real life." He scoffed. "When Rice stomped into my office thinking he was about to unveil another Watergate, it actually pissed me off. It's not like you did anything I wouldn't have done myself. Quite the opposite, in fact. You were cut out to be an agent from the old days when the badge meant more than hashtags. I mean, how many little girls do you know who would have had the courage to do what you did? Picking up that gun and shooting the man who killed your family." He leaned forward, elbows on the desk. "The balls to do that, Rose. Not many people I know would have done the same. Especially not a worm like Rice."

Rose glanced at him, then nervously looked at the file again.

"And yet," McCourt added, "the one thing I never understood in this whole thing: Why did you lie about it in the first place? It was self-defense, was it not?"

"If I were born on Beacon Hill, it would be," Rose mumbled, a comment McCourt fortunately didn't catch.

"What was that?" he asked.

Of course, she wouldn't repeat those words. Nor would she launch into a rant about how Rice had it out for her the moment she won against him in a target shooting event during training. The contempt she saw in his eyes from that day forward. The eyes of a misogynistic prick who probably went home and took out his frustrations on his abused wife. McCourt wasn't blind to social and economic injustices, but he showed little concern for them.

"I . . . was scared," she finally answered truthfully, without elaborating.

McCourt frowned, then nodded. "Did they ever find out who was behind the hit?"

He hadn't bothered to spend even a few minutes on the case files of the incident. Classic McCourt.

"They did. It was a rival gang hit. The Critters on fourth."

"Mm-hm." McCourt nodded. "Animals."

At least on that, she could partially agree. It wasn't that simple, but what the Critters had done that day went against even the hood's code. They didn't shoot her family as a revenge attack but simply because her brother wouldn't snitch about the location of a warehouse full of "goods." The real fucked-up tragedy about all this was that the Critters later joined forces with her brother's gang, the past deaths "forgiven." Her brother became a famous tale of loyalty to death.

A tale Rose refused to tell that way, ever.

Her brother's death was murder, nothing else. It was the reason she'd worked so hard to become more than just another statistic. She wanted to change the country, make it a better place for others, and she wouldn't settle for less than the best in the field—the FBI.

Rose's eyes narrowed at the file in front of her. How could such a small thing hold the power to destroy her?

"We get to see what happens only if we don't give up," her brother had always told her.

Would she let a man like Rice ruin her future and everything she had worked so hard for?

With newfound confidence, Rose grabbed the file, then looked straight at McCourt. "Am I to assume this is mine now?" she asked.

"It is. Rice won't ever be a problem again. Nor will anybody else. Sometimes, files just get lost. It happens more than you'd think at three-letter agencies."

Rose nodded, her grip tightening on the papers that held the keys to her destruction and, now, her freedom. "Why are you doing this for me?" she asked.

McCourt shrugged. "Why wouldn't I? You just saved the day, and the agency needs great agents like you. *I* need great agents like you. Trustworthy agents willing to do the job, whatever that might be. To protect the agency's best interests."

Or, more likely, *his*.

But for now, Rose was okay with this deal; asshole or not, nothing he'd asked of her so far was truly a sacrifice.

"Thank you, sir," she said, and she meant it.

McCourt acknowledged her with a slow, meaningful nod. "Well, why don't you go home and get some rest? We need you to look your best for the award ceremony."

Slowly, she rose, file in hand. With a faint smile, she turned and was about to leave when McCourt leaned forward in his seat.

"Oh, one more thing, Rose."

She turned to face him expectantly.

"That night, with Kirby," he began, his eyes piercing her like bullets, "was anybody else at the scene with you and Richter?"

The smile vanished from Rose's face. "Sir?" she said.

"Careful, Rose. Richter might think I'm an idiot, but unless he can show me his medical degree, I can't shake the feeling that something is amiss here. That procedure that saved your life—I was told that most of the doctors at the hospital wouldn't have been able to perform it. They were in awe of how a simple FBI agent without medical training was able to execute a procedure only one of their best surgeons could do, without killing the patient. Of course, I shrugged it off, supported his lies. It's the best story for them and the public. But *best* doesn't do it for me."

Rose's heart hammered against her chest. Of course, he wanted something in return from her. This wasn't just a meeting to reward the agent who'd prevented one of the potentially biggest mass murders in recent history.

This was a test.

The possibility of another copy of the file in her hand crossed her mind. Now she felt stupid. How had she ever trusted or believed in this man? She would have to be his footwoman for all eternity.

"There were also those dirt bike tire marks, which it's argued Kirby must have left while gathering his ingredients for his bomb recipe, but I find that rather . . . well, a bunch of horse shit."

Rose stared at him, her hands shaking. Would she be the downfall of the woman who'd saved her life and helped kill Kirby?

"You see, Agent Rose, trust is a two-way street." McCourt nodded at the file in Rose's hand.

Her mind raced with questions and answers, lies, worries, and regrets.

"I need to know I can trust you," McCourt added, his voice hypnotizing like that of a snake charmer. "Because if I can't . . ."

The walls of the room seemed to close in. What about the Train Track Killer? Would she become the sad prophecy Leah Nachtnebel had predicted so bluntly at Anna's crime scene? The snitch who helped the Train Track Killer by taking out his enemies?

Snitch. Her brother and mother had paid a heavy price for his silence. If silence was golden, maybe talking was diamonds?

"Because if I can't trust you, I don't need you, and if I don't need you, the FBI doesn't either," McCourt continued.

The file crinkled beneath Rose's grip. She could barely breathe, bile rising in her throat. Why did life always play her dirty? Why couldn't she just catch a break for once?

McCourt locked eyes with her, his gaze now threatening.

"So, let me ask you one more time, Agent Rose. What the hell really went down that night?"

CHAPTER THIRTY-EIGHT

Leah

I was practicing tomorrow's program on my Vanderbilt Bösendorfer on stage at the Boston Symphony Hall. My concerts had been canceled for weeks until I healed enough to sit for an hour with only moderate pain. When I finally did, I arranged a string of fall concerts to accommodate those who had refused a refund and opted for a replacement ticket— which was practically everyone.

A moderate wave of pain struck my ribcage, enough to make me flinch but not enough to stop my play.

I pushed through Chopin's "Revolutionary Étude," which demanded fierce left-hand dexterity for its relentless, stormy arpeggios, symbolizing turmoil.

Not until I finished the entire piece did I allow myself to take a deep breath. I tried to ease the pain with another Tylenol.

Crystal and Mr. Hieber were watching from the first row of seats. They were both worried that I'd cancel this weekend's concert, that I'd come back too soon.

They were right, of course, but the fuss my absence created was not in my best interest. People had laid flowers in front of my home and the symphony hall. There were so many flowers that the news stations started to pick up on the story. I needed to put an end to the drama.

I hit the last notes of the piece, sweat dripping onto the keys. Shortly after, Hieber and Crystal rose to their feet, applauding.

"Wonderful, Leah," Hieber said, his tone dripping with insincere friendliness. "We are all so relieved to see you healthy and well."

I adjusted my choker necklace, which hid the scar from Kirby's knife until a plastic surgeon could see to it.

"I'm certain you are, Hieber," I replied coldly as I rose to my feet. I planned to practice at home for the rest of the day. The only reason I had come here was to approve the tuning of the piano, as tomorrow included several important guests from the music world.

I was about to leave when Hieber rushed onto the stage. "Leah," he panted, "I wanted to ask if we might place a special guest in your personal box next to Luca Domizio's."

I raised an eyebrow at him. That was quite an audacious request considering nobody but myself had a say over this box. "And who would that be?" I asked.

"The Assistant Director of the FBI, Charles—"

"McCourt," I finished, my eyes narrowing.

This could mean trouble.

Had Rose talked to him after all?

A coincidence?

Or . . . had Liam tried to find a way out of the current situation? Was his worry about losing his daughter greater than his hatred for the Train Track Killer? How could I blame him for that?

"You know him?" Hieber asked.

"No."

Hieber rearranged his scarf. "Well . . . would it be okay if we assign him your box? Unless you have someone else in mind you wanted to invite, then—"

"You can give him the box."

Hieber smiled, likely having secured some favors in return for clearing the box for such a high government figure.

"Anything else?" I asked.

"No, no, thank you. Go get some rest. Tomorrow will be epic."

Epic.

I didn't agree with that choice of word, but I understood what he was referring to: the large live screen outside the symphony hall. To honor my recovery, the mayor himself had arranged to have the street blocked during my concert to allow a crowd to follow along on a large live screen.

My gaze moved up to the box McCourt would be placed in, right next to Luca.

The fact that I had not been arrested or questioned yet indicated he could seek a private conversation with me. But why?

"I'll see you tomorrow," I said as I made my way back to my car. The soft drizzle of another fall rain embraced me like a cool greeting. It was refreshing and grounding.

Whatever McCourt wanted, I would deal with him. I had never really met the man, yet I knew everything about him.

Selfish.

Narcissistic.

Arrogant.

While many despised those traits, I had no personal feelings toward them one way or the other. On the contrary, those traits would make handling him all the easier, as men like him could bend a thousand ways.

None of them were noble, which was fine as long as they did the trick.

CHAPTER THIRTY-NINE

Liam

Cowboy and I were south of Boston, watching the entrance of the Green Hill funeral home. Its ridiculously large and bright neon cross was nearly blinding. We were leaning against the car, the rain having just stopped. It was a bit cold, but the inside of the SUV felt claustrophobic, as if it were cutting off my air supply.

This whole thing with Anna weighed heavily on my soul. Another young girl gone. Her death made me feel like my work was pointless.

"They say stress kills people," Cowboy remarked, blowing out a stream of vape from the pen he was sucking on.

"Yup. Working with serial killers can do that. But I'm an FBI agent, not some B-list model who can quit his job and start dancing on social media."

"FBI or not, you're too old anyway," Cowboy said.

I frowned at him.

"Although the ladies might dig the whole broke-ass-down-on-his-luck agent vibe. If you get some Botox on that forehead and your eyebrows microbladed, you might be able to shave off a few years."

"What?"

I watched as Cowboy admired his reflection in the mirror of our SUV. "I just got my own brows done, and the ladies are in love with them."

"Fucking Christ," I mumbled. "You said you'd be quiet if I let you tag along."

"If you believed me, that's on you."

I ignored him. A strange silence fell between us.

"I'm really sorry about Anna," he finally said, his tone serious. "You know, you're not the only one who feels like we failed her. Like it was all for fucking nothing. I mean, why the hell did she do it? Why kill herself?"

Initially, I expected Cowboy to start laughing and say something stupid. However, when he remained silent, staring at the ground with sadness in his eyes, I placed my hand on his shoulder in a fatherly gesture.

"None of this is on you," I said as his eyes met mine. "It pains me to admit it, but you're doing an incredible job at the BAU. We're lucky to have you here in Boston."

His eyes lit up as if this acknowledgment was all he ever wanted. Then, suddenly, his gaze drifted off into the distance. "What the fuck is this shit?" he asked.

I followed his gaze to find Anna's uncle and aunt stepping out of the funeral home. They appeared worn and disheveled, with baggy clothes and faces that bore signs of hardship. At first glance, compassion stirred within me, leading to thoughts of how I could help. However, my second thought was less kind when I noticed the urn they were carrying.

Or the lack of it.

Instead of holding a beautiful urn, the older man, dressed in sweats and a bomber jacket, held a plastic bag wrapped around his wrist. Undoubtedly, the bag carried Anna's remains. He leaned over and opened the bag only to close it again with a coughing sound.

Cowboy tucked his vape away and was about to storm over, but I held him back. "It's not our place."

"They have her in a freaking plastic bag!" he protested.

"I know." The words felt like acid in my throat. "But it's not our place to tell them how to deal with a loved one."

My intention of walking over and expressing my condolences were completely dashed when Anna's uncle tossed the remains in the plastic bag into the back of a black pickup truck.

"What the fuck," I cursed, barely able to hold myself back now. This man deserved a good beating.

"People are animals," Cowboy spat.

We watched in disgust as they drove off. My heart raced with rage. For a brief moment, I saw Anna in front of me, vibrant and alive, laughing like she did with her friends on campus when I watched her a few times in the distance from my car.

"This is fucking terrible," Cowboy mumbled. "Just fucking terrible."

Without another word, he got into the passenger's side of the SUV, where he sat like a pouting child.

I took a deep breath, trying to process all of this. Deep down, I had hoped this would give me a bit of closure—shaking hands with her family, apologizing that I wasn't able to do more for her. It would have helped with the anxiety caused by Rose's absence from work and her silence in response to my texts.

But now, life had revealed itself as another bad rollercoaster ride: too many downs, none of them fun.

As I got into the car, my phone rang.

McCourt.

"Shit," I muttered, staring at the screen.

"My uncle?"

I nodded, then accepted the call.

"Can't be good this late on a Friday," Cowboy said too loudly.

"Tell Theo to keep his whining to his therapy sessions, not my phone calls," McCourt said, loud enough for him to hear. Cowboy rolled his eyes.

"Sir?"

"Where are you?"

"We were attending Anna's funeral."

"The suicide case? Why?"

"Thought it might reflect well on the FBI considering she was a survivor of the Train Track Killer."

"Good move. Will make us look sensible and caring."

Prick.

"Well, I need you to join me at the Boston Symphony Hall tonight."

The phone nearly slipped from my grip as my mouth fell open. My stomach turned a thousand times over. "S-sir?" I stuttered.

"The Boston Symphony Hall. I got tickets for tonight's performance. Rose will be there as well. It's a work thing. I'll meet you at headquarters around eight. We'll ride together. Don't be late."

And just like that, he hung up.

I sat there, staring into nothingness out the window, paralyzed. Did he know? Had Rose talked?

This was bad.

"Did he say I can come too?" Cowboy asked.

Cowboy must have overheard everything. I ignored him.

"I mean, the pianist is really hot."

My mind was a whirlwind of panic. Sweat beaded on my forehead. I envisioned it all. The worst-case scenario: Josie visiting me in prison. The best case scenario: all of us simply enjoying the concert, nothing more than a treat for his Kirby stars.

"Hello?" Cowboy persisted.

"I don't know, Cowboy, call him," I said as I started the car.

"He didn't say anything about me coming too?"

"I said I don't know!" I snapped. "Fucking call him, all right!"

Cowboy looked at me, shocked.

"I'm sorry," I apologized.

He just gave me a curt nod. "No worries. Tonight really fucked with me too. On second thought, can you just drop me off at home? I don't feel like being anywhere near my uncle right now."

"That makes two of us," I mumbled.

CHAPTER FORTY

Leah

I was wearing a new dress gifted to me by Rilloni, one of the most renowned designers in the world. Its sleek, figure-hugging black Japanese silk cascaded down to mid-thigh. I usually preferred dresses with plunging necklines and low, open backs, but this one perfectly hid the bruises on my back and chest while adding a touch of class and seduction with a hemline that boasted a flirtatious slit. Completing the ensemble was a delicate golden belt cinching the waist. It enhanced my curves and sculpted a striking silhouette, perfect for tonight's special performance.

The cool breeze of a Boston fall evening greeted me as I stepped outside to meet Mark, who had already opened the door for me. That was when I saw Luca's black limousine parked in front of my front yard's metal gate. His driver got out and opened the door to the back of the car, signaling me to get in.

I smiled at Mark, who nodded and closed my door. Then I walked over to Luca's limousine and got in.

He was in his usual immaculate tuxedo, holding a small pink flower that differed from my usual gift—a red rose.

"How kind of you to pick me up," I said with a smile. "Our quarrel pains me."

Luca looked at me, his expression hard to read. "I wouldn't have missed tonight's performance for anything in the world. Every moment

299

with you is worth a thousand lifetimes, La Imperatrice." He stretched his hand to offer me the flower. I accepted it, inspecting it curiously.

Its bloom was exquisite. Vibrant pink petals, soft and velvety to the touch, contrasting strikingly against the lush green of its stem and leaves.

"This can't be . . . a Middlemist Red," I murmured, genuinely surprised by the treasure in my hand

"I wouldn't dare bring you anything less tonight."

"But there are only two left in the world. Billionaires and presidents have failed to secure a clipping from it."

Luca observed me silently as I marveled at the beautiful flower. "They call it Middlemist Red despite it actually being pink," he said. "But the more fascinating mystery is its extinction from its native country as well as anywhere else in the world. Only two plants have survived in botanical gardens, and nobody knows why."

"What an intriguing secret it holds about its own demise," I commented, sniffing its fresh floral scent.

"Indeed," Luca said, his eyes fixed on me. "A priceless mystery right in front of all of us, yet nobody dares to push too hard in a search for answers, fearing it might be unforgiving and decide to take away even the little we are blessed to have."

I met his gaze.

"A riddle that might never be solved," I remarked with a smile. Then I grew serious. "I always enjoyed our time together, Luca. As much as I am capable of enjoying anything this world has to offer me. My ability to do so is, well, hindered."

"I know." Luca smiled, offering comfort. "I have enjoyed our time together too, La Imperatrice. My trade comes at a heavy price. Your music is the one thing still able to stir emotions in me, the one thing that keeps me from questioning if I'm already dead. I wanted to thank you for this precious gift."

I met his intense gaze with a respectful nod.

He smiled. "But now, let's shift to lighter topics. I've formed an opinion on Cziffra's obsession with Liszt, and I'm eager to hear your thoughts on it."

CHAPTER FORTY-ONE

Liam

The car ride to the symphony hall was unbearably awkward. Rose was driving the SUV, I was in the passenger seat, and McCourt was in the back. I tried hard not to stare at either one of them, attempting to act normal, but in the rare moments when neither was looking, I discreetly wiped my forehead.

Had Rose talked?

Or was this a coincidence, and McCourt genuinely wanted to reward his two "best agents" with a rare treat, just as he had explained when I met up with them at headquarters?

Neither of us was dressed in concert clothes, but our formal work suits would blend in enough to ensure we didn't stick out.

We parked the car. I was about to get out when McCourt pulled his gun from his holster. I froze. His eyes locked on me as he lifted the gun and handed it over. "Put that in the glove compartment for me, will you?"

I nodded and complied.

"Put yours in as well. We don't need them here tonight."

Rose threw me a glance before handing her gun to me.

When I hesitated, McCourt narrowed his eyes at me. "Or do we, Agent Richter? Need guns tonight?"

"Of course not," I said, placing my gun in the glove compartment. What else would I be doing with it anyway? If they planned to arrest me tonight, I wouldn't engage in some crazy shootout. I would quietly let them cuff me and take me in. No innocent guests would be endangered by me.

On our way to the balcony, McCourt trailed me and Rose as if watching our every move. This made it impossible for me to pull her aside to talk privately.

We entered the balcony where I'd sat when I'd first seen Leah play. My heart took a dramatic leap when I noticed Luca Domizio taking his seat in his balcony right next to ours. He didn't glance over. It was as if none of us were worthy of his attention.

"I heard she's quite something," McCourt said as we took our seats. He grabbed the program and skimmed it. I finally managed to catch a longer gaze from Rose, whose amber eyes looked troubled.

"Leah Nachtnebel. I've never heard her play. Up until recently, I didn't pay her much attention," McCourt continued. "I didn't really give a fuck, to be honest. I heard even the president holds her in high regard, along with pretty much every major player in DC. It takes a certain person to not only do well in this world but actually contribute to its script. That's quite something. You've got to give her that. Right?"

"Sir?" I asked, perplexed.

McCourt grinned at me. "We all have a role in this world's play, Richter. Some of us are main characters, like Leah Nachtnebel. Others are merely extras. Most don't even get to be part of the play at all. They watch from their seats and clap along like idiots. Their existence is unnoticed. Their sparks too weak to ever start a fire."

He glanced at Rose, who kept her gaze fixed on the red curtain of the stage. Then he turned and looked straight at me.

Right then, the lights went out. There was a bizarre moment of utter silence in the room, like the calm before a major storm or the eye of a deadly tornado, all while McCourt still stared at me.

The large red curtains opened to reveal the Monet grand piano. Leah walked onto the stage, looking stunning. The hall rose to its feet as thunderous applause washed over us like the apocalypse. It felt like the Olympics of the classical music world, even more intense than when I had first witnessed it. Every breath I took felt heavy and dangerous.

I broke free from McCourt's gaze and watched Leah bow. Her eyes briefly found mine as if she were telling me it would all be alright.

McCourt leaned over and said to me, "What is your role in this world, Richter? Main character, extra, or not even worth giving a fuck about?"

CHAPTER FORTY-TWO

Leah

My fingers moved on autopilot, playing Maurice Ravel's "Gaspard de la Nuit," then Bach's "Goldberg Variations BWV 988," followed by Claude Debussy's "Clair de Lune."

My thoughts had completely drifted off. The look Richter gave me was unsettling. He attempted to hide it, but the stress etched on his face was as clear as permanent ink. I had considered why McCourt was in my concert hall—everything from a post-concert interrogation to merely an admirer's attendance, which I doubted. The reality was, all possibilities were still in play, with none yet realized. There was no point in worrying. Things would unfold as they did, and I would respond as necessary, as circumstances required. It was as simple as that.

Halfway through the concert, just after I finished Chopin, Richter's intense gaze bore into me like a fresh cattle brand. Resisting the urge to meet his eyes, I focused back on the piano to begin the next piece.

Suddenly, the hall's silence broke into murmurs. They were sparse at first, but they quickly grew. I peeked out to find a man storming through the seated guests. He wore a tuxedo, yet his rugged features stood in sharp contrast to the formal attire.

Suddenly, somebody screamed right before a growing chorus shouted, "Gun!"

I leaped to my feet as chaos erupted. People rushed toward exits, and some even clambered over the stage. In an instant, the gunman leaped onto the stage, gun poised and aimed directly at me. He advanced steadily.

It was strange, but I was oddly calm. I looked for Richter. His box was now empty except for McCourt, who was still seated. His calmness left no doubt about his involvement in this. I knew everything. And now, he was asking for my head.

My gaze shifted to Luca, who stood there motionless. My days were numbered, as were my minutes, but not my seconds. So, in the final moments before I went to hell, I scanned the crowd for Richter. Why did I want him to be the last thing I saw? When I spotted him hanging off the first balcony toward the end of the concert hall, where the distance to the floor was shortest, a wave of emotions washed over me. Excitement? Joy? I wasn't sure.

Had I grown soft? Had I inconveniently and illogically attached myself to a dying breed of man? Whatever the case, I was grateful to be able to leave the world like this.

Feeling something.

Anything.

As he fought his way through the crowd of guests rushing for the exit—people falling, tumbling, screaming—our eyes finally met. I couldn't help but smile.

It didn't even matter if he'd been the one who told McCourt everything and had asked Luca to follow through on his promise to kill me. I understood why he would have done it—to protect his own well-being and, more importantly, his daughter's. Given Rose's awareness of the entire situation, I had become a liability in his eyes.

306

And although I wished he would have allowed me to at least kill the Train Track Killer first, I not only forgave him but was grateful he'd been a part of my life. Before him, I was truly dead inside. Now, I was fortunate enough to die with feeling, almost as if I had a heart like a normal human being. Nothing special, nothing broken. Just a normal model exiting the factory of life.

"Thank you, Richter," I mumbled with a smile on my lips. He was only feet away from the stage, where the gunman was now ready to fire. "Thank you."

CHAPTER FORTY-THREE

Liam

I pushed, shoved, and even elbowed, fighting my way against the tide of people desperately trying to escape.

I felt like a salmon swimming against a current of sharks; every second was a lifetime. From the corner of my eye, I caught a glimpse of McCourt calmly standing on the balcony, a smile on his face. Not far from him, Luca Domizio was sitting in his seat, his face grave and serious.

Then her green eyes locked on mine, her figure illuminated on stage against a backdrop of darkness.

The emotion in her eyes, coupled with her faint smile, shattered me. Forgiveness.

She was forgiving me. She thought I was the one who had arranged this, likely to save myself.

"Leah!" I screamed as I finally broke free from the crowd and reached the stage. "No!"

Desperation surged through me as I leaped onto the stage. The gunman to my right, Leah to my left, I did what instinct dictated.

As the gun fired, I threw myself between them, pulling her to the floor, trying to cover as much of her body with mine as I could.

The collision was harsh, and the impact on the floor stole my breath. I wrapped my arms around her, clinging tightly, attempting to shield her from further harm. A second gunshot tore through the silence of the hall.

Was I hit?

I wasn't!

Fuck . . . was she?

Silence stretched on for heart-stopping seconds before I loosened my grip around her chest and waist and raised my head. My eyes darted around only to spot Rose near the stage, looking like she was ready to take on the gunman bare-handed. Just a few feet away, the gunman lay lifeless on the stage, blood pooling around him. He had shot himself. But twice?

I looked back down at Leah as her green eyes met mine.

"Are you shot?" I needed to know.

"No," she answered, her tone shockingly calm and steady. "You?"

I shook my head. "Are you hurt?" I yelled over to Rose as I quickly got to my feet. She shook her head, her sweat glistening in the stark stage lights.

Then the gurgling sounds reached us from the damn first-floor balcony.

"McCourt!" Rose shouted as she pulled her phone from her jacket. "Agent down. We need an ambulance and immediate backup at the Boston Symphony Hall," she barked into the phone.

I gave Leah a puzzled look, then raced after Rose out of the hall to ascend the stairs to McCourt. When we reached the balcony, he was slumped off his chair, gasping for air, each breath heavy and strained with evident pain.

"Shit," I muttered as I stretched his legs out on the carpeted floor. He had taken a clean shot in the middle of the chest. His chances were slim.

I ripped off my jacket and pressed it firmly against the wound.

"Police!" came shouts from officers below.

"Up here!" I yelled back. "Rose, get them up here."

In all the chaos, my gaze dropped to the stage, where Leah stood tall, fearless, proud, and strong as always. She stood beside the dead man, her expression devoid of emotion as she looked down at him. Then her gaze lifted, not to me but to the man in the box next to us.

Luca Domizio.

He stood there, eerily still, returning her stare. Then, just as the first officers arrived at the balcony, he turned and cast a brief, dismissive glance at me and McCourt before disappearing as if all this were nothing more than a dream.

Or, in this case, a nightmare.

Chapter Forty-Four

Leah

I was sitting on the couch in my private quarters at the symphony hall, surrounded by Liam and police officers pressing for a statement.

"Can we please give Ms. Nachtnebel some space?" Liam asked. "We can go over her statement again tomorrow."

The officers left the room, though the EMTs lingered a bit longer. "Are you sure you don't want to go to the hospital for a thorough check-up?" asked one of the EMTs, a young woman with a caring aura.

"Quite certain, thank you," I replied.

She nodded, then packed up her equipment and exited with the other EMTs.

The room was now empty except for the two of us.

"You okay?" Liam asked.

"Yes."

He nodded and looked down at his hand, which was shaking. He stuffed it into his pants pocket. "You know it wasn't me who did this, right?" he whispered loudly, stepping closer.

I hesitated, then offered a faint smile. "Your actions on the stage spoke for your innocence."

"It was fucking McCourt or Rose," he muttered, his words punctuated by inaudible curses. "I saw McCourt on the balcony when all hell broke loose. He was sitting there calmly, grinning like a villain from a bad sci-fi movie. He must have asked Luca Domizio to make good on his promise to you. But why didn't he? Why did Luca turn on McCourt instead?"

"I'm not certain," I replied, "but I'll find out."

A knock sounded, then Rose entered the room

Liam confronted her. "You have some fucking nerve to show up here."

"Richter," I interjected, but he didn't back down. Instead, he closed the door behind Rose, standing in front of it as if to block her exit.

"Did you do this?" he demanded, his tone menacing. "Was it you who asked Luca Domizio to kill her?"

Rose, normally confident and bold, appeared diminished, shaking her head meekly.

"Liar!" Liam hissed.

"I swear I didn't do this," Rose said.

"So, you didn't run to McCourt like the loyal pet you are?" Liam shot back.

"Fuck you," Rose said. "I don't owe you anything." She took a step toward him. "Last time I checked, I'm not the one killing folks in secret. I'm on the right side of the law here."

"Did you tell McCourt or not, you fucking snitch? I swear, if you're lying to me—"

"I had no choice," she interrupted, her gaze falling to the floor. "I didn't want to, I swear. And I never thought that crazy bastard would try to have her killed. Honestly, I didn't even believe this whole business with Luca Domizio was real. But McCourt blackmailed me. He . . ." Her voice faltered, but one look at Richter's judgmental eyes spurred her to continue. "He has dirt on me."

"And what could that possibly be?" Richter pressed.

It took her a few deep breaths to muster her strength. "I . . . lied on my application. An instructor at the academy found out and reported it to McCourt."

"So, to save yourself a job, you almost ruined my life and had Leah killed?"

"This job is all I have."

"My daughter is all I have, and I got close to never seeing her again tonight. Might still turn out that way if McCourt survives."

Richter's shoulders relaxed as the room grew silent.

"What does he have on you?" I asked.

Rose bit her lip.

"Mind sharing that parking ticket or AI-generated college paper crime with us?" Richter asked.

"I shot the man who killed my family," she spat at him. "McCourt helped me cover it up back when my instructor approached him about it. I thought it was to help me, that he saw something special in me." Rose slumped in disappointment. "But instead, he turned me into his puppet."

"So, you told him everything," Liam said.

She nodded, her eyes shadowed with shame. "I really didn't want to. I've felt like shit ever since."

"Must have been really hard on you," Richter remarked.

"Yeah, Richter, it actually was. Especially after I'd already investigated the train track suicides. For days, I drove around, frantic. To find out that everything she said was true." Rose nodded toward me. "They all bear the ankh symbol, just like Anna's crime scene."

The air suddenly felt cold.

"It's the craziest thing I've ever seen, but you're right," Rose continued. "The Train Track Killer is still out there, playing his twisted games, and it might be a lot worse than you realize."

I rose to my feet. "What do you mean?" I asked.

"The computer files don't match the paper files," Rose said.

Richter stepped away from the door, moving closer. "That's not true. I've seen the files. They match."

Rose nodded. "The paper files printed from the computer and the computer files match, of course. But they don't match the original file of Emma Mauser by Officer Wagner."

I exchanged a bewildered look with Liam, seeking clarification.

"What original file?" he asked.

"One of the officers at the train station police noticed a discrepancy in his report," Rose said. "He was convinced the coroner had mentioned to him that he, the coroner, suspected homicide after finding rope marks on Emma's wrists."

"Rope marks? That's not in the file I read," I said.

"That's because Officer Wagner corrected his report by hand in the original file to match the computer file. We somehow ended up with his original file at headquarters."

"Larsen must have requested it and failed to notice the discrepancy," Richter concluded.

"Larsen?" Rose asked, raising an eyebrow.

"So, how can you be sure the computer file is incorrect?" I asked, sidestepping the Larsen issue.

"I called Dr. Post, the coroner. He was unaware that his report states suicide on the computer. He believes it indicates homicide."

"That makes no sense," Liam said. "Why would his file be altered on the computer?"

Rose shrugged. "I was hoping you might have an answer. You guys have been at this much longer than I have."

Liam's gaze lowered, his forehead wrinkling. "Only top-secret classified files are manipulated like that. We're instructed to ignore discrepancies when a three-letter agency is involved, for national security reasons."

"But wouldn't more families notice the discrepancies in the cause of death and raise an issue?" Rose asked.

"Some did," I said. "That's how my previous partner in the FBI first became aware of the Train Track Killer. A complaint from a very persistent family reached higher levels within the FBI. Nothing concrete has resulted from it yet, but it put the murders on my radar."

"And not much is likely to come of it ever," Rose interjected.

Both Liam and I turned our attention to her. "What do you mean?" Liam pressed.

"I mean that most of the files are marked as active investigations with instructions to block their release to the public. Nobody outside of us even knows what's really in those files. Somebody has altered them and blocked them without anybody really knowing."

"But," Liam said, "why would non-political death cases be altered by us or any other three-letter agency? They hold no information that threatens national security."

My thoughts raced. "The more interesting question isn't why they're blocked, but who's behind the blocking."

Liam's face contorted as if a sudden, distressing thought had struck him. "Kirby! He had extensive files on all his victims, information you'd normally need a warrant to obtain. It was as if they were handed to him by a government agency, And right before he died, Kirby told me that *he* was too powerful. I thought he was talking about a voice in his head, but now . . ."

Rose's eyes widened. "You're suggesting someone fed Kirby those files to manipulate him? Play him like a puppet? Maybe even tipped him off when we were closing in on him?"

The pieces of the puzzle were aligning slowly but unmistakably.

"Patel," I declared with newfound clarity. "He was a pawn that the Train Track Killer used against us. It's possible the same person manipulated Kirby too."

Rose's voice trembled with disbelief. "But how could anybody possibly orchestrate all of this? Are you saying that the Train Track Killer might be an FBI or CIA agent?"

I had considered this, but it didn't align with what we knew. "No, I don't think so. The killer's behavior is too unpredictable for a federal agency employee, who would need to maintain regular work hours and can be tracked. But it does make me wonder, who or what outside of the government could have the ability to manipulate official documents? Be everywhere at once—constantly listening and watching."

Rose and Liam stared at me, their expressions a mix of anticipation and confusion.

"Think about it," I pressed. "Leros. Emanuel and my code word. We wondered how the Train Track Killer had accessed that personal information without someone feeding it to him."

Liam mulled over my words. "What if Emanuel provided that information himself?"

I shook my head. "I'm certain that's not the case. He had no reason to do that. I paid too well, and he enjoyed his work with me."

"Then how else could he have known?" Liam asked.

Pondering this, I posed a question, "How can anybody see and hear everything without being physically present?"

"Wiretaps?" Rose suggested.

"But you need someone to actually wear them," Liam said.

"Maybe he pays for access to security footage," Rose proposed.

"Or the Train Track Killer owns a security company," Liam said. "Many security firms now incorporate indoor cameras with sound."

I tilted my head. "Jan Novak holds a significant fortune in the tech sector. But owning a security firm wouldn't grant him or anybody else the ability to alter or block FBI or other law enforcement files."

As I mulled this over, the fragments began connecting in a rapid, chaotic dance in my mind.

Then it struck me.

"The tech sector," I murmured. "Which branch in the tech industry, privately owned, remains shrouded in secrecy and is almost never discussed in the media?"

There was only one answer.

"It infiltrates every aspect of our lives," I continued, "managing the content of every moment we're captured on camera or speaking on the phone."

Liam's eyes widened. "My God. The cloud!"

"The cloud?" Rose asked, puzzled.

"It's the biggest cash cow in the tech industry," I explained. "Amazon's entire worth hinges on its cloud services. So does Microsoft's. And neither are the biggest players in the field. They hold only a tiny margin in the industry."

Richter scratched his head. "A few weeks ago, I read about a major new contract between the NSA and the largest cloud storage provider in the world."

"Which is?" Rose asked, her curiosity piqued.

Silence hung in the air.

"I see," she said, pulling out her phone to do a quick search. She read for a moment, then recoiled slightly. "Og . . . Ogledalo?"

"Ogledalo Corporation?" I repeated, feeling a chill spread through my veins.

"Ogledalo," she repeated, confused. "Does that mean anything?"

"It means 'mirror' in Slovenian," I said. "Or, metaphorically, 'ankh,' in this context."

"What?" Liam and Rose said at once.

"Ogledalo Corporation," I mumbled as if summoning a demon. "It's named after the symbol that the Train Track Killer leaves at crime scenes. The largest cloud computing storage company in the world. It's storing information from phone companies to banks all the way to the National Security Agency's darkest secrets."

"Jesus," Rose whispered. "That's a hell of a lot of power. Who in the name of God would be granted such ridiculous leverage?"

Richter did a quick online search on his phone, then shrugged. "The owner or board members aren't named publicly."

We still needed more evidence, but that strong feeling in my gut was undeniable.

The concert visits. The meeting at the Smithsonian Museum. The ability to block facial recognition. The missing files on him... and the large wealth in tech.

I walked past them and flung the door open. The hallway had already cleared of officers.

"Where are you going?" I heard Liam call after me.

Both Rose and Liam were on my heels as we moved through the hallways and into the busy foyer. Scattered around were officers, EMTs, and a few concert-goers who were being questioned. Some of them cast relieved glances my way when they saw I was unharmed.

Liam and Rose appeared hesitant about being associated with me out here, as was evident from their quick scans of the surroundings. However, they were two federal agents in a crowd of law enforcement following a shooting, so their presence wasn't out of the ordinary.

I stopped to graciously accept the well-wishes of some guests. Then I walked a few more steps, right into the middle of the entrance hall. Rose and Liam stopped next to me, bewildered, scanning the area as if I'd lost my mind. Other people were beginning to notice, sneaking sidelong glances at me.

"What the hell are you doing?" Rose asked, her gaze not meeting mine.

I tilted my head upward, directing my gaze toward the security camera of the Boston Symphony entrance hall. I looked straight into it, then smiled.

Triumphant.

Fearless.

Provocative.

"I'm just saying hello," I explained to Liam and Rose.

"Saying hello? To whom?" Rose asked. Both she and Liam were now also staring straight into the camera.

All three of us stood there, side by side, like the Three Musketeers taking on an invisible enemy from above.

"Saying hello to whom?" Rose pressed again.

"To Jan fucking Novak," Liam said on my behalf, his face shifting into that of a Viking ready to take on hordes of Roman legions.

As we all stared into the camera, it dawned on me. The real fight had finally begun. The ultimate battle that would determine my and Liam's fate and now Rose's as well. It was going to be a fight of life and death.

There was nothing I wouldn't do to win the overall war against one of the mightiest monsters alive. But if we were to stand a chance, I needed the same commitment from Liam and Rose.

It would take everything we had to bring him down.

And that was perfectly fine by me.

Let him come.

After all, we kill killers.

CHAPTER FORTY-FIVE

Jan Novak

Deep in the underground cloud computing storage center of a large compound belonging to Ogledalo Corporation in New York state, Jan Novak, the embodiment of power and wealth, sat in his windowless office. All crucial storage was underground, with the buildings above used primarily for storing parts and housing the offices of low-security-level employees. And, of course, the enormous team tasked with securing the most valuable information-gathering system on earth. One that was more valuable than gold mines. Or Area 51.

With strategic planning, Ogledalo Corporation had decimated most other cloud services by aggressively slashing its storage fees and outbidding competitors until it controlled over ninety percent of all US cloud storage. It was a mistake that its clients were too late to rectify. These clients included the CIA, the NSA, the IRS, ICE, banks, telecommunication firms, internet providers, security companies—the list was endless. Ogledalo Corporation knew what you "sexted" to your ex just as it knew who shot JFK.

Jan Novak leaned forward in his chair, examining his reflection in the mirrored walls of his office, every move captured like a window to his soul. Like a modern form of the ankh.

The wall opposite him was lined with screens as thin as glass, showcasing cutting-edge technology not yet on the market. These screens presented information from the cloud, pulling whatever he needed at the moment. The setup made his office feel like a futuristic space station.

His company employed only the brightest and most genius computer scientists in the world, often provided by the NSA itself.

Deep in thought, he swiped his finger over the touchscreen desk in front of him, all while petting his one-eyed rescue dog with his other hand.

It was early morning, but the first item on his agenda was reviewing last night's footage of the shooting at the Boston Symphony Hall.

He watched as a gunman shot Assistant FBI Director McCourt and then himself on stage during a concert by Leah Nachtnebel. Agent Liam Richter had tried to protect her, but that had turned out to be unnecessary.

But what fascinated Novak the most was the moment Ms. Nachtnebel stepped into the entrance hall and came back into view of the security camera. Looking straight up, she smiled into the lens as if she knew Novak was watching. The directness of her gaze, the knowing smile—it felt as if she was peering right at him.

He paused the footage, sitting there in awe.

There was no doubt. Her green eyes were seeking him out. This was for him. A message.

But why reveal that she'd finally found him?

"Mr. Novak," his suit-clad young secretary called out as she stepped inside. "The CIA director is waiting for you to sign the papers for the updated storage agreement."

He didn't even look at her, just waved her off. "Tell him to wait. I'm busy."

"Yes sir," she said without the slightest hesitation, then left.

Jan Novak leaned over his desk, narrowing his eyes at Leah Nachtnebel and the two FBI agents she was dragging along.

Those green eyes were staring through all the walls between them. She was smiling even though somebody had almost shot her.

He couldn't help but grin back at her. He had always feared this day would come—the day he would become the target of someone as brilliant and determined as he was. The fact that she had actually uncovered his identity was nothing short of marvelous. Especially considering the extreme measures he had taken to erase the scar on his shoulder. The skin graft surgery had cost a fortune and been performed by a team of the world's top plastic surgeons, all paid in cash to keep his identity hidden.

And yet, she had found him.

This woman.

A dark angel.

A genius.

A monster that was now coming for him. And, in her mind, there would be only one ending for a killer more powerful than the president.

That would be death.

But he wouldn't go down without a fight. His work was too important. Not the company. His other work.

"Brilliant, Ms. Nachtnebel," he murmured in admiration. "Let the games begin."

Epilogue

New York, 1981

Mojca and Anton spent hours on the train, endlessly looping the city, re-tracing the same route through New York. They sat silently, watching the sun's last rays glimmer off the high-rises surrounding them.

The joyful sound of a giggling girl nearby captured their attention. Mojca watched with a mix of jealousy and sadness as the girl's father playfully tickled her side while her mother watched with a fond smile.

As the train slowed into the station, Anton grasped Mojca's hand. "Let's get off here and head back home. One of them must be in jail by now."

Mojca nodded as his gaze lingered on the happy family across from them.

Anton tightened his grip around Mojca's hand as they got off the train and crossed the station's platform to catch the train for home.

"I think we should pick up some chocolate and chips and watch Wonder Woman tonight," Anton suggested.

Mojca's mood brightened. "Can I have some cola too?"

"Only if you promise not to stay up all night again, bombarding me with questions about Ancient Egypt and why cats lick their butts."

A genuine chuckle escaped Mojca—a stark contrast to the forced ones on the train when Anton tried his jokes too hard too soon.

As they watched the train approaching in the distance, Mojca felt a tremor in his hand. He instantly knew his own hand wasn't trembling. In sheer panic, he looked at Anton. His brother's eyes had rolled back as if a demon were possessing him

"Help, he's having a seizure!" Mojca shouted as Anton's violently shaking body fell forward onto the train tracks, almost pulling Mojca along with him. "Help!" he screamed, looking left and right at the crowd that had gathered and was now staring at the horrific scene. "Please help my brother!"

Mojca's voice shattered the silence, but no one moved.

His eyes darted to the train thundering toward them as his unconscious brother violently seized on the tracks.

"Why is nobody helping?" he cried out. Hot tears streamed down his face as a sharp pain choked his breath, leaving him gasping for air. But the large crowd merely gawked, unwilling to help, captivated by the unbelievable scene unfolding before them.

Thoughts of terror and blame raced through Mojca's mind. This was all his fault. If it weren't for him, his brother wouldn't have forgotten his coat with his medication at home.

Without a second to waste, Mojca leaped onto the tracks. The train's loud horn blared a stark warning that it couldn't stop in time. As things stood, it was set to claim not only Anton's life but Mojca's as well.

Desperately, with only seconds left, Mojca pulled at his brother's heavy body. "Help! Please help!" he screamed over and over again.

But the train drew nearer, and the onlookers did nothing but stare.

Mojca pulled relentlessly, bargaining with God and the mighty pharaohs to never lie or do anything bad again if only they would help save the one person who loved him—the one person who had always been there for him, the one reason he still wanted to wake up each morning.

The train was moments away from striking them with the force of a bomb. However, suddenly, an odd sense of relief mixed with Mojca's horror. At least now the train would take him too. Because without his brother, no soul on earth would feel the profound, hollow emptiness inside that Mojca would.

BOOK III

COMING SOON!

This is the third installment in the series, following the second book, "We Kill Killers."

If you want to get your discounted ebook preorder now, go to the link below.

https://www.amazon.com/dp/B0D5V4BG8W

By preordering, you support an author/mom dedicated to bringing original stories to readers, even when it means facing challenges in a market dominated by large publishers. Your support helps ensure that fresh, high-quality content can reach readers and promote creativity.

THANK YOU!

Dear Reader,

Thank you for reading "We Kill Killers." If you enjoyed the book, please consider leaving a review on your preferred retailer's website (like Amazon, Goodreads, Barnes & Noble, etc.). Sharing "We Kill Killers" on social media or with friends and family would also be a great help. I have a small, mom-run author/publishing business, so every click, share, and kind word makes a huge difference and means the world to me.

Newsletter: https://www.ashmanbooks.com

Instagram: https://www.instagram.com/booksbyashman/

TikTok: https://www.tiktok.com/@ashmanbooks

Join Ashman's Dark Thriller Facebook Group to Meet the Author:

https://www.facebook.com/profile.php?id=100094353614873

Contact: hello@ashmanbooks.com

Thank you for your support.

S. T. Ashman

About the Author

S. T. Ashman is a writer who once delved into the criminal justice system as a psychotherapist. This role gifted her with a unique insight into the human psyche—both the beautiful and the deeply shadowed. She considers herself a crime-solving enthusiast, often daydreaming about being the female version of Columbo, solving mysteries while rocking a trench coat. Her writing audaciously defies norms and promises to keep readers engrossed in a nail-biting adventure.

When she's not busy crafting suspenseful tales, she's chasing after her nap-resistant kids, binge-watching TV with her husband, or . . . actually, that pretty much covers it.

She aims to bend your brain, tickle your intrigue, and leave you pondering long after the last page. Come join her on her journeys.

Made in United States
North Haven, CT
01 August 2024

55662986R00202